LETTERS TO LINCOLN

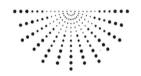

TRACIE PODGER

✾ Created with Vellum

ACKNOWLEDGMENTS

My heartfelt thanks to the best beta readers a girl could want, Alison Parkins & Karen Atkinson-Lingham - your input is invaluable.

Thank you to Sofie at Hart & Bailey for an amazing cover, I absolutely love it!

I'd also like to give a huge thank you to my editor, Karen Hrdlicka, and proofreader, Joanne Thompson.

See how pretty this book looks inside? Leigh Stone over at Irish Ink Formatting is to thank for that.

A big hug goes to the ladies in my team. These ladies give up their time to support and promote my books. Alison 'Awesome' Parkins, Karen Atkinson-Lingham, Marina Marinova, Ann Batty, Fran Brisland, Elaine Turner, Kerry-Ann Bell, Jodie Scott, and Louise White – otherwise known as the Twisted Angels.

To all the wonderful bloggers that have been involved in promoting my books and joining tours, thank you and I appreciate your support. There are too many to name individually – you know who you are.

If you wish to keep up to date with information on this series and future releases - and have the chance to enter monthly competitions, feel free to sign up for my newsletter. You can find the details on my web site:

www.TraciePodger.com

Would you like a FREE book? If you sign up to receive my newsletters, you'll receive a link in the welcome email to download my novella, Evelyn. Evelyn is one of my favourite characters and I'm thrilled to share her with you.

http://eepurl.com/clbNTP

CHAPTER ONE

I heard noises: beeping, whispered voices. It was the clinical smell assaulting my nose that had me realise I wasn't at home. I tried to open my eyes, but the light, such a bright light above me, burned my retinas. My body ached, my arm felt heavy as if weighed down.

I drifted back into sleep.

"Dani, can you hear me?"

"Dani, we need you to open your eyes, honey."

Honey?

I felt a hand on my shoulder, it gently squeezed. Why couldn't they leave me be? Did they not understand? The minute I opened my eyes, the minute I heard their words, I'd have to remember. I didn't want to remember.

"Baby girl, it's time to wake up now." Not even my dad's voice could chase the fear of waking up away.

The hand squeezed and eventually, fingertips pried one eyelid open. I moved my head away; it was an invasion. An assault on my desired numbness. I had no choice. I opened my eyes, squinting against the harsh lights above me and turned my head.

My dad sat on a chair beside me. He leant forwards, reached out, and smoothed the hair from my forehead. I winced at the sting as his fingers brushed over the stitches.

"Hey," he said, gently.

A nurse stood beside him, busying herself with a clipboard and notes. She looked up and smiled softly at me. I didn't return the smile.

I looked down at the arm that felt heavy and saw the white plaster cast, stretching from hand to elbow. Using my other hand, I placed it on my stomach. I knew.

"They…" I heard my dad say. I closed my eyes and shook my head. I knew. I didn't need his words.

It was why I hadn't wanted to wake up. It was why I'd wanted to keep my eyes closed, my ears shut off from sound. It was why I wanted to pretend I hadn't been in a car accident, I hadn't watched my husband tumble inside the car, being smashed from window to door as he tried to protect me and… I didn't want to remember! I shook my head from side to side; I tried hard not to let the tears fall. I clamped my mouth closed, so hard that my teeth hurt, to stop the scream that wanted to erupt.

I breathed hard in and out through my nose, anything to quell the nausea, the panic. But I couldn't stop it. I opened my mouth and I screamed.

I wailed until I had no air in my lungs. I screeched until my throat was raw. Tears poured down my cheeks, snot ran from my nose. I heard running feet, I felt my hand being lifted, and I felt the warmth as something soothing flowed through my veins until it reached my brain and shut off the pain, closed down the images, and the memories.

I drifted back into sleep.

&

I had no concept of time, what day of the week it was, even. I had no idea how long I'd been in the hospital. I did know my husband was dead. I felt it. I also knew my baby was gone. The daughter Trey and I had tried for three years to conceive; the daughter so precious that had come along just at the point we'd decided to stop trying. The daughter that caused my husband to fall to his knees, to sob tears when I'd told him I was pregnant. I didn't need anyone to tell me. I was hollow; my heart physically ached in my chest.

For the first time in my life; I had no purpose. There was no point to me or my existence.

I lay looking at fluorescent lighting in a stained, dirty, panelled ceiling. I turned my head slightly to look at the blue plastic curtains separating my bed from the next and wondered what poor soul was on the other side.

"Good morning, Dani," I heard.

A nurse circled the bed, looking at *things*, checking *things*. I tried to shuffle up the bed; my back was sore. I winced at the pull on the stitches across my stomach.

"Let me help you," she said, picking up a remote and raising the back of the bed.

"Are you comfortable?" she asked, placing her hand on my arm.

"Where are they?" I whispered.

She sat on the edge of the bed. "Your dad will be here shortly, he arrives bang on eight o'clock every morning."

"You know what I mean."

"I do, but I'd rather your dad was here first."

3

An orderly pushed a trolley with breakfast into the twin occupancy room. She poured a cup of tea and placed it on the tray connected to the bed. She asked if I wanted sugar, I shook my head. She inquired what I'd like to eat; I shook my head again. No amount of food would fill the emptiness I felt inside.

"Hey," a familiar voice came from the doorway.

Dad pulled the chair up to the side of my bed. "It's good to see you fully awake."

"How long have I been here?"

"Just over two weeks now," he said.

His reply surprised me. It felt like only yesterday that I'd been brought in. Tears pricked at my eyes and I had to will my hand to stay on the bed and not cover my stomach.

I watched him close his eyes, taking a deep breath in, before opening them and exhaling.

"I know, Dad."

I wanted to spare him the awfulness of having to tell me. Those tears gently rolled down my cheeks.

"I don't know what to say to you," he said, his voice cracking on every word.

"I need to see them."

He gently nodded. "I'm not sure how…"

"Honey, you're awake," an American voice sounded from the doorway.

Patricia, my mother-in-law, strode in. I saw her once, twice a year, but seeing her just then, she looked as if she'd aged twenty years.

She smiled at my dad who, ever the gentleman, vacated his chair for her. She took hold of my hand. I gave it a squeeze when I saw the tears in her eyes.

"I…" she started to speak. I shook my head.

"She knows," Dad said. "She wants to see them."

For a little while, we sat in silence. What could any of us say?

"The truck driver fell asleep, I think," I whispered. "We were laughing, Trey was singing to…to Hannah; we called her Hannah."

Patricia smiled, that had been her mother's name.

I swallowed hard and closed my eyes. "He ploughed straight into us. The car rolled down the bank, Trey unclipped his belt. He threw himself over my lap, I screamed at him not to. I screamed…"

The image of his body being thrown around like a rag doll hit me hard. The sight of his head hitting the windshield, of an arc of red covering the glass as it shattered, was all I could see. I blinked rapidly, trying to rid my mind of the image.

"He was trying to protect you and the…Hannah. He was trying to protect Hannah."

"And he died because of it."

My statement pulled us all up short. I frowned, not sure of the feelings coursing through my body. Had Trey stayed buckled in his seat, he might have lived, and I wasn't sure if it was anger or the unbelievable sadness I felt that coursed through me.

Or was it guilt?

Trey hadn't wanted to take a drive that day. He'd wanted for us to stay indoors. He had a cot to build; he had work to do. I'd been on bed rest because of high blood pressure and was bored.

I'd nagged until he gave in. *Just an hour, let's go for a drive, just for an hour*, I'd pleaded.

That hour had devastated, destroyed, ended, not just mine, but his and my baby's lives.

That hour had made a mother childless, and a wife, alone. That hour had changed my father's, my mother-in-law's and my life, forever.

"I think the police want to speak to you, when you're ready for that," Dad said.

I nodded my head. I wanted to speak to the police; I wanted that driver prosecuted. He was responsible for two deaths, and my broken heart.

I placed my feet into slippers laid beside my bed. With my dad on one side and Patricia on the other, I tentatively stood. I wasn't sure if the ache in my back was from the accident or sleeping on a bed for so long. My casted arm was in a sling. I held my hand over my stomach. That act caused a lump to form in my throat. It was an action I'd done many times to protect my bump. Now it was to protect the wound of a C-section.

I lowered myself into a wheelchair and a nurse pushed. I was grateful it wasn't a porter. We rode the lift in silence, down a few floors, and when the doors slid open my heart started to pound. I gripped the arms of the wheelchair, thankful for it, I wasn't sure my legs would have held me up.

I'd cried over the past week, so I'd been told. I'd screamed and been sedated. I'd fought, pulled the cannula from my hand, apparently. But those tears, those screams had come from night-mares and drugs.

Trey lay on the bed; a sheet covered him to his neck. Hannah, in a cot beside him, was dressed in white, angelic and serene. Blonde hair covered her head. I didn't know who to go to first. I pushed myself from the chair, I placed my hands on the bed beside Trey's head and I broke. I completely broke.

"You can pick her up, Dani," I heard the nurse say.

I picked up my baby but she felt like a doll, a porcelain doll. I held her to me, hoping to breathe in her scent, she smelled clinical, not like my baby should smell. I laid her on the bed beside Trey. I stroked the side of his face, and then her hair.

"They need to be buried together," I whispered.

The tears that flowed were my soul leaving my body. I watched it. I watched my soul climb on that bed and curl into Trey's side. I watched its arm reach over and cradle my baby. I died inside that day.

The sobs that left my mouth were the last sounds my lungs, my voice box, would produce.

CHAPTER TWO

"*W*e are gathered here to celebrate the lives of…"

I looked up at the vicar standing in front of me. Two caskets, one oak, one white, sat to the side of me.

Celebrate! She hadn't the fucking chance to live, so what the fuck are we celebrating?

Those words were screamed in my head. I hadn't been able to utter a word since that day, three weeks prior, when I'd seen Trey and my baby, cold and lifeless, in a morgue.

I was angry, I was bitter. The truck driver had been charged, death by dangerous driving, a fine, a ban, was all he'd received. A fucking driving ban! I'd thrown up at the trial when that sentence had been passed.

The vicar droned on, I tuned out. He hadn't known Trey or Hannah. He didn't know me. He spoke about Trey's life in the U.S. before he came to England. He spoke about the angels that had decided they needed my baby. If I could make sound, it would have been a snort at that one. There was no God, there were no angels—if there was, what a sadistic bastard he was.

Patricia took hold of my arm. I blinked as I looked at her. She gave me a small smile and a nod. I turned my head to the side. Pallbearers stood beside Trey's coffin, looking at me, as if waiting for some instruction. My brother had Hannah's coffin laid across his arms. It looked like a toy. I stood, keeping eye contact with my brother. I reached out, my arms straight in front of me.

Christian frowned. I opened my mouth; no sound emerged. Then he understood. He laid my baby's coffin on my arms. I was going to carry her; she was mine. I turned and walked down the aisle to the sound of sobs.

I was glad I couldn't speak; I just wished I couldn't hear. My voice was trapped inside my head making one sound only —screams.

A pallbearer took Hannah from me and laid her in the back of a hearse. Trey was laid beside her. We drove the short distance to the grave in the cemetery Trey and I would walk around, fascinated by the inscriptions on the gravestones.

Trey and Hannah were buried together, as I'd wanted. They were laid to rest in the small cemetery near the house my dad owned, on a cliff overlooking the sea.

When the burial was over, I walked away. I walked to the edge of the cliff, wrapping my jacket tight around me as a bitter wind blew off the English Channel. Dark clouds rolled over the horizon, the sea was angry. It matched my mood, and for that, I thanked Mother Nature. She was as pissed off as I was.

I wasn't sure how long I'd been standing there, looking out as waves crashed against the cliff. I felt a hand on my shoulder, before the arm pulled me into a firm chest. I breathed in the familiar scent of my dad. I swallowed back the tears, but it was just too hard.

"Cry, baby, cry," he whispered, his words caught on the wind and were whisked around us.

I gripped his jacket, my fists curled into the material. I opened my mouth to let out the silent sobs. My body shook with utter despair.

&a.

I'd left London the day I'd been released from hospital. I didn't go home, I was driven straight to Cornwall. Christian had packed up my house, Helen, his wife, had organised all the baby items to be taken to the local charity shop. I imagined that task had brought her to her knees; bearing in mind she was pregnant herself. I hadn't been able to see her, I'd shut her out, and she held no malice towards me for that.

"Let's get you inside," Dad said. He turned me gently and we walked towards the house.

Hushed voices floated around, mixed with stilted soft laughter. The house was full of people, most I knew, and some I didn't. Patricia walked towards me, she took me from my dad's arms and ushered me to the sofa. I obediently sat. I was thankful she took the seat beside me and held my hand. I didn't want to be there, I didn't want all those people to be there. I kept my head bowed. No one came and spoke to me, everyone knew of my inability to speak. I guessed they just didn't know how to deal with it.

How do you have a one-sided conversation with someone so broken their hands shook too much to even write a response?

I'd given up on the pad and pen I was supposed to carry around. I didn't invite *conversation* full stop. Other than to sit on the cliff, I didn't leave the house, there was no need to communicate with anyone, other than my dad and Patricia.

As the afternoon wore on, the anti-depressants I'd taken started to work. My eyelids began to droop. I slept more hours each day and night than I'd ever had. I'd been told it was my body's way of allowing my mind to heal. I was hoping I was dying, that I wouldn't wake up one morning to pop those little white pills. I was longing to be reunited with Trey and Hannah.

I felt an arm wrap under mine and I was lifted to my feet. I think I was carried to my bedroom, the room I'd slept in as a child. I didn't remember my feet touching the wooden stairs.

My shoes were removed and I curled on my bed. Christian, my twin, the other half of the *non-me*, pulled a comforter from the chair by the window. He placed it over me before climbing on the bed himself and pulling me into his arms. I was beyond crying at that point. I was beyond fighting to live.

I closed my eyes, thanking the pills for emptying my mind. I let myself sink into the blackness and I slept.

I slept on and off for the next week, or maybe it was more. I ate when food was placed in front of me, but I didn't taste one morsel. I ate to please my dad, Patricia, no other reason. I'd have happily starved myself.

The day Patricia had to leave, to return to the U.S., was a day I felt I lost more of Trey. Her voice, although feminine, reminded me of him. The accent, her mannerisms, kept that connection. With her gone, that last thread to my husband was severed.

Time had no meaning. I got up, showered and dressed, and I walked. For all the years I'd lived in that house, I'd never walked the many miles I had the past few weeks. I wasn't sure why I walked; I didn't want the exercise. I didn't need the fresh air. It did nothing to clear the confusion, the anger, the hatred, the sadness, and the mass of emotion that bubbled away inside me. All it achieved was time alone.

Being alone was what I desired but was too afraid to ask for. I found it frustrating not to be able to speak. Doctors had said it was a shock thing, I shouldn't push it; my voice would come back when ready. It was psychological, of course; there was nothing physically wrong with me. No one seemed to understand though. I didn't want my voice back. I didn't want the ability to speak, because I was unsure I'd be able to contain the spew of hatred that would pour out in the form of words.

In the meantime, I went back to relying on pieces of paper and a pen. I left notes; I answered questions by writing them down.

It was early hours one morning, and I'd been sitting in the chair by the bay window with the blasted pad and pen by my side when a thought hit me.

I wanted to tell Trey I was sorry. I was sorry for badgering him to drive that day. I wanted to tell Hannah that I was sorry. I was sorry for not being the mummy she deserved.

I picked up the pad and flicked to a clean page. Dawn broke, and I wrote. My scrawling handwriting covered each small page and I poured my thoughts onto it. Tears dripped, smudging the ink. Blue colouring spread out, obliterating the words. I pulled my sleeve down over my hand and dabbed at it.

When I'd written enough, I tore the pages from the pad. Not that I thought anyone would read it. I was a grown woman; I didn't think I needed to hide a diary.

I needed air; I needed to clear my head. I pulled on my Converse sneakers and snuck from my bedroom. I could hear the gentle snores from my dad's room. I knew he didn't sleep well. I knew he'd creep along the corridor to listen outside my door, hoping to hear if I spoke in my sleep, if I was unsettled. Each day, I saw the stress and upset age him more. He'd lost his wife, my mum, many years ago to cancer. He'd raised two children as a single father and done an amazing job of it. Despite my grief, I felt guilty that he had to deal with me in his old age. He should be out playing boules, or cards at the local pub. He should be walking his aged Labrador along the coastal paths. He should be able to take a leisurely stroll to the local shop for his morning paper. All the things he did on a daily basis had been put on hold, for me.

I opened the back door in the kitchen and stepped out into the morning. I pulled the zipper higher on my jacket and the hood up to keep out the biting chill. I stuffed the letter in my pocket with no clear idea what I was going to do with it. I walked along the cliff until I came to the stone steps that led to the small beach.

I sat on the damp sand, watching the waves break: white foam, flotsam, rolled closer and closer as the tide came in. An old fishing net wrapped about a buoy bobbed until the sand anchored it. As children, Christian and I would walk the beach collecting the rubbish that the sea gave up to us. We'd bag it up, keeping our beach clean. I rose and made my way to where the buoy lay. As I reached down for it, I spotted a bottle. An old wine bottle, I imagined, with a screw top. The label had long since disintegrated; the constant grinding against sand had almost polished the green glass so that it was see-through. I picked it up. A memory punched me in the gut.

Trey, as a child, had often placed a letter in a bottle and thrown it overboard when he'd been sailing with his father. He had been desperate to see how far that bottle travelled and whether anyone would reply to him. He'd told me, he'd spent weeks scouring the shore of Lake Erie when the family had visited their holiday home. He had taken me there one time, when we'd spent a couple of weeks with his mum. We'd written a note, a love note, and threw it from the small sailing dingy we'd taken out.

I reread what I wrote.

I miss you, so so much, Trey. I can't breathe through the pain anymore. I can't accept that you're gone. And I can't accept that our baby is gone, too. I feel so much guilt and I don't know how to deal with that. I made us take that drive, if I'd only listened to you, we'd be planning the birth of our daughter any day now. I'd be excited; you'd be panicking. We'd be the parents we were so desperate to be. I saw you; I came to see you and I laid Hannah down beside you. I died inside that day, Trey, and I continue to shrivel up with no purpose in life. I'm waiting for the day I'll be back with you. Do you believe that? I have to. I have to force myself that all those things we laughed at are true. We'll be together one day. The vicar said, at your funeral, that the angels had come for Hannah. I don't believe that, I don't want to believe something thought that was the right thing to do.

You were stolen from me, Trey. Hannah was wrenched from my body without my permission.

I want you back; I need you back. I love you, and you left me, you promised me that you'd never do that.

We were supposed to grow old together. We were supposed to be parents, grandparents. We were supposed to fight and love. We only had five years together, that's all. It's not enough, Trey, for me to hold on to. It wasn't enough time to have created memories to last me my lifetime. I can't do this without you.

Dani

Before I realised, I'd rolled my letter and pushed it into the bottle. There seemed to be some poetic justice in what I was doing. I screwed the cap back on and threw it as far as I could. I had no idea on the tides; I had no idea what would happen to the bottle.

I sat and watched the bottle bob about until the sun rose high enough to hide it within the shimmers. I stood and dusted the damp sand from my jeans. I walked back to the cottage and paused halfway. My mind felt a little clearer, just a tiny bit, but I didn't feel the hit to my chest that had my heart miss a beat when I pictured Trey or Hannah.

"Hey, baby, been for a walk?" Dad said, when I entered the kitchen. I nodded as I kicked off my Converse.

"I was about to do some breakfast, sit down and I'll make you a cup of tea."

I removed my jacket and pointed that I was going to the hallway to hang it up.

"You go ahead, and you might want to change your jeans, your backside is a little wet. Oh, and put a sweater on, the heating went out again, I need to call an engineer."

I climbed the stairs to my bedroom and changed. My cheeks had reddened with the cold; the top of my nose was numb. I grabbed a sweatshirt from a drawer and pulled it over my head, then headed back downstairs.

A steaming cup of tea was set on the table and I wrapped my hands around it. Dad was cooking bacon, feeding Lucy, the dog, pieces straight from the pan. She was too old to do the length of walks I'd been doing, but I missed taking her out to run on the beach. I grabbed one of the many pads and pens lying around the house.

How old is Lucy now? I wrote. I tapped the table to gain Dad's attention. He read.

"Oh, must be nearly eight now. Her poor hips aren't doing so well anymore." He smiled at her as he spoke.

He sat opposite and pushed a plate with a bacon sandwich towards me. I took a bite, not tasting it. Bacon sandwiches had been one of my favourite things, along with a large mug of tea; it made for a perfect breakfast.

"I'm going to pop up to the shop in a bit, is there anything you need?"

I shook my head. "I think you're low on that shampoo stuff you like, I'll see if they have any."

I wrote. *Any shampoo will be fine, thank you.*

He nodded as he ate. He then went on to tell me the local gossip. Sometimes I wondered if he struggled for things to say. It couldn't have been easy on him to have this one-sided conversation with me. I wanted to smile, nod, or shake my head. I wanted to laugh; knowing I'd open my mouth and no sound would emerge, but at least he'd understand, but I couldn't bring myself to. I looked at him, I heard some of what he'd said, but the voices in my head often overrode what my ears heard.

I only got part of his sentences. And it scared me. I hadn't *told* anyone for fear that I'd be put on a higher dosage of the antidepressants, that I'd be classed as *mad*. The voices were mine, multiple *mes* trying to be heard. Whatever emotion I was suppressing the most, shouted the loudest. The consequence was that I didn't really hear what was being said to me, only snippets.

Shall I make a list? I wrote. Not sure if he had just asked me what I wanted for dinner.

He smiled and nodded. Perhaps he thought this was a breakthrough, I was participating in life.

I tore a piece of paper from the pad and wrote down some basic items I thought we might be low on. In truth, I hadn't looked in a cupboard or the fridge, since I'd arrived some…I had no idea how long I'd actually been there. I didn't know the date even. I knew it was September, but that was all.

I waited until Dad had shrugged on his coat and tied his scarf around his neck. I felt that pang of guilt hit me that I'd sit in the house, while he struggled down the lane with his shopping bags. I couldn't face people trying to talk to me. When I heard the doors close, I let the tears fall. I hated crying in front of Dad, I hated to see the pain cross his face when he realised he couldn't take mine away. It wasn't a scraped knee that he would kiss and make better. It wasn't a bump on the head from a fall off a bike that he could place an ice pack to and soothe me with his words.

I was so broken inside that it would be impossible for him to put me back together.

CHAPTER THREE

I'd gotten into the habit of waking early hours and walking. I liked the solitude of that time in the morning. I liked that there was no one on the beach that would bid me a good morning and scowl at my lack of response.

It had rained during the night, the grass, as I crossed the garden, soaked into my Converse. It was probably time to dig out some boots. I walked along the beach until I came to an outcrop of rocks. I sat and breathed in deep, inhaling the salty air. As I placed my hands behind me, I felt a crack in the rock. I felt something metal.

I looked to see a bottle, my bottle, wedged in there.

At times the sea would cover the rocks, and I assumed the bottle had been washed back up to the place I'd thrown it, getting stuck in the rock as the tide receded. I pulled it out, unscrewed the cap and upended the bottle to retrieve the page I'd wedged in there. The piece of paper that fell out wasn't the page I'd initially put in there.

I held the rolled up paper in my hand, unsure what to do at first. After a minute or so, I unrolled it and read.

I found your letter and my heart breaks for you, Dani. I can't imagine the pain you must be feeling, and I'm so sorry for your loss. I don't believe in God, I don't believe the 'angels' needed your daughter, but I do believe that Trey and Hannah are together; they're not alone. I think we have to believe that, don't we?

I don't know if you'll even find this response. I walk this beach a lot. I like to think and be alone. I hope you do. I hope you get to see that someone understands just a little of what you're going through.

I won't tell you it gets better in time, it doesn't. It becomes different, bearable. But a part of us died, and that part will never come back to life. It doesn't work that way. You will heal, and it will be a new you that emerges on the other side. You won't forget, but you'll remember how to live again.

You have to, to keep them alive as well.

It wasn't signed. I turned the piece of paper over to see if the letter continued on the back. It didn't. I studied the handwriting. It was italic and as if written with a fountain pen. A small splodge of ink had dripped on the edge of the page. It was the type of handwriting I'd expect to see from an elderly person. I read it again. Whoever it was talked as if they understood loss, as if they'd experienced it themselves. Maybe it was a partner that had died. They'd been through tragedy and they'd survived.

I grabbed the small pad from the inside pocket of the jacket I wore. Dad had the foresight to add pads and pens, not only in every room of the house, but in every jacket and handbag I owned. I balanced the pad on my knee and I wrote.

I don't know who you are, but thank you. I feel your pain, too. I never expected anyone to pick up this bottle, I never expected anyone to take the time to read my letter and to reply. I'm actually at a loss as to what to say now.

You say it doesn't get better; it just gets different. Please, tell me what that means? Will I hurt this much for the rest of my life? I can't bear the thought of that. My mum died when I was a child, my dad brought my brother and me up on his own. He understands; I know he does, but it's not the same. I don't want him to feel my pain, to be reminded of his own. I don't want him to look at me with sadness in his eyes, because for the first time in my life; he can't make it all better. There are no words of comfort; there are no plasters or bandages big enough to piece me back together.

I lost my husband; we'd only been married for a short while. I lost my daughter; she hadn't even been born before she was pulled from my body. They told me she'd survived a few hours, but I never got to meet her then. I never got to feel her take breaths while lying in my arms. I never got to hold her skin on skin or kiss her forehead.

She died before I had the courage to wake up. And that's the part that kills me more each day.

I was a coward; I hid in sleep. She struggled to live, and I hid in sleep.

I can't...I don't know the words to convey how that makes me feel right now.

I have to go. I don't know if you'll get this, if you do, I'm sorry for your loss, too.

Dani.

I placed the letter in the bottle, screwed the cap tight and wedged it back in between the rocks. I had no idea if it would be found. I'd thrown mine out to sea. I didn't know where that bottle had washed up. Had he replied and then thrown the bottle back? Or had he wedged it between the rocks?

I paused. Why had I thought 'he?' There was nothing in that note to determine, yet somehow, I guessed the words to be from a man. Maybe it was the fountain pen, I didn't know anyone who used one anymore.

I stood and walked back, all the while thinking. That was the most I'd 'spoken' in ages. It felt like I'd just had a 'conversation' with someone without the use of the spoken word. I hadn't just written a few words in answer to a question. Why could I do that with a complete stranger and not my dad?

My head began to pound; I rubbed at my temples, hoping it was the biting cold and not a migraine. Or the fact I hadn't taken my medication in a couple of days. I'd been warned of going 'cold turkey' but I just wanted to see if the screaming in my head returned. If it did, I'd get back on them. I'd rather the numbness than the noise.

I itched to return to the beach. I made tea and sat outside, knowing I couldn't see from where I was, but just being outdoors made me feel closer to whoever it was. His words offered me comfort because they were honest. Time and time again I'd been told, 'things will improve,' 'one day you'll smile and laugh again.' I didn't want improvement, I didn't want laughter; I wanted understanding. I wanted forgiveness.

I needed forgiveness for not waking up and holding my daughter to my breast. I needed forgiveness for not letting my heartbeat be felt by her. I needed forgiveness for not kissing her goodbye.

I needed forgiveness for the feeling I felt when I'd picked her up in the hospital, the feeling of detachment. She hadn't felt like my baby, which was why I'd laid her straight back down. I needed forgiveness for not loving her enough in those moments.

The realisation that I finally understood the feelings coursing through me had me double over in pain. I wasn't just grieving the loss of my husband, of my daughter, I was grieving the loss of birthing a child, of bonding with that child.

It was conflicting. I loved Hannah, yet I hadn't wanted to spend time with her. I'd picked her up and laid her with her father, after holding her for the briefest of moments.

I angrily wiped tears from my cheeks when I heard the back door slide open.

"Dani, it's freezing out here, come on in," Dad said, as he came to stand beside me.

I reached for my pad.

I'm wrapped up warm. I was getting a headache. I thought this would help.

"Okay, baby, but at least let me make you a fresh tea."

I held up the cold mug for him to take. I heard the door slide open then close again. The sun was low on the horizon, and even though I dreaded to think about the temperature of the water, I could see the silhouette of a surfer standing on the sand, watching the waves with his board beside him. The summer would see surfers from around the country, the world. That beach was home to some of the best waves in the U.K., not that I'd ever mastered surfing.

"Patricia rang after you'd gone to bed, I guess she forgot about the time difference. She asked after you," Dad said, when I'd joined him in the kitchen. All I could do was nod.

"She said the weather was getting bad out there, they have a lot of snow predicted."

He poured hot water into mugs.

"Can you imagine having to shovel that amount of snow from your drive every year. Three, four feet deep, she said."

He rambled on as he poured the milk and stirred sugar into his mug.

"Anyway, I said I'd pass her message on. She's hoping to come over for a few days. I told her, she's more than welcome to come and stay here with us."

I noticed he hadn't said 'Christmas.' Not that I had any intention of celebrating. Another thing to grieve for, Trey had loved Christmas.

He placed the two mugs on the kitchen table and sat. "Anyway, I have a doctor's this morning, and then I have to go to the vet to pick up Lucy's meds. Do you fancy a walk with me?"

I reached for the pad.

Why do you need the doctor?

"Just the usual, old man check up. Nothing to worry about. It would be nice if you'd walk with me."

I looked at his face that held hope and I gently shook my head.

I'm sorry.

"Nothing to be sorry about, Dani. It's okay, I know, baby."

It must be so fucking frustrating for him. Having one-sided conversations with a daughter that had holed up in his house.

He placed his hand on my head and gently ruffled my hair, as he'd done so many times in the past.

As soon as Dad left, I retrieved the letter I'd received from my pocket. I read again, trying to picture the narrator in my mind. An older gentleman with grey hair; perhaps he had an old scratched writing desk beside an open fireplace. The paper looked to be high quality, the kind with the blue tint and faint blue lines. If handwriting could be described as stunning, his would. The letters were so perfectly joined up, on a slant and sharp. Maybe he had a convent education, or at least somewhere

24

where handwriting was taught, old school. For that moment, my mind wasn't focused on my misery but on the writer of the letter.

I analysed each word, found meaning behind the sentiment. I hoped he would reply.

✄

It was hard not to pull on my shoes and walk down the beach; it was an effort to hope that he had replied. I'd been offered counselling, I'd turned that down. What could anyone say to make it better? But just a couple of lines of pure honesty in his words had struck a cord.

I won't tell you it gets better in time, it doesn't. It becomes different, bearable.

Only someone who had suffered loss could have written those words.

Unless a therapist had experienced the same, how could they possibly expect to sit with me and understand?

I thought I heard the rattle of something metal. I turned to look down the hallway and to the front door, expecting my dad to walk in. When he didn't, I got up to investigate. On the odd occasion we'd have visitors, I would take myself to my bedroom, saving them, and me, the embarrassment of having to converse. I prayed we didn't have a visitor waiting outside for me to open the door.

I must have stood for a minute or two before I noticed it. On the mat just inside the front door was an envelope. A purple envelope. I bent down to pick it up. My name was handwritten on the outside. The writing was familiar and my hand shook as I stared at it.

I walked the stairs to my bedroom and curled into the leather chair placed in front of the window. I gently opened the envelope and pulled out a piece of paper, neatly folded in half.

Dani,

I think you needed me to reply, and I didn't want to run the risk of leaving this letter in a bottle on a beach. I didn't think you'd mind if I dropped it through your door. Of course, I know where you live. It's a small village, and I knew you when you were a child.

So, how does it become different? I can only tell you my story. The pain will subside; the numbness will chase it away. And maybe, for a while, the numbness is all you will feel. You might get scared that you won't ever feel again. I forced the feelings to come back, Dani. I did stupid things before I discovered that wasn't the answer.

Time is the only thing you have and if, like me, you're impatient, you'll find that time drags so very slowly. Let nature heal you, let time just tick away as it's supposed to.

You will survive this, but you will be different. You can't possibly be the same person. How you end up is your decision. You can drown yourself in alcohol, and hate the world more, or you can learn that life isn't fair. It's fucking shit sometimes, but there is nothing we can do about that. You can stop fighting and start accepting. Only then will you be able to come out the other side with part of you left intact. And it's that part that is the foundation from which the new you will emerge.

It's hard work, Dani. It's not easy; don't let anyone try to tell you differently. It's an effort to get up each morning, shower, and dress. It's hard work to force food into a stomach coiled so tight with acid and pain. But you have to.

Each day, without you even noticing, you are one step closer to being able to function without the crushing guilt and the endless pain.

Whether this is right or wrong, I'm pleased to have made your acquaintance. Maybe, we both need this.

If you want to reply, let's get creative. Just a short walk up the lane is the entrance to the farm. Don't worry, it's not mine, I don't live there. Outside the gate you'll see an old wooden box. It used to be an honesty box, maybe you remember. They would put a small table outside with apples; we'd drop a few coins in the box as payment. Leave your response there, Dani.

Soon enough the bottle will be taken out to sea and won't return. And I'd hate for you to think I didn't reply.

Lincoln.

Lincoln? I racked my brain; I didn't know a Lincoln, but he said he knew me as a child. Maybe he was a teacher and I'd only know him by his surname. I read the letter again. There were parts where I thought he was actually writing to himself, giving himself the advice he needed. His letter wasn't just to help me; it was to help him as well.

I read the letter through again. I paused over one part of a sentence…*we'd drop a few coins in the box as payment.* Had he meant *we* as in him and me? Or *we* as in the general public? I remembered the table with the apples, and especially liked to visit in October when the table would be filled with homemade toffee apples for Halloween.

His use of an expletive surprised me; maybe he wasn't the elderly man with the scratched writing desk, beside an open fire, that I imagined. I tried to remember the children in the small primary school I'd attended, the name Lincoln didn't ring any bells there. Not that I could remember that many names. Maybe Christian or Dad might know. But that would mean confessing to opening up to a complete stranger. Telling this *Lincoln* things they had been trying to get me to say to them. Would that hurt them?

I picked up my pad and pen.

Lincoln,

I'm pleased to know your name. I wondered if part of what you wrote was to yourself, as well as me.

I can't speak, physically there is nothing wrong with me, but I open my mouth and no words come out. I'm glad. I don't want to speak, so writing to you is the only conversation I've had since... You know, I can't remember the date it happened. It was early in the year, that's all I know. A truck drove into our car, it forced us off the road. Trey unclipped himself to protect Hannah and me; I was seven months pregnant at the time. If he'd stayed in his seat, he might not be dead. We all might have survived. At first, I was angry with him. Not now, now I know he sacrificed himself for Hannah and me, she just didn't make it. I don't actually know why. I never read any medical reports; I didn't want to know.

They're buried in the cemetery and I've never visited them. Other than to walk the beach, when I know it will be empty; I don't leave the house. I can't face meeting someone and them wanting to talk. Perhaps that gives you some idea why, for the first time in however many months, receiving your letter has lifted me a little.

You know, don't you? You know exactly how I feel. Who did you lose, Lincoln?

How long does it take? How long before I'll be able to feel some-thing again?

Dani.

I folded the letter and placed in the same envelope he had left through the letterbox. I wrote his name next to mine. I wasn't sure whether I'd make that short walk to the honesty box, but it felt cathartic to reply. I wanted to know his story; I wanted to know who he had lost and how he had survived. A small part of me felt selfish for asking him to relive that time. But then, I guessed, he wouldn't have written back in the first place if he hadn't wanted to share his story. It would have been inevitable that I'd ask, wouldn't it?

Dad had prepared dinner for us, I couldn't remember the last time I'd cooked a meal. I sat at the table with him and he chatted. Every now and again he'd reach across and place his hand on mine, giving it a squeeze. I looked at his hand, calloused from many hours of manual labour. My dad had been a carpenter before he'd retired. Most of the furnishings in the house were the product of his labour. But now the hand that held mine was riddled with arthritis, his fingers had started to curl and were bony. Soon it would be October, and although September hadn't been the late Indian summer we'd been promised, the cold winds that battered the cottage in winter would play havoc with his hands.

I studied his face as he spoke, while he ate. When did he get this old? What I remembered as fine lines around his eyes that got deeper with the laughter he always had for me, were more profound. His sparkling blue eyes were duller, filled with unshed tears. The tanned skin from days outside his workshop was paler. I should be caring for him, not the other way round.

I pushed my plate to one side.

How long has it been, Dad? I slid the pad over to him.

"Two hundred and fifty days, Dani," he said, without hesitation and completely understanding what I'd asked. "Not long enough, so don't you worry about a thing."

Two hundred and fifty days. I tried to calculate, eight months, or thereabouts. Somehow it seemed longer.

"You need to stop rushing it, baby. You know, when your mum died, I thought I'd die with her. I wanted to. I can't tell you how many times I picked up bottle after bottle of medication she'd been given. I emptied one in my hand one time. I wanted to take the lot. But I didn't. The thought of you and Chris wasn't the reason I didn't. Grief makes us *selfish,* although I hate to use that word. I didn't take them because I knew your mum would be furious at me. She would be so angry that she had no choice in living but I did. I had the choice to live; I had a choice that had been denied to her. You have a choice, Dani. You can live, or you can continue with this existence. And you know what, whatever your choice, it's okay."

For the first time in a while, I heard every word he'd said. Tears formed in my eyes. He reached over and wiped his thumb under one eye.

"Every day it kills me to see you in such pain. But I can tell you this. One day you'll wake up and the sun will shine, the birds will sing, and it will lift your heart a little. One day you'll speak, when you have something to say. Right now, you have nothing to give, so sit back and be looked after. I'm your dad, this is what I needed to live for."

He stood and cleared away the plates, not that I think he'd finished his meal; it was more so I didn't see his tears fall.

CHAPTER FOUR

"*G*oing for a walk? Watch those steps, Dani, they're getting slippery now."

Dad had seen me walk out the back door. I turned to him and nodded, I managed a small smile. He beamed back at me.

Since our *chat* at dinnertime, something had changed. I saw him through different eyes. And that tonne of weight that weighed heavily on my shoulders was lighter by an ounce or two.

I placed my hand in my pocket, wrapping it around the envelope, and I skirted the side of the house. I wasn't going to the beach; I was taking a walk up the lane to the honesty box. I paused halfway. *Honesty Box.* What I wrote, what Lincoln wrote, was about the most *honest* we'd been, I believed.

I stood by the newly painted metal gate and searched. Wedged into the hedge was the wooden box. I lifted the lid and looked inside. It was empty. I placed the envelope in and closed it, and then I walked back down to the cottage.

I didn't go in straight away, I passed the side window and saw the back of Dad's head as he sat on the sofa watching the TV. I pulled out the garden chair from under the table and sat.

How angry would you be at me for giving up, Trey? I thought. I knew the answer.

I wasn't ready to face life; I didn't know when I'd be. But I knew there were some things I needed to confront. I walked in to the living room with my pad and pen.

I can't remember what she looked like, and that hurts me.

"She was beautiful. She looked like you, the day you were born. Wait here," Dad said once he'd read my note.

I sat on the sofa and waited. A couple of minutes later, he returned. He held in his hand a photo frame. I took it from him and through the blur of my tears I looked at my daughter. Her eyes were open, big blue eyes stared up at a camera and her forehead was frowned, as if in indignation. She was wrapped in a blanket. Carved into the frame were her name, the date, and her weight.

Hannah Carlton – 03/02/16 – 3lbs2oz

How did they know her name? I wrote.

"They didn't, you told me. When you woke up, you told me her name."

I ran my finger over her face.

"That was taken by a nurse immediately after she was born."

I nodded, understanding why she looked so cross and why she was wrapped in a white blanket.

Did you see her?

"I sat with her day and night, Dani. I held her little hand. She was in an incubator thing and I watched her every second of the time she…"

Were you with her when…?

"Yes. They took her out of the incubator and I held her to my chest. Like they show on the telly. I opened my shirt and I placed her next to my heart. If she couldn't feel yours, she at least had a part of you through me. I wanted to bring her to you, even though you were unconscious; I wanted to lay her on your chest. But it wasn't to be."

I watched my tears fall onto the glass.

"I made three. Patricia has one, I have one, and that one is for you. I held on to it until I thought you were ready."

I mouthed two words—*thank you.*

"Do you want to know why you had the C-section?" Dad whispered. I nodded my head.

"You were bleeding, internally. The surgeon didn't think it wise to operate while you carried Hannah. So they delivered her, and then fixed you. I made a decision, Dani; a decision that was impossible to get right. Save you, and take a risk on Hannah's slim chance of survival, or maybe lose you both if they didn't operate."

I stared at him. He did nothing to hide the tears that fell from his eyes.

"I chose you, and I prayed every second of every minute of every day that Hannah would make it. If I had chosen otherwise, the surgeon would have overridden me anyway. Your life was more important."

I swallowed hard.

Lincoln didn't reply immediately. The day after I'd left the letter in the honesty box, I'd walked back up the lane, and although mine had gone, there wasn't a reply. Nor was there one the following day. At first, I wondered if my question had put him off replying. I walked along the beach and found the bottle missing, maybe the tide had finally taken it out.

I was still processing what my dad had told me. It had been the first time I'd learned of the details. I couldn't imagine the position he'd been put in, but there was a tiny piece of me that had hoped he would have given both Hannah and me just a little longer to see. Maybe another month on and she would have survived. But then, I didn't know if I would have had a month.

It was later that day when I walked into the kitchen and saw an envelope on the table. Dad was busy making tea. I sat and picked it up.

"That was on the doormat," he said. He didn't ask anymore and I didn't offer an explanation. I took the tea he handed me, picked up the envelope, and walked upstairs to my sanctuary by the window. I sat for a while, just looking out to sea and turning the envelope over continuously in my hand. Eventually, I opened it.

Dani,

My wife died of breast cancer a couple of years ago, now. She didn't tell me she'd felt a lump, she didn't ask me to accompany her to the doctor's, or the consultant for her diagnosis. She even started treatment without me knowing. I found out by mistake. I took a call from the oncology office, changing an appointment. Can you imagine the shock? I was so angry with her. She hadn't wanted me to worry about her. It was my job to worry about her! We fought, and I felt like a shit for walking out and slamming the door on her tears. Of course, we patched things up but I was hurt.

There will always be a little hurt inside I guess. I wasn't there to hold her hand and comfort her when she got the news. I wasn't there to question the doctors, ask for second opinions, or discuss treatment. I wasn't there when she had her first chemo session, and for a long time I felt excluded from her illness. I understand now, but it took time.

As for answering your second question—how long does it take to feel again? That's a hard one to answer. I felt anger, then sadness, then numbness. I screamed at the world for a while. I spent a long time looking at the bottom of an empty whisky bottle, wondering why I was still alive after consuming bottle after bottle.

It was six months before I realised being drunk all the time wasn't working. It was another two months before I was clean, before the shakes, the sickness, left me, and my body was cleansed of the poison I'd been feeding it. It was only then that I was able to breathe without the pain.

Shall I tell you a secret? When she started to lose her hair, she asked me to cut it off. I keep that hair in a little box. One day I intend to throw the hair into the sea, her favourite place. I can't bring myself to do it just yet.

Go talk to them, Dani. You don't need the details of what actually happened, but you do need to know one thing. I can guarantee Trey would have done the same thing over and over. Protecting you, protecting Hannah, it's instinct. It's inbuilt, part of our DNA, it's how our brains are wired. He did what came naturally to him, to us, to men in general.

You'll get there; don't put a time limit on it. There are no rules, Dani.

Lincoln.

I hadn't realised I'd been crying until a tear dripped onto his letter. Perhaps I'd already hit that numbness stage, maybe my sore cheeks had desensitised to the wetness. One thing happened in that moment. I felt. I felt his pain course through me, pushing mine to one side for a moment.

I cried for him and not for myself.

CHAPTER FIVE

*L*incoln and I wrote to each other, maybe twice a week, for another month before I felt able to visit Trey and Hannah. Over that month, he told me about his wife and I told him about times with Trey. We shared memories. Some of those memories hadn't been shared with anyone other than our dead partners. We shared secrets, fears, and we cried. He'd told me of his tears when he read my letters, and I told him of mine. Maybe it was the anonymity, but opening up through words on paper made the confusion start to dispel.

Not once in that time did Dad ask about the letters. He'd pick them up from the mat inside the door and leave them in the kitchen if I hadn't gotten to them first.

It had been ten months since Trey and Hannah died and for the first time I felt able to make a decision. First I needed to do something.

I'm going to the cemetery, I wrote, pushing the pad towards Dad.

"Do you want me to come with you?" he asked.

I thought for a moment. *I think I need to do this alone, but I'm scared to walk there myself,* I wrote.

"How about I drive you? I'll sit in the car until you're ready to come home."

The cemetery was within easy walking distance and I wasn't sure the last time Dad had used his car. I nodded though.

Dad rifled through a drawer for his keys. He held out a hand to me. It took longer to get the car from the workshop than it did to actually drive to the cemetery. As promised, Dad parked in the car park and let me walk to their grave alone. They had a head-stone; I didn't know where that had come from. I sat on the grass and ran my fingers over the marble. Engraved in silver were their names and dates.

I didn't cry that day, which surprised me. I expected to fall apart. I expected to feel that pain which had been a constant compan-ion. In my head, I talked to them. I told them about the letters and how talking to Lincoln had become some form of therapy for me. I told Trey about the decisions I was about to announce to Dad. I told Hannah I was sorry for not holding her. I told them both that I loved them, that I missed them.

"Okay?" Dad said when I opened the car door. I nodded.

He took hold of my hands between his and rubbed some warmth back into them. "Let's get you home, shall we?"

Dad pulled the car in front of his old workshop. It had been a barn used by the farm for many years before he'd bought it. It sat on the boundary of his garden. I climbed from the car and looked at the black, wooden clad building. I took hold of Dad's hand and encouraged him to walk with me. We circled the barn, stop-ping behind it to look out over the sea.

I hadn't brought my pad and I was desperate to ask him something. I opened and closed my mouth.

"What are you saying, Dani?" he asked.

I looked around. I bent down and pulled a piece of grass, I held it out to him then pointed to the ground. I walked away from the barn to a hedge, pointed to the ground again and then Dad.

He frowned and gently shook his head. I sighed in frustration.

"Wait! The land…" he said, I nodded enthusiastically.

"Is this land mine? Is that what you're asking?" I nodded again.

For some reason it seemed that it should have been something I would have known. Dad had owned the barn for years, but I'd never really taken notice of how much land surrounded it.

Dad took my hand and led me back to the entrance. He walked a square pacing out the boundary. There was plenty enough space to create a driveway and a small garden.

I pulled my hand from his and placed my palms together, I laid those palms against the side of my head, leaning in to them slightly. I then pointed to the barn.

"You want to sleep in there?" he asked. I nodded.

"It's an old workshop, I haven't been in there for years…Wait, you want to live there?" I nodded again, and a genuine smile formed on my lips.

"Well, I guess it could be converted. It would be a lot of work, Dani, and I imagine we'd need to get architects, the council, probably the bloody parish bigwigs involved. But you know what…" It was his turn to nod gently and then smile at me. "What a project that would be for us, huh?"

I took his hand again and walked back into the house. We went straight to the kitchen, and while he put the kettle on, I grabbed my pad.

I want Christian to put my house up for sale. I know he said to wait but it's time. I'm never going back, Dad. We can use that money to convert the barn; I can live there, next door to you.

I paused. I'd have hated for him to think I was desperate to leave him.

I don't want you to think I don't like being here, but I have to move on at some point. I don't want to leave you and this could be a perfect solution.

I slid the pad towards him when he sat.

"Don't you worry about leaving, or living with, me." He chuckled. "Dani, for the first time in months there's colour in your cheeks. We could burn the thing down afterwards, I wouldn't care, as long as it keeps that colour and maybe adds a little sparkle to your eyes as well. Let's do it."

I pulled the pad back towards me.

Will you ring Chris, ask him to deal with the house for me?

I knew Chris phoned every couple of days. Dad kept him informed of what was happening to me, he never told me what was happening to them. I guess they'd thought news of their baby wouldn't be welcome. I racked my brain to remember Helen's due date.

When is the baby due?

Dad didn't answer immediately. "The baby was born a few months ago, Dani. A little boy. They named him Alistair, after me, of course."

I covered my mouth with my hands, which was a ridiculous thing to do since they'd never shield the sound that *wouldn't* leave my lips.

"We all thought it might be a little too soon for you."

I shook my head. *But you missed out on the birth.*

"No, I've met Alistair, several times. Did we do wrong?"

I thought for a moment, and then gently shook my head.

I'm sorry.

"Don't be, Dani. We'd love nothing more than for you to meet Alistair, but we didn't want to upset you."

I understand. I'd like to meet him, though.

Dad smiled, I wasn't sure it was the breakthrough he imagined it was. Part of me asking was so Dad wouldn't feel that he'd have to sneak around to see his grandson. And my being at the cottage meant Christian and Helen felt they couldn't bring Alistair to him, I guessed.

"I'll call Chris now," he said. I gave him a nod.

I had no idea how long it would take to sell my house. I knew Chris had said I should have rented it out, but I hadn't been able to bring myself to do that. I knew I'd never return, and the compensation payout I was scheduled to receive, meant I didn't need to sell the house to convert the barn, but it made sense. I didn't want the pressure of being a landlady.

I could hear Dad in the hallway on the phone. While he chatted, I made more tea. I opened and closed cupboard doors; I made a shopping list while I did. I wasn't up to visiting a supermarket. To stand in a queue, or be in a crowded place filled me with dread, but I could start to do something instead of being waited on hand and foot.

"Alistair has a cold or the croup, or something. But Chris wants to visit tomorrow. Are you up for that?" Dad said when he walked into the kitchen.

I nodded and wondered if I was being lied to. Maybe Helen didn't want me to meet Alistair yet. I didn't think it would be for any malicious reason; rather, she was concerned I wasn't ready. I'd never be ready to hold another child. I'd never be ready to share utter joy at the birth, or the milestones, because I'd always wonder what we'd be doing with Hannah on her first birthday, her first Christmas. But I knew I had to.

❧

Lincoln,

I made a decision today. I'm going to meet my nephew. He was born months ago and I didn't know. I guess everyone thought they were helping me, they would have been right. I'm not sure how I'll feel, to be honest. I'm scared to hold him, to breathe in his scent.

You told me a secret in one of your previous letters, can I tell you one now?

I don't want to put pressure on you but writing to you, hearing back from you, has really helped. Perhaps it's because, although I know your name, your story, you're still anonymous. I can pour the words on paper and not worry because you understand.

Dad wants me to see a specialist, to see if they can work with me on talking. I haven't agreed yet. I'm still not convinced that I won't open my mouth and nothing but screams will emerge. I'm scared that my vocal cords won't actually work. So, for now, I'll just continue the way I am.

I've visited Trey and Hannah a couple of times now. It doesn't get any easier, and with Christmas looming, I'm sure things will get worse. Dad asked if I'd go to Midnight Mass with him; I can't do that. It would be hypocritical of me to sit in a church and pray to a God I don't believe in. I can't even do it just because it's the Christmas thing to do.

It seems that every time I write to you, I tell you only about myself. And I feel terrible about that. So, how are you? Tell me about your day.

Dani.

I folded the paper and placed it back in the original envelope. Why we'd stuck to that one envelope, I didn't know. It was grubby, frayed at the edges, and the only way to secure it shut was to place a small amount of tape on the flap. I waited until late afternoon before I walked up the lane and deposited it in the honesty box.

"There's an architect coming this afternoon, and Chris said he's contacted some estate agents who seem very keen to sign up your house," Dad said, when I walked back into the house.

I nodded but a pang of anxiety hit me. I'd have to try to communicate with the architect and that embarrassment I felt started to build.

"I thought what might be good is if you wrote a list of the rooms you wanted, that way we can give him that and let him come up with the best design." Dad had obviously pre-empted my anxiety.

I grabbed the pad and tapped the pen against the table as I thought. I wanted the barn to be an all open-plan, with floor-to-ceiling glass walls on one end. I wanted to be able to sit and watch the ocean. I wrote a list, a kitchen at one end that flowed through to a living room. I could put a dining table between the areas to break it up. A downstairs cloakroom would be handy, maybe doubling up as a utility room. Upstairs I just needed the one bedroom with perhaps an en suite.

"How about a guest room, if you have friends over?" Dad said, reading over my shoulder.

I paused. I'd received the usual, 'if you need anything, just call,' messages when the accident had first happened. I'd had the, 'you take all the time you need, your job will be here when you're ready to return,' statement from work. I didn't see or hear from anyone and my company quickly found a way to make me redundant. I wasn't sure I needed a guest bedroom but added it to the list, just in case.

For the first time, in a while, the constant nausea subsided. I couldn't say I was excited about the project but it gave me something other than my loss to focus on.

More importantly, for the first time in months, I saw a twinkle in my dad's eyes.

One of the problems I'd had, for most of my life, was suffering guilt when my actions caused someone else pain. My guilt levels were off the scale.

The fact that I couldn't speak turned out not to be a problem when the architect arrived. He spent an hour ignoring me and speaking only to my father. Dad tried to include me in the discussion, he'd look at me for an answer when a question was raised but the architect, Andrew The Asshole I called him, was only interested in what Dad had to say. That was until he found out I'd be paying his fees.

However, at the end of an hour consultation, he had a brief idea of what I wanted and seemed to think the council wouldn't object. There had been a lot of agricultural property converted to domestic dwellings in the area. A precedent had been set.

We were told that he'd have a provisional plan for us within a couple of weeks. His time frame suggested he wasn't overly busy, and I guessed his attitude might have had something to do with that.

I sat with Dad in his office and watched in astonishment as he worked his way through the local council website on his laptop. My dad, to me, was the last person I thought of a *silver surfer*.

"I know how to use a computer, I took some classes," he said, as if reading my thoughts.

His fingers paused over the keyboard; he quickly turned his head towards me.

"You chuckled!"

I stared back, frowning.

"You chuckled, Dani. You made a sound."

I shook my head and shrugged my shoulders. I heard every word I wanted to say, every sound I wanted to produce, in my head, but I hadn't been able to force those words out.

Are you sure? I wrote.

"Yes, try again, baby."

I opened my mouth. Nothing.

"You made a sound, when you didn't realise. Maybe you shouldn't *try*. But that's a good thing, isn't it?"

I was unsure. I mean, of course it was a good thing, or was it? Slowly I found myself nodding. Of course it was a good thing.

Was it a proper laugh?

"No, but it was a sound, as if you wanted to laugh."

Dad's smile grew wider and wider and I found myself smiling along with him. He reached out and ruffled my hair.

"You'll get there, baby. In time, you'll get there."

CHAPTER SIX

*D*ani,

    Today has been a busy day, thank you for asking. Busy days are often the best because we don't think too much! A fisherman took me out in his boat, to the spot I let go of Anna's ashes; it felt good. Although, I wouldn't say I was ready to completely let go of her then. We don't ever forget them but, like it has been for you, writing our letters has been a comfort, and I now feel I can start to live life again.

I moved out of our house shortly after she died. I rented for a while, but this weekend I'm going to move back in. The place needs a cleanup, of course, maybe a fresh coat of paint, but it will give me a project to concentrate on. I suspect I'll shed some tears, but they'll be accompanied with a smile and maybe laughter for all the memories we shared.

I'm glad you're going to meet your nephew; life has to carry on. I hope when you hold him, you'll be reminded of Hannah but you'll also smile at the wonder of a new life. All those 'firsts' will be tinged with sadness, but it gets easier.

As for Christmas? Do what you want on that day, remember them, cry for them. Your family will understand.

Lincoln

I'd picked up that letter late in the afternoon. For a while, I'd tried to time when I thought he'd post it through the door. There was a part of me that wanted to know the man behind the words, there was another part that didn't. What we had was a wonderful thing; we were able to confess, to bare our souls, without physically meeting. I was getting to know Lincoln through his letters and he was getting to know me. If we met, would either of us be disillusioned? I continued to wonder about his age, what he looked like, and where he lived. It was obviously close enough for him to leave a letter through the front door; I'd lived there for many years as a child, and didn't know of a Lincoln.

Maybe Lincoln wasn't his name. I couldn't imagine a reason why he'd use a false name, unless he wanted to stay anonymous. I wasn't entirely sure how I felt about that, however, asking him whether that was his real name or not wasn't something I was prepared to do. For now, the letters were a comfort to us both, no matter what name was written on the bottom.

The weather forecast for the next few days was rain and winds. I loved being by the sea in the winter, more so than in the summer. I loved to see Mother Nature at her angriest, the waves crashing against the shore, the rocks, and the cliffs. We'd get tourists all throughout the year, less in the winter, of course. I loved to walk the beach wrapped up against the elements and return home cold but refreshed.

I left Dad a note to say I'd taken a walk.

The good thing about walking the beach in the weather we were experiencing, was that it was empty. When I'd gotten to the end I

48

looked up the cliff. I could see the spire of the church and knew the cemetery was just a little way back from it. I took the walk up the cliff path and then along.

The cemetery was an addition to the overflowing one at the church. I pushed through rusty iron gates centred in a low stone wall. While I crouched down by Trey and Hannah's grave, I heard the squeak of the gate opening again. I peered around the headstone to see an elderly gentleman using a cane and wrapped up against the wind with a cream mac and matching scarf walk through. He headed in the opposite direction.

The wind was blowing my way and carried his gentle sobs with them. I didn't go to him, it would have been intrusive, and I sure wouldn't want anyone interrupting my grief. I heard him tell whoever lay beneath his feet about his week. I also heard him say goodbye, apologising for not being able to visit as often, since he was moving away. I watched as he raised a hand and wiped away a tear before he shuffled back the way he'd came.

When my knees ached, I kissed my fingertips and placed them over both Trey and Hannah's name. Before I left, I wandered over to the grave the gentleman had stood by.

Anna Nicolson-Carter

I turned, looking for the elderly man. Was that Lincoln? He'd told me his wife was called Anna. I suspected he'd be an elderly man. The birth date would suggest that Anna had died at age sixty-five, still relatively young. Although I hadn't really seen his face, the gentleman, by the way he walked, seemed to be a lot older. Lincoln had told me he planned to move back into his old home. He hadn't said where that was, though. I had no doubt we'd continue to write but the thought of him moving away saddened me. Maybe I should let him know I'd take care of Anna if he couldn't.

That thought brought me up short. Not that I had any intention of leaving the village, or Cornwall, but how do people, who have no choice, cope with leaving their loved ones behind?

Do you know Lincoln Nicolson-Carter? I wrote and pushed the note towards Dad.

He slowly shook his head, his brow furrowed as he tried to place the name.

"No, it doesn't ring a bell, why?"

I think that's the person that's writing to me.

Although Dad knew of the letters, we'd never discussed them. I decided to tell him.

I left a letter to Trey in a bottle on the beach; it seemed a good thing to do at the time. Then, the following day, I got a reply! We've been writing back and forth since.

Dad read, and then raised his eyebrows. "Wow, that's amazing. And you don't know who he is?"

I shook my head.

"I guess we could find out through the church's records, if you wanted to, of course."

Did I? I thought for a moment, and then shook my head. No, I didn't want to know. I was curious, but what we had was a lovely friendship that had developed simply through words on a piece of paper.

I thought of the name, maybe Lincoln didn't share the double-barrelled surname. Not being familiar with how they worked, did the husband adopt his wife's name as well? He could be Nicolson or Carter.

The telephone rang and Dad left the kitchen to answer it. No matter that it was a cordless phone, he still sat at the small telephone table in the hall. I guessed, learning the computer was about enough technological advancement for him to cope with.

I made some tea and handed Dad one as I passed to make my way upstairs. The walk had tired me out. In fact, pretty much everything I did tired me out. An afternoon nap had become routine, one I didn't want, as it meant I was awake earlier each morning. I sat in the chair facing the window and wondered how it would feel when the barn was done. I'd sit in the same position and look out over the sea. Dad didn't use his open fire that often, opting for the safer option of a boiler and mains gas. I didn't want that. I wanted to hear the crackle as logs spat, to have the smell of apple tree wood drifting around the house. I had no doubt my barn wasn't going to be particularly energy efficient, because I wanted the beams left exposed, but it was a sacrifice I was willing to make.

I picked up my Kindle, hoping to read a little. Nothing had kept my attention long enough and I scrutinised the description, avoiding anything over emotional. I also didn't want humour. I placed it back on the table beside me, not knowing what I wanted to read.

Instead, I picked up my pad and pen. I didn't write that day, I drew. I hadn't drawn since I was a teen, and even then, I was never quite sure if I was particularly good at it. I drew the view from the window. The layers of rock that cut into the cliff were ancient and had always fascinated me. I likened each layer to the rings of a tree trunk, giving age and a story of life. Even on a rainy day, the scenery was beautiful. The cliff face I could see was black, with a rainbow of colour streaking through, wet from the rain and glistening. The grass was a vibrant green, tinged with cream, as the gorse fought for dominance. Scattered around were the wildflowers that had learned to survive the harsh winters. Although not in abundance, they gave a smattering of colour and softening to an otherwise harsh environment.

My pen couldn't do the scene in front of me justice. I wondered if I should put some art supplies on my list of things to buy. I found sitting there and drawing relaxing, frustrating, but when I was done, I smiled at my efforts. It wasn't about to grace a wall in a gallery but I'd enjoyed the process.

It was, as predicted, a couple of weeks later that we received the drawings from the architect. That evening Christian decided to visit; he had an update on estate agents for me.

"Hey, Sis, how are you doing?" he asked, as he walked through the front door.

I gave him a smile and a hug. At first it felt awkward, Christian would speak then pause, as if waiting for me to answer. Dad took over and ushered us to the kitchen table. Teas were made and Dad showed Christian the plans for the barn. Ten or so minutes later the conversation flowed. They spoke, I wrote.

"These are the three valuations, they're all about the same, to be honest, but I think this estate agent might be better for you," Christian said, sliding a brochure across the table.

That's fine; will they let you deal with all? I wrote on my pad.

"Yes, although, you'll have to sign the documents. I'll call them tomorrow. They all seem to think the house is very desirable, but then I guess, they all say that." He laughed as he spoke.

Christian was a corporate lawyer in a *shit-hot* firm in London, as my dad called them. I had no doubt he'd take good care of me. I sat and listened as Dad and Christian spoke. An hour or so later, I interrupted them.

How's Alistair, have you any pics?

In the time that Christian had been there, he hadn't mentioned Alistair once.

"Erm, yes, he's doing great." I could see that he was holding back the grin as he thought of his son.

When are you bringing him over?

I watched his eyes flick to Dad. "He's had croup, so Helen didn't want to let him out of the house, but maybe next week?"

I'll look forward to it.

Something told me that they didn't think I was ready for a visit with my nephew and that pissed me off. I hadn't heard from Helen since the funeral; in fact, I hadn't heard from anyone. I decided to change the subject.

So we need to find a builder once these are sent to the council, don't we?

"I think it might be wise to source a builder now, he might look at those plans and have better suggestions or concerns," Christian said.

I nodded, agreeing with him.

"I'll ask around for recommendations," Dad added.

Christian left for his four-hour drive home after dinner. His visit had left me feeling despondent. Why should my grief have caused the distance that had obviously appeared?

"They don't know how to behave," Dad said, picking up on my low mood I guessed.

Normal would be good! I wrote.

He sighed as he placed his hand on my shoulder and gave it a gentle squeeze.

"Christian doesn't remember as well as you do, or doesn't want to remember, how it was when your mum passed. So, I guess, this is the first time he's had to deal with loss. We're all winging it really."

I'm going to head to bed. Thank you, Dad, for everything.

"Nothing to thank me for, baby."

I left him locking up the house, turning off the lights, and muttering to his dog.

I took a shower before sliding under the duvet. I'd left the curtains open, and once I'd turned off the bedside lamp, I looked out the window. The moon's reflection shimmered on the surface of the sea. I thought about Christian and Helen, my dad, and whether the man at the cemetery was Lincoln.

I heard a low voice coming from downstairs, a voice not belonging to my father. I climbed out of bed, and had a quick shower, before throwing on some clothes.

"Morning, Dani, this is Miller. Miller, my daughter, and soon to be owner of the barn, Dani," Dad said, making the introduction.

I swallowed hard, not expecting to have someone in the house. I held out my hand for a shake and forced a smile.

"Erm, my daughter can't…"

"Talk? Speech is overrated, Dani. It's a pleasure to meet you," Miller said with a smile as he shook my hand. "So how about we take a look at the plans and you can show me around the barn?"

His smile was warm, broad. He didn't appear to be much older than me but had that rugged *outdoor* look. Dark brown hair flopped over his forehead and I watched as he ran his hands through it, pushing it from his eyes. He wore torn, faded jeans, tucked into sand-coloured work boots. A black t-shirt was taut across his toned body.

Dad had made tea and gestured to a chair at the kitchen table. Miller sat and reached for the rolled up plans.

"So you want to convert the barn?" he said, looking at me. "Amazing spot with a great view, I imagine."

I looked around the room. Miller leant back in his chair; he grabbed the pad and pen from the countertop.

"You need these?" he asked.

I nodded. My hand shook a little as I wrote. I wasn't sure what it was that had my anxiety levels increased, other than the embarrassment of meeting a stranger and having to write instead of speak. I blinked back the tears I knew were starting to form in my eyes, while inwardly cursing myself for being so daft.

This is what the architect came up with, I wrote.

He nodded as he read. "But is it what you want?"

I shrugged my shoulders; *I guess so.*

He smiled at me while Dad took a seat beside me.

"Okay, first, architects know shit all about building," he chuckled as he spoke. "See here? We have a kitchen at the front of the building. That's great; you want the living at the back. But up here…?" he pointed to the en suite. "We'll need to get the plumbing from mid-house to the front, to line up with kitchen. Of course, it's totally possible but adds to the budget. And if your guest needs to pee in the night, they have to come downstairs, or traipse through your bedroom."

He took the pen from my hand. "You want a guest bedroom, so how about the kitchen is in the middle of the house? You have your dining area one side and your living the other. You have windows at the front and back of the barn, that's enough light for downstairs. Upstairs, we have two bedrooms, both en suite."

He scribbled on the plans as he spoke.

"Can we do that?" Dad asked.

Miller looked up, his smile and the wrinkles that appeared around his dark blue eyes were mischievous. "We can do what we like, for now. The council may have other ideas, of course."

I reached for the pen. *Why didn't the architect think of that?*

"Most have never even put up a shelf! What he's done here is what you asked, of course, but with no thought of logistics. I used to be one, so I know how they work," he said.

You were an architect? I wrote.

"Yep, for a short time, but creating something has always been my passion."

"Miller was highly recommended," Dad said.

"I don't just build houses, Dani, I create homes. You have to live here; it has to work for you without compromise, if possible. I can take you to some of my clients so you can see what I've done. What your architect has given you is okay, but with just a little more thought, or knowledge, it could be amazing."

Can you draw new plans?

"If you want me to, of course," Miller said.

I looked over to Dad who nodded. *Okay, can you do that for me, please? Then we need to submit them,* I wrote.

"Of course, I can submit them on your behalf, if you want me to. But don't make a decision until I've priced it up. You might not like my price," he laughed as he spoke.

The sensible thing would be to get new plans, then three quotes from various builders but for some reason, I trusted Miller already. He hadn't made a deal about my lack of speech, he hadn't tried to exclude me from conversation, and he hadn't been fazed at all by me.

"Do you want to show me around?" he asked, looking directly at me.

I slowly nodded, picking up the pad and pen and shoving them in my cardigan pocket.

"I'll make another cup of tea and bring it over," Dad said, giving me a nod of encouragement.

I hesitated, unsure why at first. "We can always wait for the tea, Alistair," Miller said, addressing my dad.

Miller has picked up on my hesitancy and that had me warm to him further. I smiled and gestured with my hand for him to lead the way.

Within a minute, I'd wished I'd picked up a jacket. I pulled the cardigan tighter around me, wondering how the heck Miller could stand the chill in just a t-shirt. He must have seen the shiver that ran over me. He headed to his truck and returned with a worn leather jacket, the kind a biker might wear, and a spray can.

"Here," he said, as he draped it around my shoulders. I gave a nod of thanks.

Miller talked as we walked around the building. He sprayed where the side windows would be to give me a visual of their position. He would speak, and then make a point to look at me, waiting for my written answer. I fished in my jeans pocket for the key to the padlocked door. It creaked as I pulled it open. Miller scanned the wall for a light switch. When Dad and I had driven to the cemetery, I'd waited outside for him to reverse the car out. I hadn't been inside the barn since I was a teenager.

"Wow, look at those beams, Dani," Miller had placed his hand on my arm to gain my attention. "Please tell me we're keeping those."

I looked up, following his gaze. Dark oak beams crisscrossed the ceiling above us.

"I have an idea." The excitement in his voice had me smiling. "Why not have an upside down house? Put the bedrooms down here and your living space up there. That way you not only get the view of the cliffs and the sea but those beams, as well."

For the first time in a while, I felt a bubble of happiness explode in my stomach. It startled me, if I was honest. It was too soon to be happy about anything, wasn't it? However, I found myself nodding and reaching for the pad and pen.

I love that idea, I wrote.

"I'll take some measurements, then draw up some new plans. Probably take me a couple of days, but I have a job to finish before I can start on them, is that okay?"

Of course, thank you.

"I'll get new drawings over to you as soon as I can, and use them to get other quotes in, okay?"

I nodded as I replaced my pad and pen. Miller took a walk around, pacing out and mumbling to himself. Just as Dad arrived with fresh tea, he headed to his truck, returning with a tape measure, a pad and pencil, and a camera. We watched while he measured, sketched, and photographed every aspect of the barn. He prodded walls, beams, kicked at the dusty floor and rattled the frame.

"There's a lot of wood here we can reuse, some of the structural beams might need to be replaced though, that one is rotted through," he said, as he took his tea from Dad.

He explained to Dad how he thought an upside down house might work better, and it pleased me to see that he would shift his gaze to me, to keep me in the conversation.

Miller left shortly after and Dad and I locked up. I threaded my arm through his and we walked back into the warmth of the house. It was as I listened to Miller's truck leave the drive that I realised I still wore his jacket.

CHAPTER SEVEN

*J*felt conflicted. I was excited about the build and that didn't feel right. It hadn't been that long ago that my world had been torn apart, thrown off its axis. I sat on my chair in my bedroom, looking at Miller's jacket hanging on the back of the door. I liked him, not in a sexual way, I felt comfortable around him. I picked up my pad and pen.

Lincoln,

I met a builder yesterday; he came up with some wonderful ideas for converting Dad's workshop. It's a barn sitting next door and I plan to live in it. I asked my brother to put my house up for sale; I have no intention of going back to London.

I don't know how long the planning process is, and what with Christmas just around the corner, I doubt this will start until some time in the new year but I feel excited about it. And guilty. Should I feel excited? How long should I mourn? How long should I grieve? It has only been about ten months, or so, and whether this is rational or not, I feel I'm letting them down by making this move. It's as if I'm moving on with my life, yet they never can.

Dad and I have decided to have a quiet Christmas this year. Just us. It made me sad, to be honest. Normally, each year he alternated between Christian and me but he, we, haven't been invited this year. I get the feeling they don't want me around, or rather, they don't want my misery around, and I'm starting to feel a little bitter about that. Is bitter better than the sadness?

I did tell Dad that he should call them, ask what their plans were. I'd love for him to go, and if I'm not invited, then so be it. I'll stay home. I know Dad wouldn't go without me but I don't understand what's happening. I want to write Christian a letter; I think I'll be able to explain how he and Helen are making me feel by trying to 'do the right thing.'

Do you have plans for Christmas? I should look online and order a few presents. I'm trying real hard to get into the spirit of things for Dad's sake, more than mine. Who knows how many Christmases we'll have left together.

Do you wonder that, Lincoln? How long do we actually have? I see inspirational posts on social media, people saying, 'live each day as if it's your last.' But that's not realistic. Real life doesn't always allow it. I'm getting morbid now.

I started to draw again; it was something I'd enjoyed as a teen. I'm not particularly good but I find it relaxing.

Have you moved back home already? I hope, if you have, it wasn't painful for you. I hope you had the chance to smile, maybe laugh a little as you thought of Anna.

Hope to hear from you soon,

Dani.

I spent some time reading back over the letters he'd sent. I'd built a picture of him in my mind, based on the man I'd seen in the cemetery. I picked up my drawing pad and sketched that image. I imagined him sitting at his desk with his fountain pen, beside an open fire. I wondered if he had an elderly dog at his feet that he'd pet every now and again. Did he speak out loud to the silence that surrounded him just to hear a voice, some noise?

Those thoughts pulled me up short. My dad had been alone for years. Although I'd lived four, maybe five hours drive away, I'd try to visit as often as I could but not as frequently as I should have. I knew Christian visited monthly, but my dad was like Lincoln—alone for most of the time.

It was a bright morning, the sun that snaked across my bedroom floor picked up small particles of the dust that floated around. I couldn't think of the last time I'd cleaned, and Dad didn't like to intrude in my 'personal space,' as he called it. I looked at the photograph of Hannah and the usual pang of guilt hit me. It made me question what kind of a mother I would have been. I hadn't been able to hold her, she was a part of me and I hadn't felt the connection I'd read about. I hadn't looked at her and noticed her beautiful silky strands of fair hair. I hadn't taken in her perfect rosebud lips, or her small fingers curled into fists. There had been no 'new baby' smell. I rose and picked up the photograph. I held it to my chest as if I could inject some life, some warmth, into it.

I didn't cry that morning. Maybe I was all out of tears, and there was a small part of me thankful for that. I didn't want to cry anymore. I was beginning to enjoy the numbness.

After my shower, I dressed and made my way downstairs. Dad hadn't woken, so I took my tea and sat with Lucy in the back garden. She pottered around, sniffing for visitors in the night. She whimpered a couple of times as her poor arthritic legs adjusted to the chill and movement. It wasn't long before she came and sat beside me. She rested her head on my lap and her chocolate-coloured eyes looked up at me. She looked as sad as I must have. I stroked her head and she closed her eyes with contentment.

"I wondered where you were," I heard.

At the sound of her master's voice, Lucy raised her head and looked towards the back door. She wagged her tail as Dad joined us.

I watched the wince cross his face as he took a seat. I guessed his arthritic bones were protesting at the cold as much as Lucy's were. I remembered back to a time when Dad had talked about moving away, somewhere warm. He couldn't tear himself away from the house he'd lived in with my mother, though. He was attached to the property and her memory. I wondered why I didn't feel that way.

I never thought of my house in London. Was I betraying Trey's memory in some way? I'd wanted nothing more than to run as far away as possible from the home we'd shared.

"Miller wants to take another look around the barn, with a structural engineer this time," Dad said.

I nodded, reaching in my pocket for a pad and pencil.

What does a structural engineer do? I wrote.

"Well, you want to take out one wall, there will have to be some steels in place to hold up the roof, I imagine. An engineer would have to advise on load-bearing and all that stuff. And he has to create a second floor. I like his idea of the bedrooms downstairs, though. Can you imagine, sitting up top and just looking out to sea each day?"

Who recommended him to you? I turned the pad towards Dad.

"He was born here but moved away for a while. Anyway, he did some work for Mrs. Hampton, you know her? She owns the shop. And, obviously, the vicar recommends him. I think he does a bit of free work at the church when needed. If a vicar recommends someone, you know you're in for a good thing." Dad laughed at his statement.

I'm going to take a walk over to the barn, want to join me?

"Sure. I guess we should make a start at clearing it out. Perhaps I should organise a skip, I'm pretty sure most of what's in there needs to be thrown."

We walked to the barn and opened the creaking door. A tool bench ran along one side. There were boxes of items piled high against one wall. I tapped Dad on the arm and pointed to the boxes.

"You know, I have no idea what's in those. I guess it's all your childhood things; they've been here for years. Let's get one down."

He reached up and grabbed one of the boxes from the top of the pile. He laid it on the workbench and opened it. He pulled out something wrapped in white tissue paper.

"Jesus, I remember these. Your mother had this dinner service given to her as a wedding gift. We used to laugh because it was hideous. Some old aunt gave it to her, I think. Might be worth money nowadays." He laid a white and blue plate on the bench before reaching in to grab another.

I picked up the plate. I was sure it was a design I'd seen before, usually in a quaint coffee shop. The plate had a delicate flower decoration. I turned it over. Although faded I could see that it might have possibly been made in Denmark. I didn't think it had any value other than sentimental, but I liked it.

Can I have these?

"Of course. It would be a shame to throw them away, I guess."

Sitting in my London home was stark white, modern crockery. It suited London; it wouldn't suit the barn. We put the box to one side, satisfied all it contained was crockery. The next box held my childhood possessions. I smiled as I reached in and pulled out Panda. He'd lost the rings of black around his eyes, the red bow tie that I recalled him wearing, and he was a little grubby, but I remembered him fondly.

"That was the first bear you owned. I bought that from the market on my way to the hospital…"

Dad's sentence tailed off. I knew the story; the day I was born he'd given me that. It was bigger than I was. I guessed he didn't want to talk about births. I squeezed his arm, hoping he understood the gesture. It was okay. I wasn't about to break down at his memories of my own birth. I placed the bear to one side. Aside from the usual first, sixteenth, and eighteenth birthday cards, the box contained old diaries I had never completed, notes from school friends, school reports, hair ribbon that, for some reason, had never been thrown away.

"I think maybe you should go through all this, decide what you want to do with it," Dad said.

In addition to the boxes there were tools: so many old carpentry tools in pristine condition. I remember my dad being studious about cleaning his tools after every use.

"Maybe Miller might like these," he said, picking up what looked like a wooden hammer and chisel.

"Like what?" I heard. I startled at the low tones of his voice as they echoed through the barn.

"Miller, we were just talking about you," Dad said.

Miller strode into the barn; he wore dark jeans with a checked shirt. With the scruff that covered his chin, his physique, and the tattoos down one arm that I'd noticed before, he looked like a lumberjack. That thought brought a chuckle to my mind.

"I thought you might like these old tools," Dad said.

"Hi, Dani, how are you today?" he asked with a smile. I gave him a smile and a nod in return.

He picked up one of the tools from the bench; I noticed the grazes to his knuckles.

"These are great, Alistair. I'd love to have whatever you want to get rid of. I remember my dad using one of these. I'd get a tanned arse if I ever tried to touch it," he said with a laugh.

"Your dad was a carpenter?"

"In his spare time, he taught me all that I know. He'd call himself a master craftsman, if I remember. He could turn his hand to pretty much anything."

I grabbed my pad and pencil.

Does he still do carpentry?

"No, he stopped working when… Well, he hasn't done anything for a long time, shame really. Anyway, I wanted to check on some measurements before I give you revised plans, that's okay isn't it?"

"Of course, how about I make some tea?" Dad said, as he headed to the door.

I wondered what Miller was going to say about his dad. I didn't ask, instead I watched as he placed a pencil behind his ear. There was no high-tech laser measuring devices for Miller, just a good old-fashioned tape measure.

"You know, Dani, this is going to be an amazing house. It has such wonderful vibes, there's history in these beams beyond our years. If it could only talk to us, imagine the secrets it could tell."

I liked his enthusiasm; he stroked beams as if coaching those secrets out through his fingertips.

"It reminds me of you," he said, not looking at me. "Everything has a story to tell, and sometimes we have to work around using conventional words. This beam here, it's way over a hundred years old, I imagine, and most probably part of a ship in its former life. Imagine the seas this beam has sailed on, the countries it's visited, yeah, everything has a story to tell." He seemed to be talking to himself.

I picked up my pen and wrote.

What story do you have to tell?

I didn't show him the page, though, in fact, I scribbled through the message. It seemed an intrusive question and I wondered why it had popped into my head. Miller measured, he wrote those down on a scrap of paper that he'd retrieved from his jean pocket. Eventually, he turned to face me.

"Did you think any more on an upside down house?"

I nodded. I'd loved the idea as soon as he'd proposed it.

I think that would be wonderful. I'll still be able to have that picture window at one end, though, won't I? I wrote and then showed him my pad.

"Of course. We'll take down that whole back wall, insert a beam where the floor is going to be, and it will be glass top to bottom. I'm sort of jealous that you'll get to sit there all the seasons and watch the sea." He laughed when he spoke.

There was something about his voice that comforted me. It was low, baritone, and so smooth. The kind of voice that could lull me to sleep.

Do you like the sea?

"I used to. I have a small boat but I don't use it that much nowadays. I guess I should get rid of it, it's cluttering up the front garden."

Dad returned with a tray and three teas. He handed me one and I wanted to laugh at the clichéd 'builders' mug with the strongest-looking tea I'd ever seen. I didn't need to guess who was about to be presented with that one.

Miller took a sip from the 'builders' mug and I watched as he winced a little. Whether that was the taste or the heat, I wasn't sure.

How long do you think this will take? I wrote.

"Planning could be up to three months, and that's if it's all straightforward. The conversion? I'd say about another four to five months. To be honest, I hate to put a firm timeframe on anything until we get going. I'll need to do some testing to see what foundations we have, if any. Half the time, these old barns were just put straight on the ground."

Miller placed his mug back on the tray; he pocketed his pencil and the piece of paper then rolled up his tape measure.

"Thank you for the tea. Hopefully, I'll see you in a few days with some drawings," he added.

Dad walked him out to his truck, and it was as he was driving away that I remembered his jacket. It was still sitting in my bedroom. I locked up the barn and walked to the warmth of the house.

Miller's words swam around my head. He likened me to the barn, not able to speak words but having a story to tell. I wondered what he knew about me. Had someone in the village told him? It was a traditional small village, full of gossipy women and although they wouldn't have been unkind, I guessed I would have been a source of entertainment for a little while.

As I entered the kitchen, I saw the familiar purple envelope on the mat beside the front door. Although I'd been inside the barn, I hadn't heard anyone approach the house. Dad walked in carrying the tray as I pocketed the envelope. I indicated I was going upstairs. Being out in the cold, and a restless night, had me wanting to curl up in my chair, snuggle under the comforter, and nap. Not before I read the letter, of course.

Dani,

I don't have plans for Christmas, I never make plans, for anything. To be honest, I like to spend the day alone. It's not to wallow, just to be.

I'm glad you've found a builder and it seems, through your words, that a little excitement is entering your life, something to take the focus off your sadness. That's a wonderful thing, isn't it? Having something, a project, is a great thing to do. Just for a few moments, a couple of hours, to have something other than your grief is a blessing. Grief is so tiring sometimes. I'm pleased you're able to find this to inject some energy into yourself.

I have moved, and it wasn't easy. Every room has memories, and although I'm repainting each room, I struggled. I felt like I was erasing her and I didn't want to. I'm a way on from where you are, Dani, but every now and again I'm pulled up short. I'm reminded that she shadows me, and I love and hate that in equal measure. She'd hate for me not to have moved on with my life. She'd hate for me to shed a tear at repainting a wall, removing her favourite colour. Daft isn't it?

Like Trey, Anna would be upset with every down day I, or you, have. If she were here, she'd be kicking my backside, for sure.

I'm sorry for such a short letter today, Dani. I've decided there is something I need to do, a reconciliation of sorts, and without you even knowing, I need to thank you for that.

Lincoln.

For the first time I notice there was sadness within his words, and I pondered on the 'reconciliation' he talked about. I imagined moving back into the house he shared with his wife had caused him painful memories. In that moment, I wished that we'd met, that I knew him personally. I would have comforted him, and I felt in that moment he needed someone. Maybe I was being presumptuous. Perhaps he had a circle of friends to rely on. His comment about spending Christmas alone also bothered me. I wanted to reach out, invite him to join Dad and me. I didn't want to picture him in his house all alone, even if he did have that imaginary dog by his side.

I found myself worrying for him and not for myself.

CHAPTER EIGHT

I didn't get a chance to write back to Lincoln for a couple of days. Miller arrived with a structural engineer, and I let Dad deal with that, I had some paperwork from Christian to go through. It seemed all so formal; I signed to give permission for him to deal with the sale of my property on my behalf. I signed the estate agent's contract and mailed them back to Chris. He had placed a note among the documents to inform me that he would organise a removal company to pack up all my furniture. I wondered why the need for the note and not a visit. Something seemed very off between us, I felt it. I was, like most twins, very much in tune with my brother. Although I didn't want it to be true, I believed he couldn't deal with my grief. He struggled to see how fragile life was, especially being a new father himself. It saddened me, but there was a part of me that understood. If Hannah had lived, and Christian's baby had died, I thought I'd struggle, too.

I opened the drawer of the desk in my bedroom. I'd had that desk when I'd been in school. After I retrieved the stack of letters from Lincoln, a thought hit me. Lincoln knew me; in the barn were boxes of my childhood things. I had wondered if Lincoln might have been a teacher at my primary school. Maybe, among those things I might find something that gave the names of my teachers. I doubted they would give first names but there might be something. It surprised me to learn that I wanted to know who he was. I'd been perfectly happy to keep the anonymity of the man in the words, but I was still troubled by his last letter.

I tried to remember the surname on the grave I'd seen the old man visit. Anna something. It wasn't a conscious effort to grab Miller's jacket, it was simply the first one my hand landed on. I filled one pocket with a pad and pen, in case I needed to make a note. I pulled on my boots and made my way down the stairs. Dad was still in the barn as I made my way along the coastal path, towards the church.

The rusting gate creaked as I pushed my way through. I hesitated as I came to the path that would take me to the newest section, where Trey and Hannah lay.

I'll be back in a minute, I said, in my head.

At first I struggled to remember the exact location of the head-stone. When I found it, I noticed fresh flowers and a small pile of weeds that had been plucked from under the headstone and placed to one side.

Anna had died just two years ago; that seemed, in my mind, to tie in with Lincoln's letters. Not that he'd given those details but he had said he was a way on from the source of his grief. I sat down on the cold earth beside her. I opened my mouth, it was unconscious, but I heard the squeak that left my lips. It sounded so strange, strangulated, and strained. I tried again, nothing.

I placed my hands over my throat; I wanted to see if the muscles worked. I had no real idea what part of my body moved when producing sound. I knew I should feel vibration but when I tried, I felt nothing. So I talked to her in my head.

When I was done, I rose, rubbing my hands over my backside to gain some warmth through the cold jeans. I walked over to where Trey and Hannah were. Their grave and headstone seemed so clean compared to Anna's. It was white marble, not what I would have chosen, had I been in the right state of mind to make that decision. I ran my fingers, as I always did, over their names.

I took a slow walk back to the house. All the while I thought of Trey and Hannah, I wondered about Anna and Lincoln. I was sure the man I'd seen that one time was him. My curiosity got the better of me and I turned around and headed back to the church. I pushed open the door; not knowing if the information I was seeking would be inside. The church was empty and in that moment, I was thankful. Had I encountered anyone, I wasn't sure if my embarrassment would get the better of me. Other than Miller and the architect, I hadn't seen anyone since I'd been at Dad's.

There was something serene about being inside the church, not that I was religious. It was the calmness of an ancient building, the history that whispered around me that seemed to have soothed my mind. I took a seat in the front pew.

"May I join you?" I heard. The voice startled me and I spun in my seat. A vicar stood beside me.

I opened my mouth, but of course, no words emerged. He held up his hand and smiled. He had a kind smile.

"Dani, isn't it?" he asked. I nodded my head and then shuffled up when he indicated with his hand towards the pew.

"We don't get too many visitors nowadays; it's such a shame," he said as he sat.

I patted my jacket for my pad and pencil.

I'm sorry, I can't talk, I wrote.

"I know. But you can, inside I bet," he replied.

I wasn't sure how to reply so simply nodded.

"I saw you at your husband and child's grave. I imagine that must be extremely painful for you."

All I could do was nod again.

"You know something? We don't need to verbalise to communicate, it helps, but it's not necessary. It's our actions that count."

I held my breath waiting for the 'God Talk.' He chuckled. "Sounds so bloody easy, doesn't it?" His expletive, although mild, surprised me. I smiled at him.

He turned slightly in his seat to face me and held out a hand. "Daniel, at your service. Should you ever need my services, of course."

I took his hand in mine and shook it.

I thought I might find some answers, but I don't know where to look, I wrote.

"Answers to what? Life and the universe? I'm pretty sure that might bore you to screaming point." He laughed out loud and I warmed to him.

Do you know someone named Lincoln? I think he might be the husband of Anna; she's buried outside. I turned the pad so he could read.

He gently shook his head. "The name doesn't ring a bell. Would you like to show me where Anna is?"

I smiled and started to rise. He stood and stepped from the pew, holding out his arm so I could lead the way. Daniel followed me to Anna's grave.

"Sadly, Anna was laid to rest before I came here, but there would be records. I could check for you, they are available for public scrutiny."

I tried to write while balancing the pad on my thigh.

I would appreciate that, I wrote.

"How about you give me a couple of days and let me see what I come up with?"

I nodded and smiled my thanks.

"I'll let you get on. I'm sorry I disturbed your peace, but please, feel free to just come and sit anytime you'd like."

I watched him walk back to the church. He hadn't been the vicar that presided over Trey and Hannah's funeral; I guessed that meant he was relatively new. He was young, and I wondered how he'd fare with the older, more traditionalists, that lived in the village. Not that any of that mattered, if he was able to find some information on Anna, I might get a little closer to understanding who Lincoln was.

I pulled Miller's jacket tight across my chest as I walked back. The wind had picked up and it was biting. Dark storm clouds rolled in so quickly it took me by surprise. My hair swirled around my face, and the wind caused my eyes to water, blurring my vision. I could see someone standing on the edge of the cliff, at the bottom of what would ultimately be my garden. I lowered my head and walked a little faster. A clap of thunder startled me, and I began to run. Being caught in the wind and rain at the edge of a cliff top wasn't where I wanted to be.

"Quick," I heard. I looked up to see Miller holding the barn door open.

As he spoke, so the heavens opened. The rain fell in sheets so dense, for a moment, it was difficult to see where to go. I

77

faltered, already soaked through. I felt a hand grab my arm and I was pulled along to the open door of the barn.

"Are you okay?" he asked, standing in front of me.

I pushed my sodden hair from my forehead and shivered with the cold. I nodded.

"It's a bit treacherous to walk that path in this weather."

I pulled the damp pad from the pocket.

It was nice when I went out, I wrote.

"Bad weather rolls in so quick here. You should be careful."

I stared at him. *I know. I was born here, lived here for many years.* I scribbled, annoyed at being chastised.

He chuckled. "Sorry, I didn't mean to offend. Did you know your handwriting changes when you're annoyed? So does your face, of course."

I sighed and shook my head, then smiled at him. He was just being kind, I thought.

"Ready to run for the house? Doesn't look like this is letting up any time soon, and I'm sure you'd like to dry off."

I placed the pad back in the pocket and headed for the door. I guessed that was all the answer Miller needed. He followed me as I ran, after he locked up the barn door. I stood by the back door and watched as he started to walk towards his truck. I waved, gaining his attention and beckoned him over. He jogged to the door and I gave him a T sign with my hands.

"Thought you'd never ask," he said with a laugh.

"Dani, look at you," Dad said, as we piled into the kitchen.

I shrugged my shoulders and removed Miller's jacket. I held it out to him.

"Keep it, it suits you more than it does me," he replied.

The leather jacket was dripping so I hung it on a peg next to the back door, the rain could drip onto the tiled floor while it dried out.

"I bet you two could do with a nice hot cup of tea," Dad asked.

"Definitely, thanks, Alistair," Miller replied.

I watched Miller take a seat, as if already invited, at the kitchen table. If it had been anyone else, I think it would have annoyed me. He seemed very much at home. Even Lucy rose and placed her head on his thigh for a petting.

Dad placed the tea on the table and I sat opposite Miller. Whether it was the fact he'd gotten soaked himself, or maybe, since I hadn't been able to speak, I'd become more aware of facial expression, but sadness seemed to radiate from him. He smiled, he laughed at something Dad had said, but it felt forced to me. He wasn't as natural as he normally was. His shoulders were a little slumped. I had to pull myself up, though. I'd only met him a handful of times. I didn't feel I knew him well enough to ask if he was okay.

Thunder rumbled overhead and the rain lashed against the windows. Miller drank down his tea and stood.

"I really should get going," he said, looking out the window at the deteriorating weather.

"Why not wait, have dinner with us? The rain might ease up by then," Dad said.

"Thank you, but I really need to go. Another time, for sure."

Miller smiled at me as he walked to the back door. I noticed the smile didn't quite meet his eyes.

"He didn't seem himself, did he?" Dad said, as he closed the door behind Miller.

I thought that, I wrote.

Dad gathered up the cups and walked to the sink. Although we had a dishwasher, he rarely used it.

"I like him, there's something a little tragic about him. Heard he'd had some trouble a year or so ago," Dad said.

I wrote, *What kind of trouble?*

I rose and stood beside Dad, showing him my pad.

"I don't know what caused it, but he had a bit of drink problem, at one point. That was according to Mrs. Hampton. Mind you, she's a terrible gossip. I didn't ask why."

I didn't think any more on what Dad had said. I decided to take a shower; I was still sitting in wet jeans and socks.

The smell of roast chicken wafted up to my room. Dad had limited cooking skills, and I wondered if he made more of an effort to cook a proper meal because I was there. I was sure that, when he lived on his own, he'd snacked more than cooked a full meal. I dressed in my pyjamas and headed downstairs.

I laid the table while Dad dished up our meal. A wave of guilt washed over me, I'd been waited on since I'd arrived and it wasn't fair. Dad chatted throughout the meal, just village gossip, what the weather was going to be like for the next few days, and his worry about Lucy, the dog. It was nice to listen to him; it was awful not to be able to participate.

I think it's time to see that specialist you talked about, I wrote, shoving the pad towards him.

The smile that he gave had me feeling terrible that I hadn't agreed before then. He left his meal and walked to the hall. He returned with a handful of leaflets.

"I did some research, on the interweb. We have to start with the doctor making a referral, of course. If you're sure, and I don't want to pressure you, but I can ring the doctor in the morning."

I chuckled at his term, 'interweb.' I nodded as he handed the leaflets over. It looked like he'd printed all sorts off the Internet. I placed them to one side and finished my meal. I'd take a read through after dinner.

It was as I was stacking the dishwasher that the lights started to flicker. Without worrying, I reached into a drawer and pulled out a pack of candles. It was quite usual for the power to be knocked out in a bad storm, and with the wind and rain causing havoc outside, it was going to be one of the worst we'd experienced in a while.

I lit the bottom of each candle melting a little wax before sticking them to some saucers I'd found. Although Dad had an array of ornaments around the house, candleholders weren't among them.

"I lit the fire, just in case the heating goes off," Dad said, taking a candle into the living room with him.

We sat in the living room, the TV was off and Dad, being the storm expert, powered down his computer. He told me about his theory on power surges destroying his information. I wondered what information he had stored on the computer.

"Sit with me, Dani. You're not too old for a cuddle from your old dad, are you?"

I smiled as I curled up next to him; he placed his arm around my shoulders.

"How do you feel, darling? What don't you tell me?"

His questions surprised me. I didn't have a pad or pencil to hand. He tightened his grip on me.

"I think you blame yourself. When you were unconscious, you mumbled an apology over and over. I'm guessing that was to Trey. But you have nothing to apologise for. What happened wasn't even a tragic accident, it was bloody…"

His body had tensed and I felt him take a deep breath in as if trying to calm himself. I wasn't sure I wanted to hear the word I thought he was about to use. It was a word that had run through my mind over and over. I placed my hand on his chest and rested my head on his shoulder. He gripped my hand tightly.

"I didn't know if I was going to lose you, as well. I'm not sure you agree with the decision I had to make but, for me, there wasn't a choice. I couldn't run the risk of you dying, Dani, can you understand that?"

I nodded my head against his shoulder.

"I thought you'd hate me. I agonised over that choice and what little time I had to come to it was brutal. Every night since then, I've dreamt of a different scenario. I can't apologise for making the decision I did, maybe you would have chosen differently, but I needed my baby to survive. Does that make me terribly selfish?"

I raised my head so I could look into his eyes and I shook my head. I mouthed the word, 'No.' It was important to me that he knew I understood that he'd made the best decision he could, in the time he was given. Would I have done the same had I been him? Without a shadow of doubt.

The power went out, leaving us sitting in a room lit only by candles and the flames of a log fire.

"If it's okay with you, I think I might head to bed. I feel quite tired today," Dad said.

I raised my head from his shoulder and let him stand. He looked down at me, placing his palm on my cheek. He didn't speak, but

I saw his shoulders heave as if a great sigh was about to leave his lips. He smiled.

"Don't stay up too late, you need your sleep, too," he said.

With that, he left the room. I curled into the edge of the sofa; comforted by the warmth he'd left behind. My dad had aged considerably. Trey and Hannah's deaths weighed heavily on his shoulders; I could see that. It must have been awful for him. He, and possibly Christian, would have been the only ones at the hospital until Patricia arrived. What an awful sight for them to have to face.

I sat for a while, just watching the flames flicker in the fireplace. Their dance was mesmerising, the logs crackled as if playing a tune. The flames created shadows across the inside of the chimney and the rug in front of the hearth. I loved the sound and smell of a real fire. I made a mental note to add at least a log burner on the list of things I wanted in the barn.

The thought of converting the barn excited me and I wasn't sure I should feel excited. A tear ran down my cheek when I thought of how Trey would have loved to do what I was doing. He would have taken over and I inwardly chuckled at the rows we would have had. It had been a nightmare when we'd bought the house in London. Our tastes were so different; the only compromise was to have a room each to design. He hated my stainless steel and high-tech kitchen; I loathed his wood panelled, ruby red-walled den. We were so different that we worked. It hadn't always been easy, yet we'd had some amazing times together. A pang of loss hit me between the chest and I sucked in a deep breath.

I grabbed a pad and pen and wrote. It seemed to be that whenever the loss and grief started to overwhelm, my coping mechanism was to write to Lincoln.

Lincoln,

The power is out here so I'm sitting by an open fire, writing with just candles for light. It's nice and peaceful, that is until I start to think, to remember. I'm worried about the strain I'm putting my dad under, and although he hides it well; I can see the constant sadness in his eyes. I've decided to speak to a therapist and see if I can sort out my speech issue. I know it's psychological, and for a while I was pleased. I didn't want to talk to anyone. Not being able to was a convenient way to avoid that awkwardness. But something has changed now, maybe I'm on that upward path you spoke about, but I want to talk out loud to someone.

I visited the church today, the vicar; I forget his name, sat with me. He was kind to me, and although I'm not remotely religious, I enjoyed his company. Isn't that a strange thing for me to write? I'm not sure why not being religious and enjoying his company should be connected. Anyway, it was nice to 'chat' to him and it made me realise, I actually miss conversation. I'm ready now.

I guess it will also be handy to be able to converse with Miller. I'm expecting the plans soon and there is a bubble of excitement inside me. My instinct is to suppress that excitement; it feels terribly wrong. But I can't. I want something positive to look forward to now. I'd do anything to have Trey and Hannah on this journey with me, but I'm also proud that I'm doing this myself. Not strictly by myself because I have my dad to advise, but you know what I mean. Should I feel guilty about that? Is it selfish of me?

Selfish is a new emotion for me. I've given all of myself to everyone who needed me for so long. I don't really know how to deal with this. I know you'll say it's another stage to conquer and I know that I will. There's a part of me that wants to see that light at the end of the proverbial tunnel, but there's a part of me comfortable in the darkness.

I feel like all I do is talk about myself in these letters, but it's what I needed for a while, so I thank you, Lincoln, for allowing me to do that. I'm not sure I can express how therapeutic it is.

Dani.

I folded the page and rose from the sofa. The fire was dying down and I used the poker to spread the logs a little. It used to cause me anxiety to head to bed leaving the fire alight. I remembered, as a teenager, I'd poured water over it. The smoke caused all the alarms to go off and Dad had come running down the stairs, tripping on his pyjama bottoms. I placed a guard in front of the opening and blew out all but one candle. I picked that up and then headed to bed.

The bedroom had chilled considerably; I wrapped myself in my duvet and blew out the candle, plunging the room into darkness. The clouds had obscured any light the moon would have given. Although the thunder had moved on, the rain hadn't lessened, and I listened to the patter of drops against the windowpanes. The noise was soothing and I soon fell into sleep.

I woke to the sound of a radio; I guessed the power had come back on at some point overnight. I could hear Dad singing along downstairs. His terrible voice, completely out of tune, made me smile and reminded me of when Trey and I married. Dad's voice drowned out the choir we'd paid for when it came time to sing a hymn. I found myself surprised that the memory hadn't provoked sadness, instead fondness washed over me. Another thought hit me, was I wallowing in my misery a little too much? I lay thinking; how long was too long to continue to cry? I guessed I would always grieve, but as the days wore on, I didn't cry as much. That confused me. I remembered a woman near where I'd lived; she'd worn black for a whole year when she'd lost her husband. I wasn't sure Trey would appreciate that. In fact, I remembered a conversation we'd had many years ago. He'd specifically said he didn't want black at his funeral. For the life of me, I couldn't remember what I'd worn. The day had been too traumatic and I was grateful for the loss of memory.

I rose and headed for the bathroom. I winced at the cold water that fell from the showerhead and opted for a quick wash instead. The cold water on my face revived me a little. I stared at myself in the mirror. The sadness was still etched in my skin, lines on my forehead had deepened, and my eyes were ringed with dark circles. I dragged a brush through my hair and tied it in a pony-tail, not really caring what it looked like.

"Good morning, did you manage to sleep at all? It was a heck of a storm in the end. I think there are some trees down in the lane, and I know half the village is still without power," Dad said when I entered the kitchen.

"I did."

I froze. Dad froze. I frowned, had I just spoken? I heard words in my head all the time but I wasn't sure if they'd left my mouth or not. However, judging by the look on Dad's face, they must have. I opened my mouth again.

Dad nodded gently, as if in encouragement, but no words came. It seemed that if I tried, it didn't happen. I shook my head and sighed.

"It's coming, Dani, that's all you need to think about. Now, breakfast?"

I saw the disappointment flash across his face even though he'd tried so hard to hide it. I grabbed a pad and flicked through until I came to a clean page.

I know it will. I don't want any breakfast and I'm going to go for a little walk, my head is fuzzy from sleeping so deep.

It was a lie, and I was sure that he realised that. I wanted to just get outside and scream, or walk off, my frustration. I rushed upstairs and grabbed the letter I'd written to Lincoln. I stuffed it in the envelope and pulled on my boots. I wrapped a scarf around my neck and shrugged into Miller's jacket. Dad was standing at the bottom of the stairs when I returned. Worry creased his face. I placed my hand on his cheek and smiled. I wanted him to think I was okay.

I walked up the lane and climbed over a small tree that had fallen. I guessed the local farmer would drag it out of the way with his tractor at some point. The local council tended to ignore damage in the lanes, concentrating on the major routes initially. I left the letter in the honesty box and started to make my way back. A noise had me come to a halt. I didn't want to go back towards the farm. My heart had started to pound in my chest at the thought of meeting whoever was cutting the tree. It had been the sound of a chainsaw I'd heard.

As I rounded the corner, I saw Miller. He had one boot-clad foot rested on the trunk of the tree. He wore a hard hat with a visor that covered his face. I stayed back as he lowered the chainsaw and wood chippings flew up into the air.

"Don't get too close, Dani," I heard. I turned to see Mrs. Hampton from the local shop.

I patted the jacket hoping to find a pad. Normally every coat, jean pocket even, contained one. Mrs. Hampton waved her hand as if she understood what I was trying to do and was telling me not to worry.

"It's okay," she said, smiling at me. "What a storm, huh? We're still out of power; I hope they can fix it quick. I've got all the fridges running off a generator at the moment. I'm hoping Miller can come and check I've got enough fuel when he's done with that tree."

Whether he heard us talking or not, I wasn't sure, but he switched off the chainsaw and straightened. He turned and at the same time raised the visor covering his face.

"Good morning, ladies. Here to help?"

"Here to help? Dani and I are just admiring the view," Mrs. Hampton said.

I gasped, silently of course. She had to be well into her seventies, but the naughty chuckle that left her lips and the dig from her elbow into my side, had me desperate to laugh out loud.

"Admiring the view? Maybe I should start charging for that," Miller replied. He gave her a wink. "Instead of standing there admiring the view, Dani, grab that branch for me."

I held on to the branch he was pointing to, and then looked at him.

"Maybe pull it out of the way?" he said, teasing me.

I heard it, I was sure I had. A laugh escaped my mouth. Miller looked at me but didn't say anything and I was thankful. If my voice was coming back, I didn't want a fuss made, for fear it might go again. I pulled the branch to the side of the lane.

"Ready for some more admiring, Mrs. Hampton?" Miller said, as he raised the chainsaw and pulled on the starter cord. With one foot back on the trunk, he posed with the chainsaw, resting on his knee, and lowered his visor again.

"Dani, I wish I'd brought a couple of chairs and a flask," she said.

I pointed to my chest and then down the lane, I wanted to indicate to her that I was leaving. I'd have loved to stay longer, simply to enjoy listening to her banter but I was cold.

"Come on by the shop soon, we can have a cup of tea," she called out as I skirted the tree.

"I'll be down later today, if I can get away from Mrs. Hampton in one piece, Dani," Miller said. Their laughter followed me down the lane.

I smiled as I walked home.

"That's a nice thing to see," Dad said, as I walked through the front door.

I bumped into Mrs. Hampton and Miller. A tree had fallen down; he was cutting it up. I think Mrs. Hampton has a thing for him, I wrote on a pad.

Dad laughed. "Mrs. Hampton has a *thing* for anyone. She quite scares me sometimes."

She seemed fun. I don't remember her being fun.

"She's a nice, kind person. I enjoy her company," he said. I noticed that his cheeks had coloured a little.

Maybe you should spend some time with her. I'm sure you'd enjoy a night out, I scribbled.

He coloured some more and then laughed. He didn't answer my note but busied himself making tea instead. Had I hit on something there?

Dad had been single for years, and in all that time, I don't ever remember him dating another woman. It was a shame in one way. He'd dedicated himself to being a single father but was that at the expense of his own happiness?

Seriously, invite her down for dinner one evening, I wrote. I slid the pad in front of him.

"Well, she has been, a couple of times in the past. I've been up to her house, as well. I haven't seen so much of her lately."

Because of me?

"Because of lots of things, Dani. Now, drink your tea, there's a croissant, if you want one."

I grabbed the croissant from the side and sat at the table.

You put your life on hold when Mum died to look after us, you've done the same now and it's not fair. I'm fine, you need to get back to your old life, I wrote.

He didn't answer but patted my hand when he leant down to pick up my empty plate. Maybe I'd have to force the issue a little. The fact his cheeks had coloured suggested that he enjoyed her company.

CHAPTER NINE

*T*he sound of a truck on the gravel drive roused me from a daydream as I sat in the garden, wrapped against the elements. I was thinking of Lincoln and the fact he'd be spending Christmas alone. I rose from the garden chair and walked around the side of the house. Miller was climbing from the driver's seat, his sweater was covered in bark and wood chips from his earlier chore.

"Hey, I have some plans for you to look over," he said, reaching back into the truck.

He pulled out a tube and then followed me to the back door.

"Shall I put them here?" he said, pointing to the kitchen table. I nodded my head.

He retrieved the plans from the tube and unrolled them onto the table. He used a mug to hold one side down, smoothing the paper out with his hand. I grabbed a small empty plant pot to secure the other end.

"Okay, let me walk you through. We come in through the front door and I've created a hallway with the staircase. I know you wanted all open-plan; but think about opening that door on a day like yesterday. You'll want somewhere to leave your coat, boots, that kind of stuff. I've placed two en suite bedrooms on either end, and a cloakroom in the middle, for guests. You might not want them traipsing through bedrooms to use the toilet."

I nodded and he continued, "Now, the exciting part." He slid a second plan from underneath and placed it on the top.

"Here are the stairs and the whole top floor is open-plan. We've got a kitchen at one end, dining table in the middle to create some separation, living space at this end. You've got your glass wall so you can sit and look out. Imagine walking up those stairs and seeing that space."

Miller seemed excited at what he was showing me. It certainly looked impressive.

"All the beams in the roof will be exposed to keep the character of the building. I've got the most amazing log burner in my workshop that fits perfectly here," he pointed to the sidewall. "I'd also like to keep some of the beams exposed down the walls."

I love it. It's perfect, I wrote on a pad. Miller's smile was wide. *What do we do now?*

"If you're happy with what I've done, we start the planning process. I propose that we put in a pre planning application, that gives the council a chance to state what they don't like before we submit for real. It's more cost, but in my experience, it's worth it."

Okay, whatever you think is right, I scribbled.

"Now, outside space." He pulled a third plan from the pile.

"We have to provide two car parking spaces, I suggest we place those here. At the rear, I assumed you'd want a seating area, so I've sketched this landscaping."

The plan showed a large patio, which wrapped around the side where the front door was, to the rear master bedroom.

"I think sliding doors from your bedroom to this outside space might work well. You have to take into account your living space is upstairs. If you had a party, for example, you'll be bringing things down from the kitchen. Price you have to pay for an upside down house, though."

I doubt I'll be having too many parties! What about a boundary fence or something? Do I need that?

"Maybe not immediately, but you know, at some point, your dad might sell up, so I've outlined the boundary for the council."

Miller told me about the planning process and the length of time we'd have to wait for decisions, while he did, I made tea. The planning process went over my head; my understanding was clouded by the building excitement, fighting with the layer of guilt it had to push through. I shouldn't be excited, but I was.

Is there anything we can start to do?

"Not really, other than maybe clear out the barn. I also have some quotes for you. You need to sit down and go through those. If you agree on the estimate, I'll need a signature. You've gotta sign your life over," he said with a laugh.

He stood, leaving all the paperwork on the kitchen table and drained the cup of tea he held.

"If you agree with everything, then I can get the planning under-way. There's always time to change minor details. You can send me a text if you like. My number is on the top of the quotes."

I nodded at him, pulling out a piece of his headed paper. It listed his company name, address, and mobile number. I hadn't thought about where Miller lived and was surprised to see he was the other side of the village.

Miller left and Dad and I looked over the plans. I found it hard to picture the finished article, especially the size of each room. While doing that, I thought back on my house in London.

Have you heard from Christian? I wonder what's happening with my house, I wrote on my pad.

"I haven't, I can give him a call later if you like."

I nodded my agreement. I was keen to get that resolved. There was a small part of me that wanted to go back there, for one last visit. A larger part knew that would put me back months. The memories would overwhelm and perhaps I was still 'hiding' from facing up to them. I just didn't feel ready and wondered if I'd regret that at some point. I had to remind myself, it was just a house, bricks and mortar; the memories would always stay with me.

"I think we should make a start on clearing out the barn. Maybe you'll get better perspective when it's empty. We can mark out the rooms, if you like," Dad said, I thought that was a great idea.

I pulled a jumper over my head and laced up my boots, there was no time like the present to get started. Dad and I headed out to the barn. It was decided that we'd separate up the boxes that were stacked against one wall. Three piles began to form. One belonged to me, one to Christian, and the third was Dad's. It seemed that Mum had been extremely organised with each box, they were labelled with either our name or the room the items had been cleared out from.

Dad turned on an old battery radio and hummed along to tunes as we shifted the boxes. A couple of hours later we'd sorted them.

"I guess we need to organise a skip, or something. I'm sure most of this can be thrown away," Dad said, sitting down on an old garden chair.

What about all your tools? Should we get a shed? I wrote.

"Might not be a bad idea. I'm also thinking of what to do with the car. Other than to take you to the church that day, I never drive it. It costs a fortune just to have sitting there. My old eyes aren't what they used to be, so I don't really feel confident on the road anymore."

But you'll lose your independence.

"We do have those things called taxis, Dani," he said with a chuckle.

I imagined the old Mercedes to be a classic nowadays and it was in mint condition. I hadn't driven in years, there was never the need when living in London and parking was at a premium. I felt it a shame to sell the car, though. Maybe I could persuade Dad to keep it.

We were both covered in dust by the time we decided to take a break. Dad headed into the house to make some tea, and I sat, looking up at the roof. I could see the beams that Miller wanted to keep exposed. I pictured myself sitting in my chair surrounded by their history. I wondered how old the barn was, Dad thought it was well over a hundred years. If a building could talk, I bet it had some stories to tell.

"Hello?" I heard. I looked over to the door as it creaked open. "Dani, your dad said you were in here."

Daniel walked into the barn. I stood, brushing some of the dust from my palms onto the front of my jeans. I held out my hand and he shook it.

"I was passing, thought I'd pop in and let you know I haven't forgotten your quest for information. It seems our Anna is a bit of a mystery. We have a record of her being buried, of course, but there isn't a great deal of information. I can say; her husband isn't called Lincoln. Alan is his name. Now, I say husband, he's listed as partner, so who knows?" he laughed as he spoke.

Do you know where she lived? I wrote.

"That's the mystery. Not in this village, which confused me at first. May I?" he indicated towards the chair. I nodded and brushed off a couple of cobwebs.

"It seems Anna might have been born here but moved away, abroad it looks like. Those are her ashes in the cemetery. She didn't have a service here, just laid to rest. Maybe it was her wish to 'come home,' which leads me to suspect the man you saw might not have been her husband, or partner."

I sighed with disappointment. I'd built that image of Lincoln in my mind based on his style of handwriting and the man I'd seen that day. My curiosity was piqued further, though. Who was the man who tended to her grave, if not her husband?

Dad arrived with three mugs of tea, balancing on an old metal tray. "I didn't know if you took sugar, Daniel, so brought a pot," he said. He laid the tray on the workbench and dragged out a couple of deckchairs from underneath it.

"I think you'll have to go first. If they collapse, I'd never be able to get back out," he said, handing me one.

Once I'd figured out how to actually open the thing, I tested the blue-stripped material seat for stability. I cautiously lowered myself down. Aside from some creaking, it held. Daniel stood and held onto Dad's arm as he sat. I didn't think I would get out of the deckchair without either help, or throwing myself to the ground.

"Dani is going to turn this into a house, assuming we get the permission, of course. Do you have any influence at the council?" Dad said. I nearly spat the mouthful of tea I'd taken all over Daniel's neatly pressed jeans.

Daniel laughed. "Sadly not, although I am a member of the parish council," he gave Dad a wink.

"Well, give us a heads up if you think there'll be any objections. I hear you're keen on DIY, I have some great tools here, if you'd like to take some."

I mouthed the word 'Dad' and frowned in embarrassment at him. I grabbed my pad.

I'm sure that's called using undue influence, or bribery, or something! And you promised Miller the tools.

Both Dad and Daniel laughed. "I don't indulge in any form of DIY, Alistair. I'm sure Miller will have more use for them than me."

"To be honest, Dani, I don't see any objections to the conversion. I think people would rather see these buildings lived in instead of falling into disrepair. And think about it, I'm your only neighbour and I don't object," Daniel added. "Plus, I think Miller might kill me if I did."

Dad and Daniel chatted back and forth and it dawned on me that they knew each other quite well, or appeared to. I made a mental note to ask Dad how. Daniel finished his tea and rose. He reached out his hand.

"Do you need help to get up?" he asked. I took his hand and he pulled me to my feet. He did the same with Dad.

"Daniel, it was great to chat with you again. You and Miller should come to dinner soon," Dad said.

I frowned. Were Daniel and Miller an item? I waited until Daniel had left.

What's the connection between him and Miller? And you seemed to know him well; I thought he was new here.

"No," Dad laughed. "They're brothers! They both grew up here, I'm pretty sure you might have played with them when you were little. I'm sure you would have all gone to the same school, although I think they're a little older than you. Daniel came back here when Miller got into trouble. Guess he thought he could save his soul, or something."

I remembered Dad saying that Miller had previously had problems but didn't know what. He'd said that Mrs. Hampton was a gossip and he hadn't taken too much notice.

That night, as I brushed my hair after my shower, it dawned on me that I'd been in a different frame of mind; I hadn't felt that deep sadness. Or if I had, it had been overridden by the activities of the day. I pulled on my pyjamas and climbed into bed. I'd enjoyed Daniel's company; he didn't seem to be a run-of-the-mill vicar. He was much more 'modern' than I'd normally expect, not that I knew many vicars, of course. It had surprised me to learn he was Miller's brother. There was no resemblance at all, and it would be interesting to know their ages, there didn't look to be much difference between them.

I'd left the curtains open and the moon was high in the sky. It cast a glow over the sea that, unusually for the time of year, was calm that evening. Not that the thought would have entered my head, but leaving this for the city lights, the honking cars at all hours, and the rowdiness of people on the streets, would be madness. I felt calm, peace surrounded me; Mother Nature was taking care of my soul.

I dozed on and off throughout the night. When the sun started to rise I felt exhausted. I had to force myself to climb out of bed. Forgoing a shower, I dressed quickly and headed downstairs. The only noise was the gentle snores from Lucy, who was curled up in her bed beside the boiler. Without opening her eyes, she wagged her tail a couple of times. I dreaded the day we'd have to say goodbye to her. She's been a constant companion to us all, especially for Dad, for years.

I made tea and opened the back door. Although December, it looked as if it was going to be a bright day. I preferred winter on the coast. There were fewer tourists than the summer months, obviously. As I sipped on my tea, I remembered back to my childhood. Each day outside of school would be on the beach. As I got older, perhaps late teens, I began to resent living in Cornwall. I wanted some excitement, and as soon as I could, I'd headed to University in London. It was where I'd met Trey.

I smiled at the thought of our first meeting. It had been in the university's coffee shop. I had queued for my coffee and he'd bowled in straight to the front of the line, oblivious to the complaints that followed him. When he had realised, he'd bought the coffee for everyone in the line. That was Trey all over. He was extremely generous and kind-hearted.

We'd dated for a short while, and we'd broken each other's hearts when he left to go home to support his mum after the death of his father. I didn't see him for another year, until one day he turned up at the flat I was sharing. Unbeknown to me, he'd contacted my dad and asked for my address.

I took a deep breath in, the gentle breeze rustled the dune grass, and its sound was as therapeutic as a wind chime. I walked to the end of the garden; just over the fence was the edge of a cliff. I leant on the fence and looked out to the horizon. We'd often see dolphins cruising past, leaping and playing in the surf. I squinted against the sun, hoping to see their fins.

"It's beautiful, isn't it?" I heard. I startled, spilling my tea down the front of my sweatshirt.

Walking along the coastal path was Daniel. Out of his 'vicar' clothes: he wore jeans, walking boots, and a heavy knit sweater. His hair was dishevelled, as if he hadn't bothered to brush it that morning.

Daniel smiled as he came towards me and leant on the other side of the fence.

"I bet your dad hates this footpath just outside his garden. I can imagine in the summer it's a nightmare."

I nodded; it had been an annoyance on occasions. Walkers would stop, stare into our garden, or sit with their feet dangling over the cliff edge causing Dad all sorts of anxiety.

"I walk along here each morning, I guess I can't really call it exercise. Want to walk with me?"

I nodded again, holding up one finger and pointing to the house. I wanted a coat. I jogged into the house and grabbed a light-weight jacket from the back of the door, left my mug on the counter, and picked up a pad and pen, and then joined Daniel.

I had to run around the side of the house to get to him. Years ago, there had been a gate at the bottom of the garden; Dad had gotten rid of that. He worried about people coming in, and us kids getting out. I smiled my thanks as Daniel placed his hand on my back and ushered me to the side of the path furthest from the cliff edge. It was rather an old-fashioned, gentlemanly thing to do, but I appreciated it.

"I know it's not your thing, Dani, but I can't help but stop and look at the beauty that has been created for us. I'm in awe some-times, does that sound really strange?" he laughed, and I found myself smiling at the sound.

I'd be surprised if you weren't, I wrote on my pad.

"I haven't always been a vicar. I've always been a believer, of course. Would you believe me if I told you I was in a band? I'd love to lie and tell you we were super famous, but I think Him upstairs might be a little pissed off with me if I did."

The laugh that left my mouth startled me enough to slap my hand over it.

"You know, you can laugh but not speak. I have a theory on that, want to hear it?"

I nodded, smiling at that smirk that played not only on his lips, but also around his eyes.

"Laughing is safe, words are not. You don't want to speak, maybe because you don't want to say the words that swim around your mind, that sit just on your tongue, busting to come out. But to laugh? Well, that's something different. It's just a sound, there's no fear of it turning into a word. I can imagine you want to curse, scream at God, anyone, don't you?"

I stopped walking, and he turned to face me. "I've never experienced the depth of grief you have. My mother died, but that was a long time ago. I can imagine how you feel, however, I've seen it too many times, sadly."

I feel guilty for laughing. I'm not happy, but for that one moment, I was. It confuses me, I wrote.

"I can imagine. It's okay to have those 'one moments,' Dani. At some point, those moments will be more moments, until you can freely be happy without the guilt. I'm glad I was able to make you laugh."

He turned and we continued to walk, for a while, it was in silence. We came to a bench and sat. Daniel stretched out his legs and raised his face to the sun. He closed his eyes and I watched his mouth move, as if in silent prayer.

I just found out you and Miller are brothers, I didn't know, I wrote on my pad. When Daniel opened his eyes, I placed the pad in front of him.

"Yes, I'm three years older. We were always so close growing up, but we drifted apart for a while. He was very troubled..." His sentence trailed off as he looked out to sea.

I was curious but didn't want to ask anymore. I guessed Daniel hadn't meant to divulge such a personal statement. There was a pained look on his face, and I could have kicked myself for spoiling the moment.

Daniel placed his hands on his knees, and after a deep breath in, with a slow exhale, he stood.

"I have to start making my way back. I'll have a group of old ladies, headed up by Mrs. Hampton, bashing down the church door shortly." He laughed as he spoke and I was pleased to see the humour back in his eyes.

"Honestly, Dani, I think they believe I am totally incapable of anything. I keep telling them, I was motherless when I was younger, I know how to make a bed and iron a shirt."

We walked side by side and Daniel talked the whole journey back. He pointed out different birds; he named the dune grass we passed, and had me laughing a second time with anecdotes of the 'old biddies,' as he called them, who ran his life and the church.

All too soon, we'd arrived back at Dad's garden. "It was a pleasure to spend some time with you, and I'm sure we'll get to the bottom of who Anna really is."

I smiled my goodbye and watched him walk away. I circled the house to the side gate.

"There you are, we were worried." Dad's voice carried down the garden. I turned to see him standing with Miller.

Miller didn't seem to be as happy to see me as Dad was. Although he smiled, it seemed to be forced.

Daniel and I took a walk along the path, I wrote.

"I bet the fresh air did you the world of good," Dad said with a smile.

We had a nice time, I laughed! I enjoy his company.

I nodded, shrugging off my jacket and accepting the steaming cup of tea he handed me. I turned to Miller and gave him a smile, he didn't quite meet my eyes and I frowned.

I didn't know you were brothers, I wrote, showing the pad to Miller.

There was a moment of awkwardness. "We're not close," he said.

I looked at Dad, not knowing what to say next.

"How about a fresh cup of tea, Miller?" Dad said, diffusing the tension that seemed to have mounted.

"That would be great, thanks, Alistair," Miller said.

I saw the transition. Miller was very transparent with his emotions. A wall had been erected and I knew not to ask any more questions. After all, he was my builder, not a personal friend. I felt a little disappointment in that; I'd have liked to have a friendship with him. I thought that might have made working together easier.

I picked up the roll of plans; assuming Miller had visited for a reason and laid them out on the kitchen table. I sat, expecting him to also sit. He stood, waiting for Dad to finish making the tea. I reached for my pad and wrote.

I've gone through these, there's nothing I'd like to change, so can we go ahead?

I tapped the pad with my pencil to gain his attention. The Miller that turned towards me and sat was the one I'd seen the most of. He smiled and nodded, his earlier mood concealed.

"That's great," he said.

I signed the documents to give him the go ahead to proceed and we shook hands to seal the deal. He took one copy and folded it in half; he left the other on the table.

Do you need these? I wrote, tapping the plans.

"No, they're your copies. Like I said before, I'll get started with a pre-application, that will give the council a chance to decide if there's anything they don't like before we go with the full application."

"Do you anticipate any problems, Miller?" Dad asked, taking the seat beside him.

"Not really, there are enough parking spaces. They do get a bit anxious about that. It's a sympathetic conversion to a building that's outlived its purpose. I've dealt with the planning officer many times, he's usually a good guy, never caught him on a bad day yet," he said with a laugh.

For an hour or so after Miller had left, I sat and pondered on his reaction to seeing me with Daniel. He'd said they weren't close, in fact, he hadn't acknowledged Daniel in any way. But that didn't excuse his attitude towards me. He confused me but I decided I wasn't going to worry about it. I'd keep a professional relationship with him. It would have been nice to have a couple of friends locally. Since we were probably the only three in the village under the age of sixty, it was a shame that wasn't likely to happen.

The sound of the letterbox rattling brought me out of my thoughts. Dad had popped up to the local shop as we were low on milk, or maybe he just wanted a chat with Mrs. Hampton. I walked to the front door and saw the familiar purple envelope on the mat. If I could time when I was likely to get a response from Lincoln, I'd sit by the living room window and see if I could catch who was delivering the letter. I bent down to pick it up.

I held the envelope in my hand for a while, just staring at our two names on the front. The flap was held down with fresh tape but I wasn't sure how long the envelope would survive. It was torn on one corner, frayed on another. I took the letter upstairs, wanting some privacy when I read it. Dad was due back soon.

Dani,

I'm glad you find these letters therapeutic; I do, too. I rarely talk about emotion, or how I'm feeling. It's not the done thing for a guy, we're supposed to 'get over it' or 'move on.' I was even told that I'd spent enough time mourning; it was time to pull myself together. That comment hurt, especially since it was from a family member.

Is it selfish of you to want to experience something positive? Of course not. Looking forwards is all you have, Dani. You can spend your life looking back, but you'll end up standing in one place. I don't believe you'd want that. It took me a long time to understand that concept; the drink paralysed me for a while. I did some stupid things; spoke terrible words to those that cared about me. I alienated myself, and for a long time, I was happy about that. I didn't want their pity, their concern, and I didn't want to infect them with my misery.

I'm also happy to hear you're going to a therapist. I believe you have so much to say, can you imagine how wonderful it will feel to speak out the words you want to when you visit Trey and Hannah? Those words will float off, Dani, to be heard by them wherever they are. Thoughts can only be contained within the mind. Words are free. Which is why, I guess, they are also so abused.

We lost power, too. It took until the end of the following day for us to be reconnected. Like you, I sat with the fire roaring and the candles burning. It made me think of how much time is wasted with a blaring television or the undecipherable music on the radio. It was nice to just sit and think, to read a little, and to ponder on life.

It's the third anniversary of Anna's death soon. I don't intend to hide away. Do you remember what I said about her hair? I'm going to do what she wanted, and throw it out to sea. She had such a fascination with the sea, loved being in it at all times of the year. She'd always wanted to be a marine biologist, but sadly, she'd never gotten her desired career. That was my fault.

I have many regrets; I have many wrongs to right. It's only now, and I thank you for this, that I feel able to start that next leg of my journey.

Make that appointment, Dani, let your words be free.

Lincoln.

I read his letter a couple of times. There was something maudlin about it. There wasn't one particular thing that jumped out at me, just the tone of what he'd written. I guessed coming up to Anna's passing anniversary had done that. I wondered, again, if my writing to him prompted him to think of her and her death more than he wanted to.

Even more so, I wanted to know who Lincoln was.

CHAPTER TEN

*C*hristian made a surprise visit, without Helen or Alistair. He looked tired, dark circles framed his normally blue eyes that seemed dull with stress. His shirt was unusually creased, and there was a stain on the lapel of his jacket. At first, I assumed it was the 'new baby thing,' but when he avoided all reference to Helen and Alistair, I became concerned. He'd been sitting talking about my house; the agents had received an offer for the asking price from the first viewing. Christian had thought we should refuse and see if we can achieve a little more. I wasn't particularly fussed. I told him to go ahead and accept the offer.

Periodically, Dad would look over to me. I could see the concern etched in his face. He knew something was wrong as well. Christian was often a private person but his body language screamed that all was not right.

Take a walk with me? Let me show you what we're doing with the barn, I wrote.

He didn't look up from the pad but slowly nodded. Dad gave me a very slight nod of his head, as if he'd approved of my question.

"How about I sort out some lunch while you two catch up?" Dad said.

"That sounds good," Christian replied.

We rose and donned coats before leaving by the back door. I took his hand in mine while we walked towards the barn.

I pulled the creaking door open and we walked in.

Those boxes are all yours. We haven't looked through them, thought you might like to, I wrote on my pad.

"Are you going to ever talk again?" Christian asked, surprising me.

I hope so. I'm making an appointment to see a therapist in a week or so.

"It would be nice to have a conversation with someone."

Again, his comment surprised he. He slumped down in one of the chairs beside a pile of boxes. He pulled one towards him and opened the lid. It was a bitter laugh that left his lips when he pulled out an old small, wooden, cigar box.

Christian, are you okay? I know you're not, but if you want to talk, I'm here, I wrote.

I wasn't sure if the snort was in response to what I'd said or what he'd found in the cigar box. He opened the lid and pulled out a pile of letters.

"Helen has been having an affair. I don't know if Alistair is my child or not."

His words stunned me. I sat on a chair opposite him and reached out to take one of his hands in mine. Eventually, he looked up at me, his eyes were filled with tears.

"It's why we haven't invited you, or Dad, over. The atmosphere is just fucking awful, right now. I don't know what to do about it all. I mean, I know what I want to do. If it weren't for Alistair, I'd walk. She's begging my forgiveness, telling me Alistair is mine but refuses a DNA test. That tells me all I need to know really."

Oh God, Chris. I can't imagine how you feel right now. Can you do the test without her consent? Do you need to do the test? What does your heart tell you? Does it matter whose child he is? I wrote.

"I can, and I will. But having her agree would have satisfied my mind a little. I don't think she knows who the father is. And you know what? It does matter, to me. I'll love Alistair no matter what, but it matters, Dani. I can't go through life not knowing."

What if you find out he isn't yours? How will you feel then?

"I don't know, is the honest answer. He's innocent in all this, but I can't see past what Helen has done, and I don't think I can live with her. I know I can't forgive her. I asked her what I did wrong. I work hard, provide a nice life for us, I want to know why I wasn't enough. I'm going to get Christmas out of the way and then make some decisions. She's planned this fucking big Christmas with all her family, and I'm not sure I can keep up the pretence anymore."

I was hurt by his statement. There had been no thought of Dad, or me, in their Christmas plans.

Is she still having the affair? Do you know who it is?

"No, so she says, of course. And no, she won't tell me who it is, although I suspect it's someone she used to work with."

How did you find out about the affair?

"She sent him a picture on her phone. How fucking dumb is that?" His laughter was forced and full of pain.

I didn't want to ask what kind of a picture, but it didn't sound like the Helen I knew. She'd always been so prim, and on the nights we'd spent out on our own, she'd always been the one to avoid the crowded bars, opting for a quiet restaurant instead. I remembered a conversation where she believed a mutual friend was having an affair. She'd been so scornful of that.

"Anyway, enough of my woes. What's going on with this?" he said, effectively shutting down any further conversation.

I paused for a moment. It wasn't like Chris to shut me out, but then so much had happened, to both of us. We were different people.

I pointed to one of the plans that Dad had taped to the wall so we could visualise the layout. He rose, throwing the cigar box onto the workbench and walked over. He stood for a while, cocking his head to one side as he scanned over the image.

"I think that's amazing. Whoever drew these has a great vision for this place."

Miller did them. We had an architect but I didn't like him.

I thrust the pad in front of him so he could read. Not for the first time did I become frustrated that I couldn't speak out the words.

"Dani, it's going to be amazing. A change is what we both need, I guess. I was surprised when you left London so quickly. I kind of imagined you'd want to be surrounded by the memories. I'll confess, I didn't understand it at first. You just walked away from a whole life, and I didn't know how you could do that. I understand now, of course."

He turned towards me. "I miss him, a lot."

Christian and Trey had been great friends. They spent time going to watch rugby, sipping on a pint in a bar, or playing golf. They had been skiing together. In my grief, I guessed, I hadn't thought of the impact on Christian. He placed his arm around my shoulders and pulled me into his side. We fell silent while we thought of Trey, as we looked at the plans.

"You never know, I might come and stay in that spare bedroom until I sort out what I'm doing. There's something about coming home when you're troubled that can't be beat," he said quietly.

You'd be welcome anytime, I wrote.

We walked back to the house and settled down for lunch. Dad had made soup that we ate with fresh, crusty rolls. Once we'd eaten, I gave Christian instructions to accept the offer on the house. I also asked if he could organise for me to visit the storage unit that housed all my possessions. There would be things I'd want, but I'd decided that the majority of it would be sold. I wasn't wiping my life with Trey clean; I was creating a new one. Trey would forever be in my heart, my soul, and my memories, but most of what we'd owned wouldn't fit in the barn anyway.

I stood at the door and watched Christian drive up the lane. I shed a tear for him and his situation. I shed another for baby Alistair who was caught in the middle. Dad and I sat in the living room with a cup of tea and I relayed the conversation to him.

CHAPTER ELEVEN

$\mathcal{I}$t was two days later that Christian called and told Dad that I'd effectively sold my house. He'd instructed a solicitor to act on my behalf and would be in touch when he had more news. He hadn't mentioned Helen, or his situation, to Dad at all. I dug out my mobile and charger. It hadn't been turned on for months and once it had a suitable charge, I texted him.

How are things at home?

His reply was prompt. **Not good at all. New development that I can't talk about right now. I'll come down soon, I promise.**

I wondered what the new development was and worried for him.

"I think Chris might be coming here for Christmas. Things must be really bad if he's prepared to miss Alistair's first Christmas," Dad said, when I walked into the kitchen.

Did he say that? I wrote.

"Sort of. He said he was making some plans to visit over Christmas, he didn't specify Christmas Day, and he didn't mention Helen at all."

Dad sat at the kitchen table and rubbed his palms over his face.

Please don't worry, Dad. He's a grown man; he'll sort it out. I pushed the pad between his elbows so he could read.

"I just can't believe what's happened. They seemed such an ideal couple. Why would she do that?"

I don't know. Something had to be missing in their relationship, I hope. I'd hate to think she is someone who could do that for no reason, other than self-gratification, I wrote.

Was there ever justification in having an affair? Maybe I was being too kind. To bring a child into a relationship, where the father might not actually be the father, was quite cruel in my mind. And if there was something lacking in their relationship, shouldn't they have tried to fix it, or should she have left Christian?

Dad mumbled about needing to pay his newspaper bill. He shrugged on his jacket, wrapped a scarf around his neck, and pulled a cap from a peg in the hall. His movements were laboured and when he patted his leg for Lucy to follow, they both seemed as rickety as the other. I watched from the front door as they slowly walked up the lane.

It was as I was about to close it that I saw Daniel, casually dressed, walk past. He turned and waved. I indicated with my hands the letter T, in the hope he'd understand. He smiled and nodded enthusiastically.

"It's a bloody chilly morning. I just saw your dad walking up the lane," he said, as he walked through the front door and followed me to the kitchen.

I set the kettle to boil and gathered two mugs from the cupboard, while he unwrapped himself from the many layers he appeared to be wearing.

Aren't you supposed to be wearing your uniform at all times? I wrote on my pad.

He chuckled. "I'm allowed a day off, aren't I? To be honest, it's nice to get out of that garb. Whoever invented the collar needs shooting."

My jaw clicked open and my eyes widened in shock at his comment. His laughter though was infectious, and although in my head, I laughed along.

"But if I find someone who is in need while on my walks, I do have this…" He pulled his collar from his jean pocket.

Doesn't quite go with the T-shirt! I wrote.

Daniel wore a black T-shirt with *AC/DC* blazoned across the front. I hadn't taken him for a rock music fan.

"When I first arrived, I had the radio blasting out tunes from some rock station in the church while I was pottering around. Mrs. Hampton, when she came to set out some flowers, nearly had a fit."

I guess you're not the typical village priest, or vicar, whatever the term is.

"Life isn't typical, Dani," he said with a smile. "Now, there's a local folk band playing in the pub this evening, and I don't want to go on my own, I get accosted by the old women. Do you fancy coming with me?"

I blinked a couple of times, unsure of how to answer. I didn't want to go out in public. My pen hovered over the pad; I was thankful the kettle came to a boil and I had the distraction of making tea while I thought on his request.

"Here's the plan. We sneak in, grab a beer or two, and find a corner to sit in near the band. It will be too loud for the old dears to want to come and chat." He smiled at me.

So you're inviting me because you're frightened of the old dears in the village? I teased, trying to hide the smirk.

"Of course. Although, I can't say that I don't enjoy your company. It would be nice to get out, wouldn't it? Invite your dad, too."

I thought I might feel a little more comfortable with Dad there but that seemed silly. There wasn't anyone in the village that wasn't aware of my situation. Most had been to Trey and Hannah's funeral. They talked to Dad, asked how I was getting on.

"The whole village attends, it's like a one-night folk festival. The music is often terrible but it can be so bad, it's fun. Not that I say that in public, of course."

Daniel sipped on his tea, wincing as he took too large a mouthful and burnt his lips. He was fun to be around, and although I still felt conflicted, a part of me wasn't sure I was meant to be having fun, the thought of listening to terrible bands with him sounded appealing.

I nodded. *Okay, I'll come.*

"That's fantastic. I'll swing by about seven."

Daniel finished his tea and left. It took as long to wrap himself up, as it had to drink his tea in the first place.

At seven o'clock promptly, Daniel knocked on the door. Dad had decided a night in the local pub with folk music wasn't his idea of a good time so decided to stay home. It was with shaking hands that I opened the front door. I was greeted with the familiar smile and a hand to help me into my coat.

"Ready to save me?" he asked. I nodded, patting my pocket to reassure I had a pad and pen with me.

Daniel held out the crook of his arm, encouraging me to take it. He patted my hand when I did, laughed, and we started the walk to the village green. The Black Lion was a historic building. Even at five feet and two inches, I had to duck my head to walk under some of the beams. It had been a while since I'd visited the pub, and the last time had been with Trey. A pang of sadness hit me in the centre of the chest and my breath caught in my throat.

"Breathe, Dani," Daniel whispered, alerted to my discomfort.

He took hold of my hand, and at first, I froze. I hadn't held anyone's hand other than my dad, Christian, or Trey's for a long time. Whether he sensed my hesitation or not, I wasn't sure, but he let go and placed his hand on my lower back to guide me through the bar to the only vacant table. I took a seat with my back to the wall and scanned the bar. The first band was about to strike up, and I noticed many people smile, or wave over to me. Daniel asked me what I wanted to drink, I opted for a glass of wine and he left me to stand at the bar. I felt sorry for him; he was 'assaulted by those old dears' constantly.

I caught sight of Miller at the other end of the bar, he looked over to me, and although I smiled at him, it wasn't instantly returned. I frowned at him, hoping he'd understand that I was concerned. He hadn't been himself for a couple of weeks. I saw his shoulders rise and fall, as if he'd taken a deep breath; he pushed himself away from the bar and weaved his way through the throng queuing to get to my table.

I had just taken off my coat and fished around in the pocket for my pad and pen. Miller took the only available seat next to me.

"Hey, it's nice to see you out," he said, giving me a genuine smile then, or so I thought.

It's been a while! Daniel invited me and I thought, why not? I wrote.

"Sorry, that took forever. Miller, can I get you another?" Daniel asked as he joined us.

I noticed that awkwardness between them and wondered, again, what their deal was.

"No, thanks. Just having the one and then I'm leaving," Miller replied. Although he'd smiled at Daniel, it didn't appear to be genuine.

A short silence followed. Daniel placed my wine on the table and I smiled my thanks. He stood to one side, not having a spare chair, and Miller didn't offer him the one he was sitting on.

"So, how are things?" Miller asked me.

Okay, I showed my brother the plans for the barn. He was very impressed with your vision, I wrote.

Talking about his work seemed to perk Miller up a little. "I'm glad he approved," he said.

"Miller is an amazing architect," Daniel said, smiling at his brother. The smile wasn't returned.

"Yeah, well, I better get going. It was nice to see you out and about, Dani," Miller said. He stood, downed the rest of his pint, and simply nodded to his brother before he left.

Daniel sighed, and then took the vacated seat.

You two don't seem to get on, or is that too personal for me to say?

I kept the pad close to me for a little while, wondering if I should show Daniel what I'd written. It made no difference, he'd obviously seen.

"We did, for a long time. We were very close as children, but then something happened, and I think Miller didn't feel that I supported him enough. He's a very stubborn man; he alienated himself from the family for a while. There are things we disagree

118

on. But let's not worry about that now, we're here to laugh at the terrible music and pretend it's the best thing we've heard in ages."

Before I could consider a response, a wailing drowned out any noise inside the bar. I looked towards the 'stage,' which was nothing more than a small raised platform made out of pallets, to see a man on a violin. Although it wasn't like any violin I'd ever seen before, it looked homemade.

The wailing was short-lived, thankfully, only to be replaced by the not so dulcet tones of a man who looked, and sounded, more drunk than sober. It was hard to actually hear what he was singing about, and when I looked over to Daniel, I could see a man desperately trying to hold back the laughter.

His cheeks had reddened and his eyes watered. I could see the tension in his jaw as he ground his teeth together to keep his mouth closed. The addition of a tambourine was the tipping point for him. Daniel bent over double and laughed so hard he had tears streaming down his cheeks. It was hard not to join in. Although I didn't make the sound, I covered my mouth with my hand and my body visibly laughed along with him.

A chuckle started on the table beside us, and like a tsunami, that chuckle built and flowed from table to table, until most of the people sitting in the bar were laughing. The man kept *singing*, the tambourine kept tinkling, and at the end people stood and gave a round of applause. I wasn't sure it was in appreciation, though.

"I'm sorry, but that was about the funniest thing I've seen, or heard," Daniel said, wiping his eyes on a napkin.

We sat through another band, one that, thankfully, was quite good. I'd been sipping on my wine and Daniel chatted, as much as he could with the noise of the busy pub obliterating his words.

After a little while I grew hot and uncomfortable. I think my limit on being in public for the first time in ages was slowly approaching. Perhaps Daniel saw, or felt, my discomfort.

"Shall we get out of here? It's getting rather stuffy," he said.

I nodded and pulled my coat from the back of my chair. It was too warm to put it on, so I waited until we walked through and out the front door. The chill that hit me had me shiver. Daniel took my coat from me and held it open. I shrugged into it. We took a slow walk back to my house.

"Any more thoughts on Lincoln?" Daniel asked.

It wasn't always the easiest to write while I walked so I just shrugged my shoulders.

"I must admit, Anna intrigues me. It's not often that we have so very little information in the church on our guests." He chuckled at the use of his words.

I'd begun to think the gentleman I'd seen wasn't Lincoln after all, although I still had an elderly man in my mind when I pictured him. I thought back on his last letter and the sadness I'd picked up from his words. I was due to write to him and wondered if it would be right to ask him to meet me. Would it dispel the mystery around him? I appreciated his letters, his words comforted me, and although I was concerned for him, if I met him would we get on in real life?

We arrived back at the house, and I gave Daniel a smile in thanks for walking me home.

"Well, here we are. Thank you for spending the evening with me. It was nice to get out and it not be a work call," he said.

I reached for my pad. *I enjoyed myself; I didn't think I would, so thank you for inviting me.*

"We'll have to do it again some other time," he said. He gave me a smile before leaving.

The hallway and the kitchen light were left on, but I suspected Dad had already gone to bed. He seemed to retire to his bedroom earlier and earlier lately. I made my way to the kitchen and switched the kettle on to boil. The glass of wine had left me with a dry mouth. I made my tea, patted Lucy on the head, and then took my mug upstairs.

Once I'd changed into my pyjamas, I pulled a wrap around me and snuggled into the chair by the window. I placed the tea on the small wooden table and picked up my writing pad.

Lincoln,

I can't help but detect sadness in your last letter and I'm concerned about you. I don't know if you have friends locally, but if you ever felt you'd like to meet up, I'd enjoy that. I felt the loneliness in your words, although I might be way off the mark. Forgive me if I am. I know you said that it's Anna's anniversary coming up, and I wondered if you'd like some company on that day? I'd hate to think of you sitting alone. You've become impor-tant to me, your words have given some clarity to the mess that is my mind, and I'd like to think I could be a friend to you.

I went to the pub tonight with Daniel, and Miller was there. I hope you don't think I'm gossiping, but they don't seem to get on, and that worries me, too. They're brothers, and as much as I'd like to see if I can help to repair their relationship, I think it would be seen to be interfering. Sometimes, I feel that Miller doesn't approve of any time I spend with Daniel, and I don't know why. I don't think we have the kind of relationship where I could ask why. After all, I guess he is just my builder, and although he's friendly, and I find him great to be around, he does keep his distance. I think I'm just trying too hard, hoping to be friends with them both.

I heard some terrible news. My sister-in-law is, or was, having an affair. My brother is devastated. He opened up a little to me, but I can sense there's so much more he'd like to say. We're

121

twins, I can feel when he's not right. That was the strangest thing to get to grips with when we were children. It's like a sixth sense that we have. More that I have, I guess.

I'm rambling on, aren't I? I meant what I wrote, if you'd like some company, I'd be honoured to be your friend.

Dani.

I read the letter a couple of times, hoping that I didn't come across as someone needy for a friend. My sentiment was genuine; I wanted to get to know the man behind the words.

I folded the letter and placed it in the envelope, ready for leaving in the honesty box the following morning. As I climbed into bed, I thought of Miller and his strange behaviour. A little nagging doubt crossed my mind. Was he upset that I was spending time with Daniel? Maybe he felt there was a reason that I shouldn't. Daniel had said that Miller felt he hadn't supported him enough and curiosity was burning a hole in my mind.

CHAPTER TWELVE

"$\mathcal{I}$ think we should get a Christmas tree," Dad announced over breakfast.

It's three weeks away yet, it won't live that long, I wrote on my pad.

"I don't mean right now. I've been using that old plastic one your mum bought years ago. Half the branches are missing; it's a semi-bald tree stump now. There must be a tree farm, or wherever one gets a real tree from, locally."

There is a field of Christmas trees somewhere along the Atlantic Highway, I remember seeing it.

"We'll do some investigating. I know they have small ones in the garden centre, but let's go all out this year."

I wasn't sure I wanted to go 'all out' but I understood that Dad was trying to distract me from any negative thoughts. If it were up to me, I'd just stay in bed all day and ignore it.

"I mean, if you want to, of course," he added.

If you want a real tree, we'll get a real tree. It will be nice to spend some time to decorate it. You have decorations, I take it?

"Somewhere, probably in the loft. I think I'll have a look later today." His smile was broad.

The ringing of the telephone distracted him and I watched him walk to the hallway. I inwardly chuckled that he'd sit in that hallway on the old-fashioned telephone table and talk on the cordless phone.

"That was Christian, he's driving down today. He didn't sound good at all. I think he plans on staying over for a couple of nights. I'll have to get the spare room sorted."

Dad seemed flustered and I wondered if Christian had said any more in their telephone conversation.

I'll help, what needs doing? I wrote.

"The bed might need a change, I can't remember when it last was, not that anyone has slept in it for ages."

I placed my hand on his arm and patted my chest. I wanted him to know I'd do that. I headed upstairs to what had been Christian's childhood bedroom. It had since been decorated many times, from memory. As I passed the linen cupboard, I grabbed some fresh bedding.

I opened the bedroom window, just to blast a little fresh air into the otherwise stuffy room. The radiator had been left on full and the room felt very oppressive. Once I'd changed the bed linen, I closed the window and decided to give them a wipe over. I didn't think they'd been cleaned in a while. A layer of dust covered each surface, and yet again, guilt flowed over me that I hadn't been the best at helping around the house. I heard a bumping up the stairs and went to look. Dad was dragging the vacuum cleaner behind him, and also holding a bucket of cleaning items. I took the vacuum from him. Between us, we cleaned up the room.

"That's a little more welcoming," Dad said once we'd finished.

I didn't have a pad close by so could only smile. Dad patted my shoulder as we left the room. I decided I'd give the other rooms a quick go over and took the cleaning bucket from Dad. I ushered him to the top of the stairs, so he'd know to go and relax and let me get on with it.

It took me a half hour to clean the bathroom and my bedroom. I hesitated outside Dad's bedroom door, trying to remember the last time I'd been in that room. I took a deep breath and pushed open the door. His bed was neatly made and standing proud on his bedside cabinet were photographs of him and Mum, Christian, and me. There was one photograph, a close up of my mum smiling, that was the closest to bed. I could imagine my dad wishing my mum a goodnight, just before he would reach over and turn off the lamp.

I gave the room a vacuum, dusted, and fluffed up the cushions on the bed. The room had a familiar scent, a flowery perfume. Memories flooded my mind, I remembered my mother smelling that way. On the bedside cabinet was an old bottle of perfume, it was nearly empty and I wondered if that had belonged to my mum. Perhaps Dad sprayed it in the room to remind him of her. I made a mental note of the perfume.

Later that afternoon, just as the sun was starting to lower, I heard the sound of a car pull onto the driveway. I looked over to Dad, who was reading his newspaper for the second time that day.

That might be Chris, I wrote, tapping his newspaper to get his attention.

Dad nodded and rose. I let him open the front door and strained to hear a mumbled conversation.

When Christian walked through to the kitchen, I wanted to gasp. His hair was a mess, those dark circles framed eyes reddened with unshed tears. His hand visibly shook. He slumped into a chair opposite me and lowered his head into his hands. Dad stood to his side with his hand on Christian's back.

"She's been having an affair for two years. Two fucking years and I didn't know a thing," Christian said. He hadn't looked up, but a tear dripped through his fingers and landed on the kitchen table. My heart broke for him.

"Did she tell you that, Son?" Dad asked.

Christian nodded his head. "I found some things, she had no choice but to confess it all. Dad, I smashed the house to pieces, I was so angry, and now I don't know what to do."

"Did you hurt her?" Dad said, his voice had lowered to a whisper.

Christian looked up sharply. "No!"

"How have you left it with her?" Dad asked.

"I can't go back there. It's finished. She's betrayed me in the worst way."

Christian looked at me with such devastation in his eyes that it startled me.

Christian, what is it? I wrote, sliding the pad across to him.

"I need…I need an hour or two to get over the journey. I have a couple of bags in the boot." He stood from his chair but wobbled.

"Sit down, Son, I'll fetch them in," Dad said.

I'd never seen Christian so distressed. His breathing was heavy, as if he'd just finished a run. I rose to fill a glass of water for him. He drank half of it down without taking a breath. He had kept his head bowed as I took my seat opposite him. I reached forwards to hold his hand. His grip was so tight my skin whitened. Something was very, very wrong.

I heard Dad place a couple of bags, or possibly suitcases, by the bottom of the stairs. Christian released my hand and stood.

"I have such a headache. I need to lay down for a little while," he said. I nodded and watched him walk out of the kitchen.

It was a few minutes later that Dad came back into the kitchen. He had a stricken look on his face.

Did he say anything more? I wrote.

Dad took the longest breath, exhaling so slowly before closing his eyes.

"Let's give him tonight, I think he's going to collapse in that bed. He's emotionally exhausted right now. Do you think I should ring Helen?"

I don't know. I guess she'd know he'd come here, wouldn't she? What do you think he meant when he said he smashed the place up?

Christian didn't have a violent bone in his body. I remembered as children, I was the one to fight his battles because he wouldn't. It wasn't that he wasn't capable, he was a fit man, a fit child back then, but he had no desire for confrontation, even if that meant taking a beating from the schoolyard bully.

"I think he punched some doors, smashed a few ornaments, or something. He said he threw a vase across the room; it smashed the mirror on the wall. That's not like him, Dani, not like him at all."

You need to sit down, let me make you a cup of tea, and we'll wait until Chris is ready to tell us more.

Dad sat as I stood to make the tea. I thought more about what he said about calling Helen. Once I'd made the tea, I fetched the telephone from the hallway and laid it on the table. I stared at it for a while. Would Christian feel we were not supporting him if we called Helen to ask if she was okay? She hadn't made any effort with us, and thinking about it, she didn't call Dad, ever. Christian was the one who would call.

When did Helen last visit you? I wrote.

"I don't know, long before…you know? Could even have been last year. Why?"

I'm just wondering why she's kept her distance.

"Because she's been cheating on my son. Maybe, hopefully, she feels guilty enough not to want to face me," Dad said with such vehemence in his voice.

I'll get dinner started, what do you fancy? I wrote, hoping that a change of subject, for the moment, might lessen some of the sadness in his eyes.

"I don't mind. I don't think Christian will be up to eating much. How about some of that soup you made the other day?"

I gave him a smile and nodded.

Christian didn't come down for dinner. I'd taken a tray up to him, but he was sleeping so soundly I decided to leave him alone. If he woke later, he could always reheat the soup. Dad seemed to be on edge for most of the evening, deciding to retire to bed earlier than normal. He gave me a kiss to the top of my head and told me not to stay up too late. I settled on the sofa with the television on low, not really watching a movie that I'd joined halfway through. My mind was on Christian.

I believed Dad was right in his reasoning for Helen keeping her distance. She'd certainly kept that distance from me since Trey and Hannah's deaths. We'd assumed it was because she hadn't wanted to upset me with the birth of Alistair, but I wasn't so sure anymore. I pondered on what Christian would do with regards to Alistair. Being in Cornwall was a long way from London. The more I thought about it, what would he do with regards to work? He'd have to return to London at some point.

I switched off the television and made my way to the kitchen. I let Lucy out for a last pee while I waited for the kettle to boil. A camomile tea would settle my brain from its overactivity.

It was as I crossed the upstairs hallway, heading to my bedroom, that I heard a sob. I paused beside Christian's door and closed my eyes. My hand hesitated over the handle until eventually, I pulled away. As much as I was longing to comfort him, I knew what it felt like to feel utter devastation and the need to be alone at times. The decision left me very unsettled for the rest of the night, though.

CHAPTER THIRTEEN

I was standing at the back door sipping on my tea when I heard the shuffle of feet behind me. I turned to see Christian looking worse than he had when he'd arrived.

I raised my mug in the hopes he'd understand I was offering to make him some tea. He didn't reply, just simply nodded. He sat at the kitchen table and let his head fall back a little, looking up at the ceiling. His sigh echoed around the quiet room.

"Take a walk with me, when we've had our tea," he said, his voice sounded so pained.

I nodded and gave him a small smile.

I placed his cup in front of him and wrapped my arm around his shoulders. With one hand, he held onto me. He didn't speak while he drank and he didn't let go of me, either. Once he placed his empty cup back on the table, he stood. I gathered my coat and scarf from the back of the door, and while I waited for him to retrieve his, I checked my pocket for my pad and pencil.

Christian walked back into the kitchen and kept his eyes lowered until he reached the door.

"I guess Lucy doesn't do walks anymore, does she?" he said, looking over at her curled form in front of the boiler.

I shook my head, not knowing if he could see me or not.

Christian opened the back door and we stepped out into the chilly morning. We walked around the side of the garden and through the gate. We turned left. Had we gone the other way, we would have ended up at the bench, and perhaps, we could have sat and talked for a while. Instead we headed towards the church.

Christian didn't speak for a while, I heard him take in long deep breaths; perhaps he thought the nippy air would clear his thoughts. Eventually we came to the small stone wall that circled the cemetery. Christian stopped walking and rested on the wall.

"I know who she was having an affair with," he said, not looking at me, but staring out into the distance.

He didn't wait for me to find my pad to reply. "I found a photo she'd sent, it was old, that's how it all started. The receiver had a nickname and I didn't twig at first. She admitted the affair right off, said it was a one off thing, the usual shit one says when caught out. But then, the other day, I found some letters hidden in the bottom of the closet in the spare bedroom. I was trying to find some old trainers that I used to wear for the gym, they were more comfortable than my new ones."

He paused, as if wanting to check himself.

"Anyway, I found some letters, signed off with a nickname and then it hit me. I knew the name. I confronted her with the letters; the dates went back two years, Dani. Two fucking years they'd been screwing. I asked her if Alistair was mine." At that point, he looked at me with tears coursing down his cheeks.

"She said, no. I'm not sure how she can prove it, unless she's already had Alistair tested. I flipped, I tore the letters and threw them on the fire, and she fucking had the gall to cry and try to retrieve them from the embers. I know why, of course. It's all she has of him, I guess."

My mind wasn't keeping up with the speed he was speaking, but a sinking feeling began to form in my stomach. I placed my hand on his arm and squeezed, I wanted him to look at me. He did, and I wished he hadn't.

Anger laced his face, but not just anger. Was it pity? Was it disbelief, even? Because I was sure disbelief reflected back at him from mine. I stared at him for the longest moment, waiting. He opened his mouth to speak; the words didn't come. He closed his eyes and I watched the teardrop roll so gently down his chapped cheeks. Cheeks already so tear-stained the skin was red and sore.

"Trey is the father of Alistair," he said.

I don't think I moved, my body froze, other than my heart, which pounded so hard I could hear a pulse in my ears.

"I didn't want to tell you but it's going to come out. I'm divorcing her, she admitted it, I fucking…"

A scream bounced off the walls and the trees that lined it. It echoed back from the expanse of space to one side of me, where the cliff ended and the sea raged beneath it. My vision clouded. I saw Christian stand straight but that was all. I felt hands on my arms but I twisted myself free. The scream continued and it confused me. I wasn't sure where it was coming from, initially. It was only when my throat became so sore, and my mouth dry, that I realised it was from me.

"No," I shouted, surprising myself. "No. No. No."

"Dani, please. I'm so sorry. I have all the evidence; she admitted it. I found photographs."

He hadn't mentioned photographs before. I believed every word he'd told me, then.

I ran into the cemetery and fell to my knees in front of Trey's grave. I pounded on it with my fists, I scratched at his name until my fingernails broke and bled. Blood smeared, giving me the satisfaction that his name was being obliterated from the white marble.

"You fucking piece of shit. How could you? How could you be buried with my daughter after what you'd done?" Despite realising it had been me that screamed, my tone of voice shocked me.

I clawed at the earth under the headstone. I didn't want my baby in the ground with him. I dug up the plants I'd laid and threw them across the way. All the time I cursed and shouted at him.

I fell back on my arse and kicked at the headstone, smearing earth over his name. That was until Hannah's name caught my eye. I reached forwards, trying to clean the mess I'd made over her precious name. I pulled the sleeve of my jacket over my hand and rubbed as hard as I could. Then I attacked the earth again. I grabbed handfuls of earth and threw them. I pulled at the grass that had grown trying to…In fact, I wasn't sure what I was trying to do.

Arms reached around from behind and by the strength, I knew them not to belong to Christian. I was lifted from the ground and hauled backwards. I fought. I didn't want to stop my digging. I screamed some more and dug my nails into my captor. I kicked backwards satisfied at the grunt as I caught a shinbone.

"It's okay, I've got you," I heard. I recognised the voice but not why Miller was trying to stop what I was doing.

"Let me go!" I shouted.

"No, trust me, Dani, please?" It was a pleading that I wanted to obey but just couldn't.

"Get him away from my daughter!" I screamed, my voice becoming so hoarse from excessive use after so long of silence.

"Dani, I'm going to set you down now, and I want you to look at me, okay?"

Miller lowered me so my feet touched the ground; he turned me, still holding on as tight as he could. I stared into his face, one as grief-stricken as I imagined mine to be.

"Breathe, Dani."

I gasped for air, and then the sobbing came. I collapsed against his chest; thankful he was holding me up. I didn't want to fall on the grave of a traitor. I didn't want to be that close to him.

Miller wrapped his arms around me so tightly I couldn't move. He rested his chin on top of my head and I could hear him whisper but not make out the words.

We stayed that way for what felt like ages. Eventually, exhaustion overwhelmed me and I passed out.

I heard myself crying, sobbing, but my body felt so heavy and my eyelids remained firmly closed. I knew I was being carried, I could feel Miller's chest under my cheek. I could hear voices, Christian and Miller, and another that was distant. I was jolted as Miller jogged along, I assumed. I knew I was back home, the gate gave a familiar creak and then it was warm.

I was laid on a bed, mine by the lavender scent I'd place on the pillow to aid sleep. I curled into a ball. I felt my boots being removed. My jacket was tugged from my body and a comforter was placed over me.

"Baby?" My dad's heartbroken voice penetrated my sobs. I reached out and took his hand. I wanted him to know I'd heard him.

After a while I opened my eyes, they were sore, sticky, and swollen. My dad sat on a chair beside me, and behind him, Miller sat on the floor with his back resting against the wall.

"Dad?" I croaked out.

"Oh, my baby. I'm so sorry, so so sorry," Dad said. His voice broke and fresh tears streamed down my face.

Miller stood and walked over; he sat on the edge of the bed and pushed back some sodden hair from my forehead. It was a gentle gesture that I wasn't sure the meaning of.

"I'd like to come back later, when you've had a chance to talk to your family. Is that okay?" he asked. His low-toned voice rolled over me, comforting. I nodded my head.

I watched him leave. "Where's Christian?" I asked.

"Downstairs. I can't console him. I've tried. Oh, God, I don't know what to do," Dad said, and the tears that then rolled down his cheeks crucified me.

I glanced at the clock on the bedside cabinet. It had been four hours since Christian and I had left the house. Had I slept? I straightened myself and sat up.

"Let's go down, Dad," I said.

He nodded, not making mention of the fact my voice was back. Shock had taken it away, and shock had brought it back, at the worst possible time.

Christian stood when he saw me at the doorway, he rushed forwards but then hesitated, not sure what to do. I stepped into his arms and wrapped mine around his waist. We held each other and we cried yet again.

"I swear, I didn't want to tell you, but then I was scared how you'd feel if I'd kept that from you as well," Christian whispered.

"You had to tell me. And now you have to tell me all of it," I said.

"I don't know…"

"You *have* to. I need to know, Christian. I need to know everything."

I heard a door open and gently close, I assumed Miller had slipped out to leave us alone for a while. Dad placed his hands on our backs, encouraging us to sit. He used to do that when we'd fallen out as children. We had to sit opposite each other and talk it out. Then we had to hug. I guessed we were doing it in reverse order.

I watched his eyes widen in fear, his jaw grinding in anger, and the tears fall in sadness. He was going through every emotion at the same time. I took his hands in mine as Dad sat at the end of the table, not wanting to sit directly beside either one of us, but to be able to reach out to us both at the same time.

"Tell me," I said.

"I told you I found a photograph she'd sent, she was half-naked, well, she had her knickers on, nothing more. It was a pic taken before she was pregnant. The name of the recipient was Kitt."

I frowned. Kitt didn't ring any bells in my mind.

"I didn't twig. She let me believe it was someone at work; they hadn't had sex just some flirting that had gotten out of control. I sort of believed her, at first. I was bitterly disappointed, hurt, but she'd just had Alistair, so I put it on the back burner for a little while."

I guessed that answered why we hadn't seen them, or been invited to visit.

"She changed, I thought she had pre-baby blues, then post-baby blues, or whatever it's called. Now I know it was grief."

If I had been a dog, or a cat, or whatever animal, it would have been so visible that my hackles had just risen at his statement. I felt the hairs on all parts of my body stand on end in utter rage.

"She doesn't fucking get to grieve for him!" I said. I felt Dad reach forwards and place his hand on my arm. I pulled my arm away.

"She doesn't have the right to grieve," I repeated.

"No, she doesn't. But she did, and I mistook it for something to do with the pregnancy. Now, in hindsight, it should have been obvious the baby wasn't mine. He looks nothing like me at all."

I noticed *the baby* and not the use of his name.

"Does he…?" I turned to Dad; he'd met Alistair.

Dad sighed and gently shrugged his shoulders. "I can't say, for sure. He's fair-haired and blue-eyed."

"So was Hannah," I said quietly.

"So are you, and you," Dad said, looking between Christian and me.

Christian and I were both dark blonde, I guessed the formal term would be. Our eyes were blue but with specks of brown. We'd often laughed about our strange eyes; pleased they were a mix of our parents. Dad had brown eyes, Mum had blue.

Christian shook his head.

"Tell me more," I demanded.

"I found letters going back two years. Some of it was just general chat, some more explicit. One or two detailed what fucking fun they'd had on a weekend away."

I tried to remember times when Trey had been away, either it had been golfing with his buddies, but then Christian was usually included in that, or it had been work. I started to laugh, bitterly.

"How fucking clichéd. I guess they told us it was a work thing when instead they were sneaking away to fuck each other." I'd spat the words out and caught the wince that had Dad's eyes partially close and his brow crease.

Christian didn't reply.

"What did she say, when you confronted her?" I asked.

"She couldn't do anything other than admit it. I asked her if they were in love, she wouldn't reply. I screamed at her, I punched doors, threw things. Then I asked her if Alistair was mine and she said no. She looked at me without any fucking emotion on her face, and said no."

At that point Christian broke down again.

I was numb, stunned into paralysis. I wanted to reach forwards and comfort him but I couldn't.

I'd lost my baby; she was buried just a half a mile from me. Yet Trey's blood still ran, his DNA, his genes, were being kept alive through an adulterous relationship.

It was too much for me to take in at that moment. I let go of Christian's hand and I stood. On shaking legs, I walked to the counter. I needed to do something and I wanted to laugh out loud as I switched the kettle on to boil. How very fucking British of me!

I placed my hands on the counter and stared at the white-tiled wall. One tile had a crack. I focussed on the crack in a wall of symmetry, of pristine. I wanted to laugh. The more I looked, the more the crack stood out against the perfect. The irony wasn't lost on me. I thought I had the perfect marriage. Trey was my soul mate; we were the symmetry, the pristine. Yet there had been a fucking large crack, which, like that tile, I hadn't noticed until then.

The steam from the boiling kettle obliterated the crack, and I pulled mugs from the rack and made tea. My throat was sore, I wasn't sure if that was crying, screaming, or lack of previous use. I actually wanted a cup of tea, something to warm the ice inside my body and fill the hollow in my stomach.

"She sobbed at his funeral. I didn't think it strange, at the time," I said, as I placed three mugs on the table. I sat.

"She had no right to sob. She had no fucking right to grieve for him while I was. That day should have been mine, and mine alone. I shouldn't have had to share grief with her," I added. Bile rose to my throat.

I wasn't sure I was making sense to Dad and Christian, but it was crystal clear in my mind. I was burying my husband and my child that day: a husband and child that had been wrenched from me in the most horrific way. And I hadn't been allowed to be the one who was entitled to grieve the most. She had not only stolen my husband, as such, but she's stolen that day as well.

There had been many times I'd wished that day had never happened, I'd prayed it would be wiped from my memory, and for a while it had. In that moment, though, it all came flooding back. How she'd sobbed, while sitting in the middle of the front pew. I remembered how her hand shook as she walked to his coffin and placed a single rose on the top, yet she'd ignored Hannah. Her single sob as his coffin was lowered into the ground resonated around my mind. It all made sense.

"I feel sick," I said, darting from my chair and towards the back door. I needed fresh air.

I pulled the door closed behind me, knowing that in a minute or so, I'd be shivering with the cold. I wanted to be alone, just for a moment, and I hoped the blast of cold air would wipe those memories from my mind.

I gulped in air to quell the nausea. I wrapped my arms around myself, not for warmth but for comfort, and I closed my eyes. I felt myself sway a little, but I didn't care. I could fall where I stood, it didn't matter.

Two of the five years Trey and I had been married had been a lie. The thought tore through me.

I heard the back door open and a leather jacket was placed over my shoulders. Miller stepped in front of me, having returned, and although my arms weren't in the sleeves, he zipped it up, protecting me against the cold. I didn't speak, I didn't smile, but I did look at him.

He stared at me without speaking, without blinking, for the longest time.

"Rips you apart, doesn't it?" he whispered.

It was all I could do to nod.

"The lies, the deceit, the betrayal. If you let it, it will erode your soul, Dani."

"You're talking from experience?" I asked.

"Yes. I was married for years. She was having an affair; I didn't know the guy personally, so I guess that makes it a little easier than your situation. You wanted to know why Daniel and I didn't get on? She confessed to him, he kept her secret. I can't forgive him for that."

I wanted to say that, as a vicar, he had no choice, but it wouldn't have made any difference. There was also a part of me that sympathised with Miller; family should be stronger than anything else, including faith.

"I'm sorry," I said.

"Don't be, it's not your sin to apologise for. Now, shall we get you back in?"

"Will you stay, just for a little while?" I asked. I wasn't sure why, but I needed him at that moment.

"Of course. Christian has gone back upstairs. Your dad is hovering over who he should be with right now."

We walked into the kitchen and I had to wait for Miller to unzip the jacket since my arms were trapped inside. Dad was resting against the counter with his shoulders slumped.

"Go and sit with him, Dad. He needs you," I said.

"But..."

"I'll sit with Dani," Miller said.

I didn't want to sit in the kitchen, the heart of the house, the place where we always sat. It was tarnished, for the moment, with sour words and bad memories. I walked into the living room and slumped into the corner of the sofa. I curled my legs up under me.

Miller poked around the fire, trying to reignite the embers. He threw on some kindling wood and gently blew until flames started to flicker. I watched as he placed some logs on top before he stood and sat beside me.

"I'm not going to ask you what happened, but Christian told me some. I guess he needed to get it all out. I called him out on where he delivered the news, though. I'm not going to apologise for that," he said.

"I imagine it was coincidence we ended up at the cemetery."

"All the same, you should have been told here, in the safety of your own home."

If anyone else had criticised Chris, I would have been bristling, but I wasn't. I didn't agree with what Miller had said, but I was thankful that he was thinking of me. I doubted any time would have been a good time to hear that news, and no place would have been more of a comfort than another.

"I made a mess of the grave, didn't I?" I said quietly.

"I can fix that tomorrow for you."

"I'd appreciate that. I don't want to go there. I don't want Hannah to be there with him, either."

"I don't think there's much we can do about that. Maybe in time you'll feel differently."

"Time. That word meant something a little while ago. I thought I was finally coming to terms with what had happened to them, and now? All the pain, and more, is back."

"It's a different pain though, isn't it?"

I thought for a moment. "Yes and no. I felt betrayed when he left me, when he died. I was angry with him for a long while. Angry that he'd risked his life by taking that seatbelt off. Now I'm betrayed all over again, and there's no outlet, if you know what I mean."

"Explain to me."

"I can't confront him. I can't look into his eyes and see whether he'd tell me the truth. The worst part? I can't ask him if he loved me, or whether he loved her more."

Had Trey fallen out of love with me and in love with her?

"You made a baby together, perhaps that tells you something?"

"He made a baby with her!" I snapped, regretting that I had. "I'm sorry, I didn't mean to snap at you."

"Don't apologise. What I mean is, if he hadn't loved you, would he have done that?"

"I don't know. Which one of them was a mistake? Hannah or Alistair?"

The thought that Hannah had been a mistake, an unwanted baby by him because he hadn't loved me enough, tore through me. I wanted to double over to ease the pain that had formed in my stomach and radiated up into my chest. My heart physically hurt as it shattered inside.

Miller shuffled closer to me. He took my hand from my chest, I hadn't realised it had been covering my heart, and he held it in his. My instinct was to pull away, it was wrong to hold another man's hand, but I needed the comfort from him. We weren't friends, as such, I had hoped we could be, and he had been off with me of late. But right then he was just what I needed: a stranger to listen to me, to not judge, and offer some guidance.

"What do I do, Miller? What did you do?"

"I died inside for a while. I shrivelled up, lost my masculinity because I thought I wasn't man enough for her. I fucked around, just to show her, or maybe me, that I was desired and that she had it all wrong. I drank, I fought, I smashed things, and then I put them back together again. I spent a long time putting me back together again. And so will you."

I snorted. "I might pass on the *fucking around* if that's okay, although right now, a large glass of whisky would go down well."

He chuckled and somehow, despite my pain, I smiled at him. It was a bittersweet smile. He rose from the sofa and crossed the room to a small dark oak sideboard that housed an array of old-fashioned, crystal cut decanters. He pulled out the silver stopper from one and sniffed.

"I think this is okay," he said, pouring a measure into two glasses. "I don't suppose you have ice," he added, raising the lid of a white ceramic ice bucket decorated with flowers.

I remembered that ice bucket standing pride of place back when I was a child. It had to be over twenty years old and even then, I think it had come from a charity shop. It certainly looked like something that would have graced a 1970's living room.

"I'll fetch some," I said, starting to uncurl my legs.

"Stay there, I can find the freezer."

I heard Miller mumble to Lucy before returning with four ice cubes in his hand; the water had started to drip through his fingers. He placed two in each glass and then carried them back to the sofa.

"Whisky, no idea how old it is. We might end up with a stinking headache, and it won't be a hangover, more that it's off, but…" He handed me a glass.

The liquid burned not just my lips and mouth, but my throat and all the way down to my stomach. I dreaded to think of the cauldron of acid that was bubbling away, having aged whisky in the mix.

"I want to get drunk. I haven't gotten drunk in years," I said, taking another sip.

"You don't, trust me. Being drunk is not a good place to be when your head is full of shit. The shit turns into a sewer, and on top of it all still being there in the morning, you'll feel fucking ill."

"Then maybe just enough to numb the pain and the thoughts," I said.

"Trouble with that is, the *just enough* isn't enough the next time round. The *just enough* becomes two, three glasses, then half a bottle, a full bottle. Before you know it, you're so reliant on more and more alcohol, you can't function."

"Is that what happened to you?"

"Yes. I lost myself in the devil that is drink for a long while."

"But you're drinking now, and you had a pint at the pub the other day."

"I guess, I'm one of the lucky ones. I didn't drink because I was addicted to the alcohol, like you; I just wanted the numbness. When that stopped working, I needed a different *fix*. I can have a drink now, it doesn't make me want more."

"What was your different fix?"

"I guess I threw myself into creating things. I brought things to life, changed people's lives. I just worked, seven days a week. I moved back here and eventually I met someone else."

I stared at him. He hadn't mentioned having a partner before.

"You're...?"

"Not now. Now, it's just me. And we don't need to talk about that. Tonight is about you."

We sat for a moment in silence, with just the crackle and spit of the logs on the fire.

"I feel so lost," I said, staring at the orange and red flames, listening to a hiss and watching a fleeting streak of blue as sap seeping from the logs caught.

"I know. And right now it won't make any difference if I tell you that you're not. You have a supportive family around you. You can't get lost if you have that, and friends, because we won't let you."

"You're very philosophical, aren't you?" In fact, he was a pretty deep person overall.

He shrugged his shoulders. "I don't know about that. My dad is the philosophical one."

"Is he still local?" I asked.

"Yes, he lived at the bottom of my garden..." he chuckled as he spoke.

"I guess in a house of some kind," I said, interrupting him.

"Yes, we built a little bungalow together, a while ago now. It was nice to work alongside him again. We'd fallen out for many years. I didn't speak to him, or Daniel, after Pam left. Like I said, I felt betrayed by them both for a while."

"How did your dad betray you?" I understood how he felt about Daniel, but he hadn't mentioned his dad.

"He supported Daniel's decision not to tell me. He could have been the mediator, it would have absolved Daniel from whatever crime it is to speak out about a confession, but he didn't."

"How did your dad know if she confessed to Daniel?"

"Because my dad was the parish priest before Daniel. He might not *practice* or whatever the word is, I'm not remotely religious, but, I guess, Daniel confided in him, thinking he would give him answers. I get that Daniel was troubled and he was torn. But he chose his faith over me, and that didn't sit well with me. I can't honestly say I'd have done the same had I been the priest."

"Was it your dad at…?" I didn't want to say the words.

"No, he retired and until Daniel came here, there was a temporary vicar. Do they have temporary vicars? I don't know if that's the right word, but you know what I mean."

I had settled into the corner of the sofa again and the whisky was having the desired effect of numbing my brain, and my legs. It wasn't the largest shot but I wasn't a drinker, and perhaps, if it was a little aged, it was also more potent.

I rested my head back and closed my eyes. "I like this whisky," I said, letting the alcohol wash over me.

"Do you think, if you tried, you could forgive Daniel?" I asked.

"If I tried, maybe, but there's more to it than that. For now, though, I think you're about ready to pass out."

"I'm not drunk," I said, opening my eyes.

"Didn't say you were, but I bet you're fucking exhausted. I'll leave now, let you get some sleep."

I reached to place my glass on the coffee table; instead Miller stood and took it from me.

"Don't get up, although don't fall asleep there, either. When that fire dies down, you'll be cold."

"Pam was a silly woman. You're a very considerate man," I said, and then clamped my mouth shut for fear of having overstepped the mark.

"Yep, that she was," he said. He walked through the living room door and I heard the kitchen tap run, I assumed he'd rinsed the glasses.

"I'll see you tomorrow," he called out, as he walked out the back door.

I listened for the rumble of his truck engine and the crunch it made driving over the gravel and then sighed. I stretched out my legs and pulled the old throw from the back of the sofa over me.

It had to be early hours of the morning that I woke, stiff and cold, as Miller said I would be, after the fire had died out. I climbed from the sofa, still clutching the throw around me and made my way to bed. I was thankful that at least I'd had a few hours of dreamless sleep, and had no doubt the whisky was to be thanked for that.

CHAPTER FOURTEEN

ootsteps along the hall woke me. I lay still and listened to the shower run in the bathroom, then the buzz of an electric razor before the toilet flushed. I guessed it to be Dad, not expecting that Christian would be bothered to shave. I swung my legs over the side of the bed and sat for a while. Like a movie in slow motion, the events of the previous day filtered through my mind, and the sickness I'd felt washed over me again. I looked over to the chest of drawers to see a photograph of Trey and me on a holiday somewhere. We were laughing at something, we looked young and in love. I walked over and laid the photograph face down. I didn't want to see his face.

The footsteps crept past my door and continued down the stairs. I heard the radio being turned on and a tap run as Dad filled the kettle for his morning tea, I imagined. My legs ached, my whole body ached as I stood and grabbed a fresh towel from the stack on a chair.

Once I had showered and dressed, I joined Dad in the kitchen.

"Did you manage to sleep?" Dad said, as he slid a pad over to me.

"On and off," I replied, not needing the pad.

"I wasn't sure…" He indicated to the pad, I guessed he thought I'd gone mute again.

"Like I said, shock took my voice, shock gave it back," I said, noticing the bitterness in my voice.

"I suppose we should cancel the speech therapist appointment, but I wonder if you'd still like to talk to someone."

"I don't know that I need to. What can anyone say to me, Dad? My husband had an affair, fathered a child, and then died."

"I don't know what to do to make this all better." Dad turned away from me and I wondered if that was so I didn't see the sadness that settled over his face. He busied himself making tea.

"There's nothing you can do, I don't think. We just have to work through this ourselves, I guess."

For a moment we were silent, and I watched his shaking hand lift the kettle to pour hot water into the pot.

"Your voice is different," he said quietly.

"How?"

"I don't know, raspier, I guess. I imagine it will take some time to get back to normal."

"I don't think any part of me will ever be normal again," I replied, taking the mugs to the table.

Dad joined me with the pot of tea and poured.

"No, I don't suppose you will."

"Something I remembered during the night, Chris said the name in Helen's phone was Kitt. Trey has never been called that, to my knowledge. Do you think Chris has it wrong?"

"He said Helen admitted it was Trey."

"Convenient, though, since he's dead."

Was I trying to find a reason that she could have lied? The more I thought about it, the more I wondered. There had been absolutely no evidence that Trey had been having an affair. Not that I was aware of the times they were together, but surely I would have noticed something, wouldn't I? I didn't believe Trey to be so devious, so calculated, and so good at concealment he could have had a two-year affair and fathered a child without one wobble in our relationship.

"Ring Patricia for me. Ask her if Trey ever had a nickname. I'm not sure I can speak with her right now, just in case I break down. I'd hate for her to know what *might* have happened."

"Are you doubting Christian's story?" Dad asked.

"Not Christian's, Helen's. I want some proof, Dad. I want evidence that Alistair is Trey's son. I need that."

The previous day I'd been ready to dig his bones from the grave he shared with my daughter, and I wasn't sure what had happened overnight, but I couldn't just accept her word. By having an affair in the first place, she'd proven herself not to be trustworthy, or was I clinging on to some mistaken belief that I had the perfect husband?

I sat bolt upright in my chair. "I need to go to the storage unit, where my things are."

"What do you hope to find?"

"Evidence, Dad. If they exchanged letters, where are the ones she sent to him?"

"Do you want to put yourself through that?"

Dad's comment surprised me.

"Not only did I lose him in an accident, for which I have no closure because it was all so sudden, I can't confront him. I can't look at him and get an explanation, he can't tell me it's all lies."

"Or the truth," Dad said quietly.

"Do you believe her?"

Dad sighed deeply. "I just don't see why she would have named Trey, knowing the devastation it would cause. Why not make up a stranger that no one knows? Surely that would have been easier, wouldn't it?"

"Because Christian can confront a stranger, he can't confront a dead man."

My voice became raspier the more upset I was becoming. I took a large swig of my tea.

"It's too convenient, Dad. Can't you see that?"

"Of course I can, I'm just not sure that you aren't grasping at something just to be let down, feel even more hurt when the truth comes out. I'll ring Patricia a little later, at least we'll start there."

"I can't be more hurt than I am right now, but thank you. I think I'll take a walk, if you don't mind. I need to clear my head."

Instead of walking the coastal path, I wrapped up and left the house by the front door. I walked up to the honesty box concealed in the hedge by the farm gate. My thoughts went to Lincoln and an urge to write to him, to speak to him face-to-face overcame me. He'd understand my need, I was sure of that. I stood for ages, just looking at the cracked and paint chipped wooden box. Childhood memories flooded back. There would be a small table underneath with fruit or vegetables bagged up. Sometimes boxes of eggs would be stacked, and I remembered one time when Christian knocked the table and a couple of boxes fell. The eggs smashed on the ground and we were both so upset by what had happened that we ran back home to empty our piggybanks and put the coins in the box. I was sure that Christian even wrote an apology note.

"Woo hoo," I heard. I turned to see Mrs. Hampton walking down the lane.

She waved and her pace quickened to catch up with me.

"I thought that was you. What are you looking at?"

"Nothing, I was just thinking," I replied.

She skidded to a halt and stared at me. Her smile grew broad.

"Dani, you can…"

"Yes, I guess that block in my brain decided to shift. It hurts to talk too much, though."

"You need to keep a scarf wrapped around your throat. Oh, and honey and lemon with hot water, keep drinking that. Maybe an inhalation of steam as well. You need to keep your throat very well lubricated. When I was in the choir, we had to do all sorts of exercises to keep our vocal cords in tip-top condition. I'm sure I've got some notes written down somewhere. I could drop them down, I haven't had a cup of tea with your dad for a while."

I was unsure if the *drop them down* was out of concern for my vocal cords, or the need for a cup of tea with my dad. Either way, I found myself smiling at her.

"That would be lovely, and I know Dad would love to spend some time with you over a cup of tea."

"He would? Well, that's settled then. I'll be down this afternoon, I'm sure I have a cake somewhere. Does your dad like cake, or you? Do you like cake?" she corrected herself just in time.

"We both like cake. However, I might be out, I have some errands to run, so you might have to suffer Dad all on your own, would that be okay?"

"Oh, of course. It's a shame you won't be there, but I'm sure I can entertain your dad for a little while."

I tried not to laugh as she shuffled back up the lane, without so much as a goodbye. She had been a welcome break from the shit whirling around my mind for a few minutes.

I continued to walk, taking a right down a very narrow lane. I hadn't walked the lanes for years and struggled to remember where it would lead me. Overhanging trees shaded most of the lane, and the dip in temperature as I walked under the tree canopy was noticeable. I wondered if Mrs. Hampton might have had a point in wearing a scarf. I could feel the cold air catching in my throat. It was so quiet, and I noticed the absence of bird-song. I guessed I was used to the sound of the ocean when walking the coastal path; this route was eerie. I rounded a bend, pleased to note I was walking in a square, not that I thought I'd get lost.

A lone dog, probably a working dog from the farm that framed either side of the lane, wandered past me. It took no notice, other than to give me a cursory glance. One eye was blue and the other brown, its tongue was hanging out, as if the dog had just finished a hard session of sheep rounding. I watched it dart through a gap in a hedge too high for me to see over. The bleat of sheep suggested the dog was back to work.

I continued on my way dodging puddles, cow shit, and mud, I guessed a tractor had recently driven down the lane. Eventually, I took another turn and found myself further past the church than I imagined. I remembered that Miller lived this side of the church, or was it Daniel? Or maybe, they lived together. One of them had said that if the church hadn't been there, we'd be neighbours. There was a small collection of cottages, and if I remembered correctly, there would be a path down to a slipway. Years ago, Christian and I would watch small boats be hauled up the slipway and buckets of fish placed on the ground. The locals would take tourists out fishing from this point, and I wondered what had happened to finish all that.

I weaved through a couple of cottages looking for the slipway. I sat on the edge of a wall that bounded the slipway and what, I remembered, had been a very small harbour area. Beside me was a collection of lobster traps, coiled rope, and a neatly folded fishing net. Such was the nature of the locals; they could leave their means of fishing, knowing it wouldn't be stolen.

The sound of an engine disturbed the peace. I turned to see a trailer holding a small boat being reversed down the slipway. I stood, knowing there was plenty of space but wanting to make sure the driver of the vehicle could see me. I saw his elbow resting on the open window and when he looked out, he smiled at me.

"What are you doing here?" Miller asked.

"Needed a walk, haven't been around this way since I was child, I don't think."

"Has it changed much?"

"Yeah, I'm sure there was a pub, or a restaurant, or something over there."

Miller continued to reverse until the trailer was partly submerged in water. He left the engine running but climbed from his truck.

"Do you need some help?" I asked.

"I've got this, but thanks. And it was a fish restaurant, if I remember. No menu, you got whatever the boats had brought in that day."

"That's right. Although I don't think we ate there much, but I remember sitting outside."

I watched as Miller partially unstrapped the boat before tying it to a metal pillar on the side. He then released the boat gently into the water, before jumping back in the truck, and pulling the trailer out of the water.

"Want to do something?" he said, leaning out of his window.

"I thought you were going out in your boat?"

"Not today, that thing hasn't been on the water in years. I thought I ought to see if she still floated first. Come on, get in."

I rounded the truck and climbed into the passenger side. "I should tell my dad I'm still out." I patted my jacket knowing full well I didn't have a mobile phone on me.

"I can give him a call, if you want, or you can use my phone."

He reached forwards to a small compartment on the dashboard and produced a battered black phone that he handed to me.

"You know, I can't remember my home phone number. How awful is that?" I said.

"Well, you don't generally call yourself. And you probably just have it programmed in your phone, so you don't need to remember it."

He took the phone back and with one eye on the road he scrolled through his contacts; the phone was ringing by the time he handed it back to me.

"Dad, it's me. I'm using Miller's phone because I didn't take one out with me. I'll be back later, okay? I didn't want you to worry. Is Chris up?"

"He is, although he's not talking too much. Do you have a coat, are you warm enough?" Dad said.

"I do, and I am. I'll call you later and let you know what I'm doing."

We said our goodbyes and I placed the phone back into the compartment on the dash.

"I've got to drop the trailer off first, then I want to take you someplace," Miller said.

We pulled into the driveway of a house I could not have imagined Miller to live in. It was a chocolate box cottage, with wisteria growing up the front and hanging over a small wooden porch. He reversed down the side of the cottage and told me to wait while he unhooked the trailer. He was gone no more than a couple of minutes before returning.

"Is that your house?" I asked.

"It is. Needs a lot of work inside," he said with a chuckle. "So how are you doing today?"

In one way I wished he hadn't asked, I'd have to remember and up until that point, he had been a welcome distraction.

I sighed, loudly. "Uh Oh, that doesn't sound good," he said.

"How do I know she's telling the truth, Miller? Surely I would have noticed something in my marriage. They were together two years, how did I miss that? There's a large part of me that thinks this is all too convenient. He's dead; he can't answer any allegations. What's to say she picked him instead of the real one so Christian couldn't confront whoever it was?" I knew I was rambling but all my fears seemed to tumble out.

"What does your gut tell you?"

"My gut? My gut went into meltdown when they died, I couldn't trust one instinct of mine right now. Half the time, I don't know which way is up. I spend most days lying to everyone, and myself, about how I feel. Right now, either I'm in denial of something so bloody obvious, or I'm right. Figure that one out." I laughed at the absurdity of it all.

"Christian said that she admitted it, he found some letters, or something?"

"He did, but the contact name in her phone was Kitt. Trey never had a nickname. Not once in five years had I heard that name being used by anyone. I mean, what kind of a nickname is that, anyway?"

"What about the child?"

"She said that Trey was the father. How would she know, for fact? Chris didn't say that she'd had some sort of test done, but she was certainly screwing two men at the same time. I'm going to book an appointment at the storage facility, I want to see if I can find anything."

"Who packed up your house?"

I paused and stared at him. He glanced over when I hadn't answered as quickly as he expected.

"They did."

Did that mean that any evidence that could have been in my belongings would no longer be there?

I slumped back in my seat. "I don't know what to believe. Like I said to Dad, if it's true, the last two years of my life has been a lie."

"I can understand you wanting proof. I'll go with you to the storage facility if you want, maybe a guy, or someone uncon-nected, might spot something you'd miss."

"That's kind of you. I have no idea where it is, I can only assume in London somewhere. Christian sorted it all out. I accepted an offer on my house, I'm hoping that will go through soon, but I don't want to go back there. Especially now."

Miller held out a bottle of water that he'd retrieved from the pocket in his door. I looked at him, my brow in a frown.

"You're getting a little high-pitched, I don't want you to screw up your voice. It's nice to hear you talk so much."

I took the bottle from him and swigged at it. "Do you think I'm talking too much?" I asked.

"I think you have every right to talk too much right now. You've not been able to for months. I imagine you've got a lot of words to get out."

I hadn't taken any notice of where we were headed until we bumped over a few sand dunes and weaved our way along a small beach.

"Are you allowed to drive on the beach?" I asked.

"I don't see anyone about to stop me." He gave me a wink.

I could see a small shack ahead, it looked pretty rundown but a metal chimney protruded from the top, and smoke bellowed out. Miller pulled the truck to a halt alongside it. The shed was larger than I had originally thought and I saw a handmade sign on the front.

"The Smoke Shack?" I questioned.

"Best smoked fish you'll ever find. Best smoked meats, as well."

Miller opened his door and began to walk around to my side. He hadn't finished crossing the front before I was out and zipping up my jacket. He held out his hand and I took it without thinking.

"Follow me," he said.

He bashed on the side of the shed before walking to the door at the other end. It was opened by a guy who looked like he was still backpacking around the world in the 1970's. He had long, straggly hair that matched a beard I was concerned about. I was sure I could see food among the bristles.

They did that man thing—a sort of handshake, chest bump, and called each other 'bro.' It amused me.

"Dani, this is China."

"China?"

"Don't ask, China, this is my friend, Dani. I don't believe she has ever tasted what delights you have going on today."

"Well, you better come on in then," China said.

I was taken aback. China, and it was the strangest name I'd heard, had the poshest voice I'd ever encountered. He had pure, crystal cut glass pronunciation. We followed China into the shack and I had to dodge fish and meat hanging from a rack suspended from the ceiling. I would imagine the Environmental Health Department would have a field day, should they ever visit. The smoke I'd seen earlier seemed to come from a floor-to-ceiling wooden cabinet. He opened the top door and slid out a wooden rail. Fish hung from the rail. He unhooked a pair of what I assumed to be mackerel and laid them on fresh napkins before handing them to us.

"How about some ham? I've been experimenting with this one. It's smoked, obviously, with a homemade marmalade coating. I need to know how the marmalade works for you."

China started to carve some meat from the leg of ham.

"China did an amazing tea-smoked ham," Miller said, tearing off a piece of ham and popping it into his mouth.

I pulled a little of the fish from the napkins and it was just wonderful. A burst of oak, of a subtle charcoal, and of course, the mackerel not only coated my taste buds but the scent drifted to my nose.

"This is good!" I said.

"Now, if you'll excuse me, I have many things to get done today," China said, ushering us to the door.

"He might be the best smoker in the area, but manners, despite his very privileged upbringing, are not his forte," Miller said, laughing.

I followed Miller out onto the beach and the door was slammed shut behind us.

"What a strange man," I said.

"Yep! Smoking fish and meats isn't all he smokes," Miller said, laughing.

"Hold this." Miller handed me the ham while he opened the rear door of the truck.

He pulled out a blanket and spread it on the ground by the wheel.

"Sit," he said.

We sat with our back resting on the truck wheel and ate. The breeze caught my hair and many times I had to stop eating to pull strands from my mouth. Miller stretched out his legs and fished around in his pocket. He pulled out an elastic band, which he handed to me.

"You carry a hairband around with you?" I said, astonished.

"I happen to have an elastic band in my pocket. It bound the mail today and I just slipped it in my jeans, not thinking."

"Well, I appreciate it, thank you."

I placed the fish on the blanket and tied my hair back at the nape of my neck.

"So…" Miller said, swapping the fish for the ham.

"So…" I replied.

"I spoke with the planning officer. I wanted to get a feel of where they are with regards to applications. Doesn't appear they have a huge list to work through, but I don't see us getting an answer this side of the new year."

"Okay, I guessed as much."

We fell into a comfortable silence for a while.

"How do you do a DNA test?" I asked.

"You'd need a sample of hair or saliva, I think. Why?"

"I'm going to insist on a DNA test, see if Alistair is Trey's son."

"Can you do that?"

"I don't know, I mean, I guess I can. Why wouldn't I be able to?"

"I'm not sure, I can't imagine anyone can request one. Would she agree?"

Without warning, a sob welled up inside me. "How the fuck didn't I know?" I said between tears.

"Oh, Dani. Maybe you just didn't see any signs because there wasn't any. Why should you know? If it's all true, they were very clever about it."

Miller took the food from my hand and placed his arm around my shoulder, I gently fell against him and cried.

We hadn't spoken since we'd climbed back in the truck and started the short journey back to my house. I stared out of the window, not seeing any of the trees or the fields as we passed. I just saw his face on the day I told him I was pregnant. It was utter joy. Or was it? He'd covered his mouth with his hands and tears had formed in his eyes. I remember laughing at his inability to speak. I closed my eyes at the memory, wondering if I'd gotten it very, very, wrong.

"We're here," I heard. I'd been so focussed on my thoughts, I hadn't realised we'd already returned.

"Thank you for this morning, I needed that. Just a couple of hours of normality, or escape from my normality, I should say."

"Any time. I wish I could do more to help."

I nodded as I climbed from the truck and walked the few steps to the front door. I turned to watch him drive away.

Dad and Christian were sitting at the kitchen table when I walked through. Dad gave me a small smile but Chris hadn't looked up.

"There's tea in the pot if you want one," Dad said.

I grabbed a mug from the draining board and added a splash of milk before sitting and pouring the tea.

"Helen has agreed to a DNA test. Although she's adamant who the father is, I've told her I'll take her to court if she refuses," Chris said.

"Can you do that? Take her to court?"

"I don't actually know, but I am a lawyer so the threat was enough. There are so many things to think about. I mean, I changed my will to leave money in trust for him. I need to rectify that."

I didn't answer immediately, I wasn't sure how. Christian's bitter tone of voice displayed the anger we both should feel, but Alistair was an innocent party. Chris had been his father for the first few months of his life.

"Can Helen survive, financially, without you?" Dad asked. It was a question on the tip of my tongue as well.

"I don't care, Dad. She chose the path she's walked down, maybe she should have thought about that before."

His words were callous and so unlike Christian. Of the two of us, he was the more compassionate, the empathic one who'd never walked past a homeless person without leaving a pound, or picking up a damaged bird to bring home and nurture when we were children. I could only assume it was the hurt and anger talking.

Dad went to speak and I gently shook my head at him. Christian turned towards me.

"You can understand, can't you? You must feel as angry as I do."

I had to think on my words carefully. "I'm angry, Chris, but it's a different type of anger, I think. I don't have Trey here to curse and shout at, to demand answers from. I'm all spent in the hatred department. I was angry at Trey for unbuckling that seatbelt, I was angry with him for dying. I'm numb and I'm extremely confused. I can't channel my anger towards anyone, so I'm swallowing it down as much as I can, right now. Mostly, I feel such an overwhelming sense of sadness and disappointment. And betrayal like I've never felt before."

Helen had been my friend before she started dating Christian. We'd known each other in university and often socialised. She was the straight one, although fun-loving, she was always so cautious to the point of carrying a rape alarm, having a safety contact on speed dial, and prearranging all her taxis. She wasn't a risk-taker at all.

As much as I felt the stab in my heart at Trey's betrayal, I also felt the knife she had twisted in me as well.

"Until I have evidence, Chris, I'm trying to contain my feelings. You said the nickname in her contacts was Kitt. I've never heard of Trey being called that."

"I have. When we were away skiing one year, he was chatting to a woman at a bar, nothing untoward, but he gave his name as Kitt. I didn't really think anything of it, at the time."

"You didn't think my husband chatting a woman up in a bar and giving a false name was odd?"

"No, that's not what I mean. We were getting drinks, she just started talking to him and he replied, being polite, I imagine. I took the drinks back to the table and he followed shortly after."

"Christian, he gave a woman his name, false or not, that isn't polite chit-chat with a stranger at a bar."

Was I overreacting? I couldn't recall a time I'd had a brief conversation while buying drinks that needed an exchange of names.

"Did you ask him about it?" I asked.

"No. I didn't think any more of it, until I saw the name on Helen's phone."

"Which skiing trip was this?"

"A couple of years ago, I think."

"About the same time he's supposed to have started this affair."

Had Trey taken on a fake name for Helen's contact list and decided to use it elsewhere?

"You don't want to believe me, and I can totally understand that, Dani. Trust me, I didn't want to believe it either. I have wished and prayed that it would have been anyone other than Trey. He was my best friend as well as your husband. He was family to us both. If her affair had been with a stranger, not that my decision to leave would have changed, but I think I could have stomached it a little easier than I can right now," Christian said.

"When Alistair was born, why was I not allowed to see him?" I decided to ask a question that had been playing on my mind for months.

Christian reached into his jeans pocket and pulled out his wallet. He slid a photograph of Alistair from inside and handed it to me.

"I imagine Helen thought you might see a resemblance," he said.

Alistair was dark-haired and brown-eyed. Christian was blond and blue-eyed. Helen was dark-haired, also with blue eyes. The only one of us that had brown eyes was Trey.

"I don't see a resemblance, to be honest, but Hannah had blue eyes, so I don't think there is one colour more dominant than another. I think that's an urban myth," I replied.

"Maybe, maybe not. I thought Helen was suffering from depression, but was she? She was the one who seemed to block all contact, and Dad only saw Alistair because I didn't tell her I was collecting him for a visit. Now I know it wasn't depression."

He gave me the consideration in not telling me she was grieving, and I silently thanked him for that.

"I'm going to tell Patricia, Christian. I want to ask her about the nickname and no matter what we think or feel, Alistair is possibly her grandchild," I said.

"She could also supply DNA for testing, I imagine," he replied.

I thought Christian had a good point. I had no idea where I'd get whatever was needed for a sample of Trey's DNA.

"I'm going to take a nap, I have a terrible headache coming on," I said.

I didn't have a terrible headache coming on, and it was a daft thing to say. How does one know just how terrible the headache was going to be? I wanted some space, time to breathe and collect my thoughts.

Sitting beside my bed was the letter I was yet to post to Lincoln. I opened the envelope and pulled out the note. A need to rewrite that letter had me grab the pad and pen and settle in my chair beside the window.

Lincoln,

I don't really know where to start with this letter. I've just discovered that my husband was, possibly, having an affair with my sister-in-law. Not only were they having an affair, but also he fathered her child. I can't articulate how that makes me feel right now.

There is a part of me that doesn't believe it. I mean, it's all too convenient, but deep down I know it's true. Christian, my brother, discovered evidence, and his wife admitted it. I don't know what to do, to be honest. I went to his grave and I tried to scratch his name from the headstone, I even dug up the earth. I don't want him in there with my baby, and I know that doesn't make any sense at all.

What I can't get out of my head is, was one of those children a mistake? And how would I feel if it was Hannah? I hate Helen, and I'm jealous that Alistair, her child, is alive and my baby isn't. I haven't told anyone this because I can't rationalise it. I shouldn't be jealous of a baby, an innocent, who didn't ask for all this shit. It pains me so much to think Trey's flesh and blood survives but is not mine. And then there's another thought that runs through my mind...I wouldn't want any part of him.

I screamed, Lincoln, and I haven't stopped talking since. My voice is different, so Dad tells me, and it hurts to talk too much. I so wanted to be able to talk when I had something good, something positive, to talk about. Now it's all about Trey, Helen. Christian is living here and his pain tears me up inside. I catch him looking at me sometimes and there's a strange look in his eyes. It's as if he's wondering why I didn't know. Two years Trey and Helen were supposed to be having an affair. Two Years! How did I not know?

I've racked my mind to think of anything that would have given a clue, even in hindsight, and I can't think of one thing.

I'm going to call his mother later; she lives in the U.S. I think she deserves to know she has a grandchild, or so I'm letting everyone believe. In truth, I want to know if she knew. I want to hear her call out her son, although I know that's also unreasonable.

I'm lost, Lincoln. More lost than I was before and I don't know if I'll ever find my way back.

Dani.

I folded the page, slipped it in the envelope, and before I could change my mind and decide it wasn't fair to unload on him, I left the house to post the letter. I snuck back in the house and crept up the stairs. I could hear Christian and Dad talking, but I didn't want to be part of their conversation for a while. Christian was going round in circles, and I could sympathise, but I needed distance from his distress to concentrate on my own.

I'd been putting up a front, covering up my real thoughts. I wasn't sure how I was supposed to feel. I'd cried, I'd screamed, but I didn't know what to do next. I wasn't sure how to move, let alone forwards. I was stuck, yet momentum had me spiralling. For the past however many months, I'd only been able to deal with one thing at a time and that had worked just fine. Now I felt as if I had been hit with an information overload from all sides: some of it was bouncing off and some was being absorbed. I pretended to be rational; inside I was anything but.

A tap on the bedroom door woke me. I hadn't realised exactly when I'd fallen asleep but my neck ached from being curled up in the chair. It was dark outside and for a moment I was disorientated. The door gently opened and Dad popped his head through the gap.

"Are you okay? I wondered if you wanted some dinner?" he asked.

I straightened in the chair, wincing at the pain in my knees after having my legs bent underneath me.

"I don't think I can eat right now. I might make a sandwich or something a little later."

"Are you hiding away?"

"Not hiding, just trying to think, or not think. I can't decide which one I prefer."

Dad came into the room and sat on the bed.

"I can't imagine what you're going through, right now. It was enough to lose them, and I thought you were coming to terms with that. Now this…"

"I can't get my head around it all, Dad. I've been trying so hard to think of any times I had suspicions, or even a hint that he was having an affair, and I just can't. Either I was so blinded by him, or an absolute fool. To know part of my marriage, or maybe all of it, who knows, was a lie, fake, is just too hard to comprehend."

"Do you think Trey loved Helen?" Dad asked.

"I've no way of ever finding that out. She'll say yes, of course, but did he? And that's the hardest part. I won't ever know the truth, just her version of it."

Dad patted my arm and stood. "I'll leave some chicken aside, in case you want to make a sandwich with it later," he said before leaving me alone.

I picked up my mobile phone, still connected to the charger on the bedside cabinet. My hand shook as I held it, and I stared at the number two beside the messages. I knew who they were from, and although my finger hovered over the screen, over the button, I forced myself not to press. Those were the last two messages that Trey sent me. I hadn't needed to open the messages when they'd arrived, as they'd flashed up on my screen anyway.

I swallowed down a pang of anxiety and scrolled through my contacts until I came to Patricia's name. There was a moment of pause before I clicked on her name and lifted the phone to my ear. The long distance ringing seemed so familiar yet was the scariest thing I'd heard. The phone rang and rang. I was about to disconnect when she answered.

"Hello?"

I found at first I couldn't speak initially.

"He…hello. Patricia, it's…"

"Dani! Oh my God, Dani, is that you?"

"Yes, it's me." I choked on my words.

"Oh my. I can't believe I'm talking to you. How have you been? I really wanted to visit before Christmas but I haven't been well enough."

"What's wrong, Patricia?"

"Nothing too serious, but I'm not well enough for the flight. Dani, I can't believe we're speaking. I talk to your dad frequently, of course, but nothing beats hearing your voice."

I could hear the tears through her words.

"Patricia, I wished I was calling you for a catch up, just to chat to you. I'd planned that when I could talk again it was because I had something to look forward to, something positive to tell you, but I don't. I'm going to come straight out with this and it's going to be huge shock for you. Trey was having an affair, with Helen, my sister-in-law. Or so she says. The worst part, Patricia, Helen has told Christian that Alistair is Trey's son."

The silence that I received extended beyond what I expected, to the extent that I took the phone away from my ear and looked at the screen. I was expecting to see the call had disconnected.

"Patricia?"

"I'm here. I just…"

"I know. It's come as a huge shock to me as well. I thought you ought to know for several reasons. Alistair is your grandson, but right now, I'm struggling to believe it. I've got a request and a question for you, but I'd fully understand if you wanted me to call you back and…"

"I knew, Dani," Patricia had interrupted me.

"You knew? What did you know?"

"I knew about Alistair. Helen had told me, but please, Dani, I didn't believe her. I found her to be a vicious and vindictive woman. I honestly did not believe her."

It was hard to hold the phone to my ear, as my hand was shaking so hard.

"You should tell me what you know," I said, trying hard to keep any aggression from my voice.

"It was at the hospital, and it was really late. Way beyond visiting hours, if I remember. Trey had…he'd just passed. I needed the restroom, I felt so sick. When I came back she was on her knees by his bedside sobbing. I thought it strange that she had been allowed into his room. It was a nurse, Dani, that told me. Helen had told the nurse that he was the father of her child, so they allowed her to see him. I don't think it was his regular nurse, because she knew you were down the corridor. I confronted her, of course. I asked her why she'd lied to the nurse and why she was sobbing at his bedside. At first, she tried to dodge the question, and then she told me. She said that Trey was her baby's father."

Patricia paused and I could hear her blow her nose.

"Please, go on," I said, although her words were tearing me apart inside.

"I told her that I didn't believe her. She held up her hand and had some strands of his hair. She told me that she'd prove it. She spat the words at me, Dani. Her face contorted into anger. I asked if Christian knew, she said that he did. But again, I wasn't sure that was the truth."

"She had his hair in her hands?"

"Yes, or rather, she said it was his. She was going to hold on to it until the baby was born. I didn't know what to do; I hope you believe me. As time wore on, I made a decision; right or wrong, not to mention it to you because I thought you'd been through enough. I need you to understand when I say, I would never have tolerated my son having an affair, and I would have had no hesitation in calling him out on that. I didn't get the chance."

Patricia was openly sobbing and the miles that kept us apart intensified that desire to wrap my arms around her because I knew it wasn't a possibility.

"I need to ask one question, if you don't mind. Would Trey have ever called himself Kitt?"

I heard the sob that caught in her throat. "Kitt was my husband, Trey's father's name. Or nickname, I should say."

"I thought his name was Henry?"

"It was, he hated it so used his middle name, Kitt."

I'd never met him. When we'd had conversations about him, he'd always used the name Henry.

"That name was in Helen's phone. Christian remembers Trey using it once on a holiday. But there's more. Trey and Helen exchanged letters, or at least Trey wrote to Helen. Christian found them, he hasn't told me exactly what was in them, he decided to burn them in front of her."

"I don't know what to say, Dani. I'm heartbroken for you right now. I don't know if I did the right thing by staying quiet. I guess, in my heart, I hoped it was all fake. I'm so sorry."

"It's okay, please don't apologise, I'd have probably done the same thing had I been in your situation," I lied.

"What will happen now?"

"Christian is saying that he's going to divorce her. As for Alistair? I don't know. He's your grandchild, all that's left of…" The sob that caught in my throat forbade me from continuing.

"I can't…I'm not sure I want to deal with that right now. Does that make me terrible?" she asked.

"I don't know what I'd do, either. However, you have the choice, and no one would think any less of you if you decide to have a relationship with him."

"To do that, I'd have to have a relationship with Helen, and that's really not something I can see happening."

"Maybe you can write to Alistair, send cards and gifts. Helen could keep them for when he's older." Even I doubted that Helen would do that. "Or send them here, Patricia. I'm sure we can get them to him at some point, when he's old enough to understand he has extended family."

I wasn't sure why I was offering that service, but I needed to get to the point where I didn't view Alistair in any way other than a baby caught up in someone else's mess.

"I'll need to think about it all. It's just too much to take in right now. How on earth are you coping, Dani?"

"All I can say is, I'm just about coping. I'm so angry, but I'm also so confused as well. I keep thinking about our life, to see if I can remember any clues, and there's just nothing that springs to mind. Right now, I hate how he's made me feel, I hate that he's not here to answer to any of this."

"I can understand that, I think I'd feel the same. I know he loved you, Dani…"

"Not enough, Patricia, not enough," I said, interrupting her.

I could not listen to anyone tell me Trey loved me. If he had, this would never have happened. I didn't believe it was possible for him to 'love' two people. I would never again accept that he had respect for me, certainly in the latter years. To respect me, would have meant he'd either stayed faithful, or left if he wasn't happy.

"I need to go, Dad is calling for dinner," I said, lying again.

"Okay, despite the nature of our conversation, it was so good to hear your voice."

"I'll try to get to visit you in a few months. I guess I have to deal with things here, first."

"That would be wonderful, I'd be thrilled to see you."

We said goodbye and I laid the phone face down on the bedside cabinet. I didn't want to see those two unread messages from him. I didn't want the temptation to scroll through the many photographs stored on there, either. I closed my eyes and let more tears fall gently down my cheeks. So it was true. My husband had been having an affair, and like Christian felt, had it been with a stranger, I might have been able to stomach it a little easier.

I died just a little more inside that evening.

CHAPTER FIFTEEN

*C*hristmas week was fast approaching and with it, Christian's mood deteriorated. I noticed Dad being cautious around him, the slightest mention of Helen or Alistair, or even Christmas, seemed to set off the explosion that had been building inside him. It was awkward, unsettling, and the atmosphere was thick with tension. There came a point when I felt my feelings were brushed aside, and although it wasn't a competition on who was hurting the most, his anger was over-riding anything anyone else felt. I'd lost my cheating husband and my child; Dad had lost his only grandchild. Yet our emotions had to be kept in check.

Christian travelled to London a couple of times, returning late at night the same day. He hadn't travelled to see Helen but to check in with work. He'd decided to take an extended holiday, but I wondered how his boss felt about that. I was sure they'd be sympathetic to a degree, but having 'lost' my job when the sympathy had run out, I didn't hold much hope in Christian returning to work full-time if he didn't get himself back into gear.

He'd told me that he'd appointed a divorce lawyer to start proceedings, and had chuckled that he hoped paperwork would be served on her on Christmas Eve. That level of nastiness just wasn't Christian, normally. He was determined to leave Helen with nothing financially; even though I'd pointed out she'd be entitled to half their house at least. His words that day had stunned me, 'that bastard child will get nothing from me.'

Dad and I decided to sit in the garden wrapped up for warmth, and with a cup of tea.

"Do you still want to get a Christmas tree?" I asked.

"Do you?"

"I don't know."

"Neither do I. Is it wrong of me to be getting angry with Christian? I mean, both of you have been through a traumatic time, but his anger is just escalating."

"No, it's not wrong. It's as if we don't count, just his feelings. It's getting irritating, to be honest. How about we escape for an hour or so to the pub?"

"I haven't been to the pub for a long time. Let's do it. But we can't exactly go without inviting him, and right now, I'm not sure alcohol and his mood are a good mix."

"Maybe you're right," I said with a sigh. It felt so wrong to be planning to sneak out of the house without him, but his depression was tiring us all out.

"I mentioned a counsellor to him but he wasn't even prepared to listen," Dad said.

"I don't think Chris is the counselling type, to be honest. I think he has to work through this in his own way. What about his friends? I know he's taken some calls, but maybe we could get in touch with a couple and see if they'd invite him out, or something."

"Dani, he's thirty-five, I'm sure he'd be pretty annoyed if we pulled a stroke like that."

"Well, I think I might take a walk, do you want to join me?" I asked.

Dad gave me a secretive smirk. "I have to do some shopping, up the lane."

"At Mrs. Hampton's? She came down the other day for a visit, didn't she?"

"Yes, and she did. She's invited me visit her."

"I think it's nice," I said, giving him a smile.

I rose from my chair, leaving my cup on the table, and waved over my shoulder, as I headed to the side of the garden and out of the gate.

It wasn't a conscious decision to take a left towards the church, but I guessed something was calling me that way. When I found myself in the same spot I'd learned about Trey, I paused and sat on the wall. At first I looked out to sea, hoping to maybe see a dolphin or two. The urge I felt to go to Hannah's grave was strong, but I couldn't spend time with him. A thought came to me.

I walked to the gate and towards the church. The door was locked and disappointment washed over me. I'd sort of assumed the door would always be open. At the end of the cemetery, in the furthest corner away from where Trey lay, was a bench. I decided to sit for a while. There was something serene about being in the cemetery, so much history was inscribed on the stone and marble headstones.

The creak of the iron gate brought me out of my thoughts, and I held my breath when I saw the elderly gentleman I believed to be Lincoln walk in. He headed, without looking towards me, to Anna's grave. That time, I was close enough to hear him. He placed one hand on the top of her headstone and used it to help him lower enough to lay flowers.

"Hello, my lovely. I'm sorry not to have visited in a while. I've been a little poorly and we had some trouble at home," he chuckled as he spoke.

The wind picked up and rustled the leaves on nearby trees, masking his words.

"…I'm not sure what to do about it. I tried to tell him he's not doing a kind thing, she won't appreciate it if she finds out. But he doesn't listen."

Whether I should have been or not, I was interested in what he was saying. He seemed to be looking for guidance from Anna and I wanted to shed a tear for him. I smiled as he made to stand, placing his free hand on his lower back to ease a pain, I imagined. When he turned he caught sight of me. He wrapped his scarf a little tighter around his neck and smiled at me. I smiled back.

"May I? My old bones give me such pain in this cold weather," he said, indicating towards the bench.

"Please, join me for a while. Give those old bones time to acclimatise," I said.

He chuckled as he lowered to the bench.

"Funny how a field full of dead people can be one of the most peaceful places on the earth isn't it? But then…of course it would be peaceful, it's not like they can talk, is it?" he said, and then started laughing.

His laugh was infectious and I soon joined in.

"Are you visiting your wife?" I asked.

"I am, but she's not there."

I turned to look at him, the skin around his eyes had creased a little further as he squinted and his lips smirked in mischief. I frowned.

"You're probably going to want to run a mile when I tell you this, but I will tell you because you seem like an understanding person." He patted my knee when he spoke, but it wasn't in way that had my skin crawl.

"Tell me," I said.

"My wife didn't want to be buried, she believed the graveyards are so full up it was unfair, and sooner or later, we'll all be piled on top of each other. So she was cremated and I scattered her ashes. But I wanted a place I could come and talk to her. No one visits Anna, ever. I cleaned up her headstone, weeded a little, everyone deserves a nice resting place, and I pretend it's my wife there."

"Wow, that's a…"

"Strange thing to do?"

"No. I think it's actually a nice thing to do. Anna gets company, you're tending to her grave, and you get the comfort of having somewhere to sit and communicate with your wife."

I remembered that Daniel had said Anna's husband wasn't named Lincoln, and I'd half given up on the idea that the gentleman I was sitting beside, the one I'd seen that time, was him. However…

"My name's Daniella, but everyone calls me Dani," I said, turning on the bench slightly to extend my hand.

"Lincoln, but everyone calls me…well, Lincoln. Pleased to meet you, Dani."

I froze with my hand held in his. His humour threw me; it was the only thing that didn't match my image of him.

He smiled and I searched his face for any sign of recognition, there was none, and I gently removed my hand from his.

"Do you come here often?" he asked.

"My...my daughter is buried here," I said.

"I'm sorry to hear that. No one should have to bury their child, it must be terribly painful for you."

"It is. You know she's actually buried with someone I'd rather she wasn't, and I came here today to see how one goes about exhumation."

"Exhumation?"

"Yes, you know, remove the..."

"I know what it means. Dig up the coffins and move them some-place else. I won't ask why, unless you want me to, of course. I get the sense you have a lot of words inside you that need to come out."

There was something familiar in what he'd just said.

"Lincoln is an unusual name, I bet there aren't that many around," I said, still fishing.

"My father was Lincoln, so is my son. So I know of three of us," he replied, still chuckling.

Although I was disappointed that he possibly wasn't the Lincoln from my letters, I was enjoying his company.

"Do you live locally?"

"No, I used to. Now I'm in the old people's home about a mile from here. I quite enjoy it really. The nurses are nice."

Somehow I thought he was trying to convince himself more than me.

"Do they look after you well?"

"They do, they're so pushed though. I'm quite able to take care of myself, unlike some of the other poor souls in there. And of course, I do escape as often as I can. They'll be hunting the grounds for me because I don't tell them when I'm off on a travel."

I watched as he pulled up the sleeve of his overcoat to check on the time.

"I guess I ought to get back, I've been gone an hour now."

"How will you get back? A mile is a long walk," I said.

"Oh, I have a car."

He rose and adjusted his coat. "It was a pleasure to talk with you, Dani. Hopefully, we'll do that again, soon."

I stood and shook his outstretched hand. "I enjoyed meeting you, too. And I'd love to chat again, soon."

He nodded before smiling and walking away, leaving me a little bemused.

Was that my Lincoln? Could he have pretended not to know me to keep our letter exchange the enigma they'd become? He'd never mentioned my casual request to meet in person and maybe, if he was in a home, he wouldn't want to. But then he said he had a car. I spun on my heels, there hadn't been the sound of a car engine starting, and I hadn't heard one the first time I'd been at the cemetery and he'd walked in. I raced for the gate but by the time I'd gotten there, he was nowhere to be seen.

I took a slow walk home and through the back door into the kitchen. No one was around but sitting on the table was some mail. On top of the pile was a purple envelope. I took the mail, a large mug of tea, and headed upstairs, opening the purple envelope as I did.

My dearest Dani,

I really don't know what to say to you. I cannot imagine the pain you must be feeling right now. I totally understand everything you are telling me: how you feel, and the confusion you have. It's a living nightmare, I imagine. I'm usually thrilled to receive a letter from you, the last few have shown an upbeat in your thinking but this...I'm blown away a little and my heart is breaking for you right now.

So you're lost? I don't doubt that for one minute, but you can come back from this. How? By finding that inner strength that I know you have. It will be hard, but you can do it. You ask what child was a mistake. I don't believe Hannah was. Not that I have any experience in this, but I can't imagine a planned pregnancy with a mistress was in your husband's mind. Are you sure she didn't entrap him? Not that I guess it makes much difference.

It's so hard to know what to write to comfort you. There's a part of me that wants to ask you to find some comfort in the marriage that you remember, in the Trey that you, and only you, spent time with. You say you didn't know, doesn't that suggest that perhaps there weren't problems in your relationship? I know that might sound strange. What man has a perfect marriage and an affair? A confused one, a selfish one, a man who maybe found himself in a situation he couldn't get out of. Or am I making excuses for him? If he were alive, Dani, I'd punch him on the nose, for sure.

I think the only way to move forwards is to find some level of acceptance. Perhaps, in time, forgiveness, but that's a big ask. I'm confident, Dani, that you will get over this, you'll find your way again.

You have a future, a house to build, and a life to live. You can live that life to the fullest, or you can be swallowed up in your grief and anger. I don't recommend the latter. You were given a second chance, Dani; you have to make use of that. I know that is way easier said than done, but he's gone, sadly.

Would it have been any easier if he were still alive? Maybe, but maybe not. Sometimes, not getting answers is actually the better way. What would have happened if you'd heard the words that you most fear? This way, you can hang on to the belief that he did love you, despite what he did, and that he planned for Hannah. Hang on to that, Dani.

Your friend,

Lincoln.

It was the first time Lincoln had addressed and signed off the letter in the way he had. I believed that was because he was so sincere in what he'd written, and he viewed me as his friend. He was fond of me, enough to change his method of addressing me.

I read the last paragraph over and over. Could I hang on to something I wasn't sure was true? Could I make myself believe that? Until the moment Christian had told me, it was exactly what I believed, anger washed over me. Trey was dead, Hannah was dead, and did I really need to know what I'd been told at all? Christian could have withheld some information, for my sake. He could have left me mourning the loss of my husband, a perfect marriage, and my child. Lincoln had said, 'sometimes, not getting the answers is actually the better way,' maybe not knowing at all would have topped that.

I put Lincoln's letter to one side. Underneath was a large white envelope with the estate agent's logo across the top. I held it in my hands, deciding whether I needed to deal with it at that moment. In addition, there was a small, plush, and obviously expensive one. The envelope had that slight velvety feel that suggested quality. There were no sender's details. I turned it over and slid my thumb under the flap; it opened easily.

I slid out a single sheet of paper and unfolded it. I wasn't sure what I was reading at first, or rather, I couldn't absorb the content. I read it again, and one more time.

Helen had instructed a solicitor. It seemed that her child, Trey's child, could be entitled to part of his estate. Trey hadn't left a will, and I'd naturally assumed, as his next of kin, what was his, became mine. I shook my head. How could she? I strode from the room and banged on Christian's bedroom door before flinging it open. His room was empty. I stomped down the stairs to find the house as empty as it was when I'd returned home. I knew where Dad was, but not Christian.

I paced the kitchen, desperate to screw the page in my hand into a small ball, to throw it on the fire or at least the gas hob. I couldn't destroy it I knew that, but I needed to show it to some-one, a solicitor that could act on my behalf. I had no intention of calling the parasites as instructed. It had been just a few days, and the bitch was already after what she could get. She hadn't even given me a chance to get used to the idea she was not only fucking my husband, but he'd fathered her child. No, she had to go in for the kill while the wound was gaping. I wanted to scream as many obscenities at her as I could, but I knew, I'd never give her the pleasure of my anger. I'd never speak to, nor see her, again, I'd hoped.

"Hey, I thought I saw you," I heard.

I spun round to see Miller at the back door.

"What's happened, Dani?" he asked, I imagined he'd seen the anger, or the horror, or whatever expression, on my face.

I thrust the page into his chest, not daring myself to speak. He read.

"What a bitch," he said, shaking his head. "Do you have a lawyer, other than Christian, of course?"

"No, but I'm about to find one. Know a good one? Someone so fucking ruthless, nasty, you know the kind you see on the television?"

"As it happens, I know a great company. Took me to the cleaners, I think they'd be perfect for you."

I frowned. "When my wife left, she got absolutely everything from the house to the car, and even the dog. I miss that dog. She had one shit-hot lawyer."

"I don't want that lawyer, just one like him."

"It was a her, a total ball-breaker, she was. I even asked her one day if she was a man underneath the tight skirt and the gaping shirt. She had more masculinity and less empathy than any bare-knuckle fighter I've met."

"You've met bare-knuckle fighters?" I asked, more interested in that part of his statement.

"Many, but let's get back to the lawyer. Seriously, Dani, this woman is ideal. She doesn't give a shit about feelings, or children in your case, dogs in mine. The only thing she wants is to win every case she takes on. Now, I don't know if she would be able to defend you in this, or whatever it is that has to be done, but it might be worth asking her."

"Okay, how do I meet the ball-breaker?"

"I'll find her details. I know I still have some paperwork lying around."

I pulled a chair away from the table, wincing as the legs scraped against the tiles and then sat.

"How about I make a coffee? Mind you, you only drink tea, don't you?" Miller said.

"Coffee or tea, I don't mind."

I scanned over the letter again while he made coffee.

"What happened to your dog?" I asked.

"Sam was his name, I'd had him as a puppy and before her. She took him to spite me; she hated dogs. She moved into a town, didn't look after him, and he got run over. She didn't even tell me until I receive a vet's bill for his euthanasia."

"What?"

"Yeah, bitch of the year award was split between the lawyer and her then."

"Did you pay it?"

"No, of course not."

"What happened?"

"The vet tried to take me court for non-payment until I showed them the divorce settlement that clearly stated she had received custody of the bloody dog."

"That's shocking."

"Not as shocking as that," he said, placing a mug in front of me and taking the page out of my hand to read again.

"Can she do this? I mean, Alistair is Trey's child but an illegitimate one."

"I don't know, is the answer."

I sipped on my coffee in silence.

"I came here to let you know I've had some unofficial feedback from my man at the council. He doesn't think there would be any objection to the plans, other than to show a clear provision of parking for this house."

"What does that mean?"

"We've left it that there is communal parking but if you sell this house, say your dad moves on or…We have to show there is enough space for two cars for this house without obstructing the two car parking space you need for the barn."

"I don't have a car, why do I need two car parking spaces?"

"Because the council insists on it. Although, it's technically one point five cars for a two-bedroom house."

"Okay, so you'll do what?"

"I think a slight readjustment in landscaping is all that's needed. To be honest, Dani, it's my fault. I know about the car parking, I should have allocated for that."

"Well, it doesn't matter because we can alter it easily enough, I take it?"

"Yes. It's already done. But, the good news is, I think this planning application will sail through."

"Talk about sailing, did you go out in your boat?" I wanted to talk about anything other than the letter he was still holding.

"It's not technically my boat but my dad's. And no. It's still afloat though, so that's a good sign. There's something I feel like I need to do, and I need the boat to do it," he said, cryptically.

I didn't feel I could ask what, he'd already lowered his eyes to the letter as if cutting off that line of conversation.

"I spoke to Patricia, Trey's mother. She confirmed the affair, and the baby. Apparently, Helen had been to see Trey when we were in the hospital. She told Patricia that she would prove that Trey was the father, and she'd pulled out some of his hair. I guess for a DNA test?"

"I imagine so, but what the fuck was she thinking?" Miller shook his head in obvious disgust.

"Is Christian divorcing her?" he asked.

I nodded. "Then that might explain this. If he forces the sale of the house, assuming she can't buy his half from him, she's going to be desperate for money."

187

I wasn't sure those words made me feel any better about it, at all.

"Christian isn't responsible for Alistair, but I don't see how Trey is, either. He was dead before Alistair was born."

"I don't know how it all works, Dani. This letter is just to open up a line of discussion. It doesn't say what she wants, or even what she's entitled to, if anything."

"Do you think I'll have to go to court? I'm not sure I could do that right now."

"I doubt anything would happen for months yet. Let's just get you some representation and see what advice you get."

"You're a good friend, Miller, thank you. I need a friend right now. But can I ask you one thing?"

He nodded as he took a sip of coffee.

"I know you said you and Daniel weren't close, but you seemed to act strangely towards me when I was with your brother. Why?"

"I wasn't aware that I had, I'm sorry if you thought that. All his godly stuff puts me on edge, I guess."

"I'm not sure that is the truth, but fair enough, you don't want to talk about him, I get that."

"It's not that I don't want to talk about him, as such, there's history there and it upsets me."

"Okay, I'll leave it there."

He smiled his thanks and drained his coffee cup. "I need to get going, I have a job that should have been finished a month ago, but the homeowners keep changing their bloody mind. I'd like to get paid before Christmas!"

"What are you doing for Christmas?"

"I have no idea and it's only a week away." He laughed.

"If you're at a loose end, you can come here. I'm sure we could do with some cheering up."

"I'll let you know in a day or so, if that's not too short notice."

"No, that will fine."

He said goodbye, patted Lucy, who sat by the back door, and left.

I sat and read the letter for the umpteenth time. A stream of expletives left my lips as my anger grew. Who the fuck did she think she was? The least she could have done was to give me some time to come to terms with what had happened. A thought hit me. Christian had revelled in the fact that he was serving divorce papers just before Christmas. Did she know and this was a retaliatory gesture? I hoped the ball-breaker that Miller spoke about could deal with this.

If Trey was alive, and I'd discovered he had a child, I would be horrified if he made no attempt to financially support that child, but this felt different. He was dead, he didn't have life insurance so the equity from the sale of the house and the compensation yet to come from the Criminal Injuries Compensation Authority was all I had. I had no idea if he even knew Alistair was his child. In fact, none of us knew for sure.

I thought back to when we'd discovered Helen was pregnant, just a few months after I was. He'd shown the usual surprise and congratulated both Christian and Helen, in fact, he'd taken Chris out for a drink and to 'wet the baby's head,' albeit prematurely. I can't imagine anyone doing that if they thought their mistress was pregnant. I was sure I would have seen some form of panic or distress in him.

CHAPTER SIXTEEN

a decision ran through my mind enough to have me shrug on my coat and leave the house. I walked with purpose back to the church. Although the door was still locked, I knew Daniel lived next door. Beside the church was a small cottage, and I sighed with relief when I noticed a gate to the side of his small garden that led straight into the cemetery. I knocked on the front door and held my breath. If I had the wrong house, perhaps the homeowner might know where he lived.

Daniel opened the door and I wanted to laugh. His hair was standing on end, in all sorts of directions; his t-shirt was covered in paint, as were his hands. And he wasn't wearing trousers but a floral pair of, what I hoped, were swimming trunks and not pants.

"Dani, hi, come on in," he said, moving to one side.

"I can see that you're busy, I can come back another time, and maybe I ought to make an appointment since this is 'church' stuff," I said.

He stared at me. "It's good to hear you speak. I heard about your recent troubles, and I can't tell you how sorry I am about that."

It occurred to me then that I hadn't seen him since I'd discovered the news.

"And 'church' stuff? Like serious church stuff because it is my day off, as you can see," he said, sweeping his arm down the front of his body. The smirk he gave confirmed he was joking.

"Honestly, I can always come back."

"No, come on in. I've been repainting the cottage, terribly, I could do with a break."

I walked into the hallway and the smell of fresh paint nearly made me gag.

"How much paint have you used?" I said, eyeing a paintbrush so loaded with paint it was hard to see the bristles.

"I guess DIY is not really my strong point, but sadly, the church doesn't pay enough for me to enlist the help of a decorator."

"What about Miller?" I asked, following him through to a small kitchen.

"Ah, Miller. Have you seen inside his house? He might build beautiful homes for people but he has no time, and rightly so, for his own house."

He hadn't answered my question.

"Tea?" he asked.

"That would be lovely."

"Okay, you take a seat, if you can find a clean one, and then we can chat about 'church' stuff."

"It can wait, I really should have made an appointment."

"No appointments necessary when I'm doing the work of the Lord," he chuckled.

"I don't know if the Lord would be overly happy with my request."

"Mmm, that sounds like a confession is required. Do I need to get dressed up?"

I laughed. "No. Thank you," I said, as I took the freshly made mug of tea from him.

Daniel sat opposite me at a rickety, pine round table with mismatched chairs. A table way too large for the small kitchen.

"So what can I do for you?"

"Exhumation. How do I go about it?"

Daniel spat the mouthful of tea he had just taken across the table.

"Oh, Lord, I'm sorry," he said, grabbing a tea towel to mop it up. "So, exhumation..."

"You might think I'm being totally irrational, but I don't want Hannah in the same place as Trey."

Daniel looked at me for a little while before answering. "You can apply for a licence to exhume a body, of course. You do that with the government. Then it will be up to the parish to determine costs. I have to say, I've never been involved in exhumation simply to move a body. I know it happens, sometimes people move away and want to take their loved one with them, but that's usually when ashes are buried."

He took a sip of his tea, all the while staring at me over the rim of his mug.

"Can I put something to you?" he said. I nodded my head.

"Right now, the level of anger you feel is justified. The shock of what you discovered must be off the scale. I don't know what your religious belief is, whether you view those graves out there as simply a place for a body to be buried and the soul has left for a better place. Sometimes, I walk around the headstones, I find it comforting, but I'm often saddened when I see a child all alone. I don't want to force my opinion on you, that wouldn't be fair, but I would like to ask you where your decision stems from. Is it anger? In which case, could you give yourself a little more time before making that decision?"

"I don't want him to have my child, whether that be in the ground or whatever 'better place' they are in," I whispered.

"Do you have that right? To deny your child her father?"

I looked sharply up at him.

"Is that what you think I'm doing?"

"Isn't it? Maybe I'm talking out of turn here, but along with all the 'church stuff,' I vowed I'd always give an honest opinion with my *flock*."

"I'm not sure I'm one of the *flock*," I said, hearing the indignation in my voice.

"No, but you are my friend," he answered simply.

I took a deep breath. "I'm not sure I believe, Daniel. I don't know if there is a 'better place,' heaven, or wherever. I want to visit my daughter, I don't want to be reminded of him every time I do."

"I can totally understand that." He leant forwards and took one of my hands in his.

"Exhuming a body is not only costly, but potentially distressing, Dani. What you saw go into the ground isn't going to look the same when it comes out. Now, I don't suppose you'll want to be there, but you're responsible for what happens to both Trey and Hannah. That's a lot of effort and thought to go through, I just want to be sure you're up to that right at this moment, and this isn't a knee jerk reaction."

"If there were problems in our relationship, any hint that he wasn't happy, I think I would come to terms with all this easier. But he was with her for two years, at that time, our marriage was going from strength to strength. The deceit is the worst thing. He was leading two lives, Daniel. He doesn't deserve peace, forgiveness, or whatever is supposed to happen."

"I can point you in the right direction for the application, all I ask is that you give it another couple of weeks and see how you feel then," he said.

"Okay, I can do that. I don't think I'll change my mind, though."

He nodded and let go of my hands. I missed the warmth and comfort holding my hand had offered me.

"How far have you gotten with the barn?" he asked.

"Miller has sent in the applications, now it's just waiting for approval, or not."

"What will you do if you don't get it?"

"I'll stay with Dad for the time being, but after that, I don't know. I guess I'll see if I can buy a little cottage or something."

"Be nice to have you stay around."

I gave him a smile and finished my tea. "I ought to get going."

"If you fancy another night at the pub, or maybe a meal out, just give me a shout," he said as he walked me to the front door.

"Thanks, I will."

I liked Daniel, I enjoyed his company; I hadn't liked his opinion or advice. I guessed he was talking to me as a friend, and he felt he had the right to, but it wasn't quite what I'd wanted to hear.

I wandered back along the lanes, thinking on his words. Whether I liked them or not, he had a point. Did I want Hannah buried on her own? I hadn't thought much about any of the people in the cemetery, I hadn't thought about souls and heaven, and all that nonsense. Or was it? Did it comfort me to think Hannah was someplace nice, with someone who would love her? But then I'd come back to that one question that bugged me. Which child was the mistake? It could well be that neither was, but how realistic was that? I just didn't see Trey wanting two children, one with his wife, and one with his mistress, being born just a few months apart. While I was on bed rest, he was fucking my sister-in-law.

I shook my head to clear the thought and swallowed down the nausea that bubbled to my throat.

My hatred for Trey intensified, that transferred to Helen. The first thing I would do is respond to the solicitor's letter, asking for evidence. I wanted to see a medical document that proved Trey was Alistair's father. I had no doubt about the affair, but I wasn't going to make it easy for her at all.

Christian was stomping around the kitchen when I returned, he held the letter I'd received in his hand; I guessed I'd left it on the table.

"What the fuck does she think she's doing?" he shouted, waving the letter in the air.

"Trying to get money for her child, I guess."

"We need to get a solicitor to fight this. She shouldn't get a fucking penny, from either of us."

"I have that sorted."

"How?"

"I'm quite capable of finding a solicitor, and Miller knows of a great one who might be able to help. Firstly, I'm going to respond and ask for evidence that Trey is the father."

196

"What do you mean?"

I thought it was quite obvious. "We don't know Trey is the father, she said he is, but she hadn't proved it to me."

"She told me he was, isn't that enough?"

"Absolutely not. You could be father, we just don't know."

"How can you trust this Miller guy, he's just a builder, isn't he?"

I wasn't sure that I liked the tone of his voice when he used Miller's name.

"Who also happens to have become a friend. If the person he has in mind isn't able to help, I'll let you know."

"You need a lawyer that practices in family law," he said.

"Thank you, I'll find out if she does."

"I think it's disgusting she thinks she can get away with this," Christian said.

"You're trying to leave her penniless, Chris, I imagine she's looking out for her child in any way she can."

Christian spun on his heels and stalked towards me. His attitude caused my heart to skip a beat and not in a good way.

"So this is my fault, is it?" he said, waving the letter in front of my face.

I reached up and took the letter from his hand.

"I didn't say that. Chris, you're not the only one that has been devastated by this, yet you seem to riding roughshod over Dad's feelings and mine. You're angry; I get that. Don't you think I am as well? Don't you think I'd like to rip every strand of hair from her head? But I know it takes two to have an affair, one happens not to be around anymore, otherwise I'd want to do the same to him."

"I just don't know how you can be so calm about all of is?"

"Calm! You've no idea whether I'm calm or not because you are so wrapped up in your own misery you can't see beyond it. My daughter died, Chris. She was taken from me before her time, I didn't get to see her, to smell or hold her while she was alive. She didn't get to spend more than a few hours on this earth. She didn't get to know me, her mother. My husband fucking your wife is nothing compared to that. So if you think I'm calm, one, you don't me as well as you should, two, he's dead, there's nothing I can do about that. I can't divorce him, I can't shout or scream at him. All I can do is keep breathing, that's when you're not here suffocating us with your anger."

By the end of my speech, I was shouting.

Christian's face was puce, I assumed with anger. His mouth was flapping open and closed as if my comments had rendered him mute.

"Do you know where I've been today?" I asked, calmer. He shook his head.

"I went to see the vicar to find out what I had to do to exhume Trey because I don't want him even in the ground with my daughter. Is that what you'd call calm?"

"Can you do that?" he asked, not answering my question.

"Apparently I can apply for a licence, whether I'd get it or not, I don't know. I don't even know if I'll really do it. I'm angry and I'm making rash decisions, like you."

"What rash decisions am I making?" He slumped into a chair as he spoke.

"She's entitled to half the equity in your house, yes? You're trying to wrangle a way out of that. I understand, I do, Chris. She's hurt you in the worst possible way. But you can fester in that for years, or you can divorce, give her what she's legally entitled to, and start your life over. Is she morally entitled to anything? No, of course not. You're the injured party, so am I. I intend to solve this issue as quickly as possible, get on and build myself a new house, and a new life."

I wasn't entirely sure when I'd come to that decision. The more I thought, the more I wanted just to put some form of closure on this, resolve it in my mind, and concentrate on something positive. I was sick of the misery that flowed through my veins.

I walked up the stairs, wanting to get my mobile phone. As I sat on the edge of the bed, I remembered I didn't have Daniel's number. But I did have Miller's.

"Hi, I'm sorry to call, but I wondered if you had Daniel's telephone number?" I asked when he'd answered the phone with a greeting to me.

"I do, but it's on my phone, and I can't put you on hold while I find it, I don't think," he said. "Why?"

"He invited me out, and right now I need to get out."

"Oh. You'll have to let me call you back." There was something in his voice that worried me.

"Are you okay?" I asked.

"Sure, let me call you back." He cut off the call, rather abruptly, I thought.

I sat for a while, holding the phone in my hand. It shouldn't take as long as it was for him to write down a telephone number and call me back.

I rose and walked to the chair by the window, it was my favourite spot in the whole house. I sat and looked out to sea. Someone had erected a Christmas tree on the beach; I knew there would be one in the square and wondered when the 'turning on of the lights' ceremony had been. I remembered going to that religiously as a child. We'd sing carols and drink hot toddies, child-friendly hot toddies, of course. It also occurred to me that I hadn't bought one gift, sent one card. I checked my phone for the date, I wasn't even aware of what that was. Christmas Eve was just three days away. I felt a tear prick at one eye when the phone vibrated in my hand.

"Sorry, I took another call and couldn't get rid of them. Anyway, do you have a pen?" Miller said.

"I do, but, and I know this is a strange request. Are you busy tomorrow?"

"I can spare some time, what's up?"

"Would you run me into town? I've just realised the date and I haven't bought one gift yet."

He laughed softly. "I don't suppose anyone would be too worried but, yes, of course I can. What time?"

"Mid-morning, maybe?"

"I'll pick you up at eleven."

"That would be great, thank you. I don't trust myself to drive, and trust Dad's car even less to get me there and back."

"When did you last drive a car?"

His tone of voice was so comforting; I rested back in the chair and let it wash over me.

"Years ago, I might look at getting an automatic."

"I'll give you a lesson in the truck. There's not much damage you can do to that beast," he said.

"I can't drive your car, what if I crash it?"

"Then the insurance will repair it. Tomorrow, eleven, okay?"

"Eleven, and thank you. I really do appreciate it."

We said goodbye and it didn't occur to me until some minutes after, I hadn't taken down Daniel's telephone number.

CHAPTER SEVENTEEN

Christian was gone when I woke the following morning.

"Did you two fight?" Dad asked, when I walked into the kitchen.

"We had words, why?"

"He's decided to stay with a friend in London for a few days."

"A few days? It's Christmas Day in a few days."

"I don't think he's thinking straight enough to know what month it is, let alone how close to Christmas. Can I say something that's probably a terrible thing to say?"

"Go on."

"I'm a little glad. I think he needs someone to talk some sense into him. He's gotten so angry it's consuming him, and he's beyond our help. I get the anger, I really do, but it's so hard to live with. I never know what to say for fear of it being the wrong thing."

"That's not a terrible thing to say, Dad. He can't see beyond his own upset, and I understand how selfish, unintentionally, that makes us. I include myself in that, Dad."

"Dani, you've had much more to cope with this past year. I'll be glad to see the back of it, to be honest."

Dad had always been one of those guys who truly believed a new year would bring a 'new' year. I remembered at midnight on New Year's Eve, he'd raise a glass to us all and tell us to leave whatever problems we had behind as we counted down to the first day of a new month and a new year. He'd make us write down our troubles, and on the stroke of midnight we'd throw the paper on the fire.

"It's not that I'm unsympathetic to his situation, I just don't know what to say or do for the best, and it seems no matter what I try, it's wrong. I've never seen him this angry before. He flew at me..."

"He what?" I asked, my voice rising on each word.

"Verbally, Dani, not physically. Although I had to leave the room, in fact, I left the house hoping to diffuse the situation."

"You cannot be driven from your own home, Dad, by someone's anger. He got angry with me over a letter I received from a solicitor. Helen is 'investigating' whether she can get some money from Trey's estate. I think, legally Alistair might be entitled to something, but Christian flew off the handle about it. He thinks I'm too calm about it all," I said, shaking my head.

"You have always been the thinker and he's always been the one to act without thinking first. He's become so bitter that it worries me he won't be able to come back from that."

"He will, Dad, and hopefully some time with his friend might do him the world of good."

Dad patted my arm, as was his way.

"Is there anything you want from town? I'm popping over there at eleven, just for a couple of hours."

"No, I don't think so."

"When I get back, we're getting those decorations from the loft, okay?"

"Well, I already did. I put them under the stairs."

"Then we'll get them out, dust them off, and go get a tree."

I was out in the front garden when Miller arrived. He reversed into the drive and I climbed into his truck.

"I really do appreciate this. You can leave me there and I'll get a bus, or something, home."

"You'll have to think of the 'or something' since there isn't a bus route here. And you're welcome. I wasn't up to much anyway."

"Daniel was painting when I visited him, you could always help your brother?" I said, gently.

Miller looked over at me with raised eyebrows.

"You and Daniel seem to be getting on extremely well, something I should know?"

I frowned at him, but then realisation dawned on me. "What? No! He's a vicar."

"He's allowed a partner."

"I don't…No, we're friends, I think."

"You think?"

"Can we just change the subject? Now, Christmas Day, did you think any more?"

"I haven't, sorry. Daniel does his church stuff, and then he goes to an old people's home for lunch and another sermon, or carol concert, I can't remember."

"Talking about old people's home. Did I tell you about the letters I receive?"

I knew Miller had handed me the envelope one time, but I couldn't remember if I'd ever told him what was in it. As much as I hadn't known him for a long time, he had seen me at my lowest and I believed I could confide in him.

"I don't think you did."

I told him about Lincoln. Miller kept his eyes firmly on the road, but I noticed his jaw work from side to side.

"And then, I met a Lincoln in the cemetery, although I don't think it was the same Lincoln. How odd is that? What are the chances of two Lincolns in this area?"

The truck swerved and I grabbed the handle on the door.

"Jesus, what was that?" I asked.

"Sorry, I thought that badger was about to run out of the hedge. You okay?"

I hadn't noticed a badger, and weren't they nocturnal? "Yes, I'm fine. You startled me a little, that's all."

Miller was mumbling, and I swore I heard the word 'badger.'

"Miller, what's wrong?" I asked.

"Nothing, sorry. I just hate to run something down if I can help it. I'd rather scratch the fuck out of the truck," he said, smiling over to me.

He seemed back to his old self, the one prior to my tale of the two Lincolns. I wasn't done though.

"I think the Lincoln in the cemetery might be the Lincoln who writes to me, but he didn't want me to know. Do you think that's possible?"

"I don't know. Did you ask him?"

"No, he showed no recognition when I mentioned my name. Something else; he said he was in a home that was a mile away, and he said he had a car. But I'm not sure there was a car outside the cemetery, I certainly didn't hear one being started, that's for sure."

"Maybe he was parked a little further down the lane," Miller said.

"Could have been but...I don't know, there's something intriguing and I really want to get to know the Lincoln that writes to me, personally."

"Why?"

"Why?" It seemed a strange question to ask. "I feel like I connect with him. I can't explain it, Miller. There's just something in what he says, in the words he uses. I feel for him, and he gets me. I'd just like to meet him."

"What if he's not what you're imagining him to be?"

"I don't think he will be, but I'd still like to meet him. I did mention about meeting in one of my letters, but I think I'm going to actually set up a meeting. I'll tell him I'll be in one place at a certain time, and if he would like to meet, he can turn up. If not, it's fine, we can just keep on writing."

"All sounds like something out of a book," Miller said with a chuckle. "Anyway, what do you need in town? I need to know, roughly, where to park."

"Oh, I noticed my dad kept a bottle of my mum's perfume. It's nearly empty and I'd like to replace it as a gift. I'll buy something for Christian, although I don't think we'll see much of him for a while. He's so angry at the moment, it's taking its toll on Dad."

"I can imagine. Okay, I'll park in the pub car park, that's pretty central."

"Honestly, you don't have to wait."

"I'll grab a pint or something, maybe do a little shopping myself. We'll pick a time to meet back up, sound good?"

"Sounds good."

I left Miller and walked to the small department store, hoping to be able to find what I was looking for. I browsed the perfume counter and was pleased to see a single bottle displayed on its box.

"Can I take that one, please?" I asked.

The saleswoman smiled and asked if I'd like it gift-wrapped. I nodded as I fished around in my bag to find my purse. With the perfume in a small bag, I browsed the men's clothing. I'd noticed Dad wearing the same jumper over and over. He washed it, of course, but I wondered if he was low on clothes. He was never the type to go shopping for himself. I picked up a jumper that I thought he'd like.

I had no idea what to get Christian, or even if we'd see him. I wandered over to the books, hoping something might inspire me. I knew he had loved to read and I'd bought books he'd been pleased to receive in the past. I picked up a couple and read the back. My eye caught the yellow cover of a humorous book. I held on to it, wondering if it might bring a smile to his lips. Any other Christmas and I would have had a list of things that I thought my family would like to receive. That year, I was totally uninspired, other than the perfume and a bloody jumper. I bought the book, more to have something to wrap up and put under the tree I was yet to organise.

I walked the longer way round to the main doors, avoiding the baby and children section. Just the sight, from a distance, of pink and blue, white and yellow, miniature clothing hanging on rails had my heart miss several beats.

208

I slowly walked along the high street, dodging the women in a mass panic, buying their last minute items, and men idling along with no clue what to get their partners. It took me a moment to realise why my vision was blurry. The coldness that followed the tears as they tracked down my face was the only indication I was crying.

I turned on my heels and with a lowered head, quickly made my way back to the pub.

By the time I rounded the corner, and the pub came into sight, I was running. My heart rate had accelerated and I struggled to get my breath. I didn't think I was particularly unfit and panic started to well inside me. My head felt fuzzy, noise seemed to swim around me until it became undecipherable. I barrelled through the doors and came to an abrupt halt. There weren't that many people in the bar, but those that were all seemed to turn their heads to look at me. I scanned the area not seeing Miller before backing out.

I leant against the bonnet of Miller's truck, taking in deep breaths and with my eyes closed.

"Hey, what's wrong?" I heard. I didn't need to open my eyes to be able to know who the voice belonged to.

"I think I just had a panic attack," I said between my deep breaths.

"Jesus, Dani," he said.

I felt him step close and then his arms wrapped around me. I leant my forehead against his chest and with every deep breath in I inhaled his scent. It was earthy, manly, and it gave me something to focus on. He didn't speak, just held me tight.

"I thought I could do that," I said quietly.

"Do what?"

"Shop, be normal. I just wanted some gifts, but as I was walking down the high street I started to cry and I'm not sure why. And then I panicked."

"It's busy today, Dani, maybe it's a little soon to be surrounded by so many people. You've been pretty isolated for a while."

"It's been months and months, in fact, nearly a year. I should have been able to walk down a street and buy gifts."

I seemed fixated on the fact I hadn't been able to buy gifts.

"It's okay, no one is going to expect too much from you. Don't overthink this. What did you get already?"

"I got my dad perfume, it was my mum's favourite, and I think he uses it to spray his room, to remember her. And a jumper, I got him a new jumper. Erm, I got Christian a book, but I don't think we're going to see him and I'm sort of glad. He's so angry right now, Dad and I just want some peace."

I seemed to be speaking at a hundred miles an hour.

"Then you've done all you need to do, haven't you?" He smiled at me.

"I didn't get cards, or wrapping paper, or…"

"Dani, forget about cards, they go in the bin anyway. Send letters if you want to send anything at all. I'm sure I'll have a cupboard full of wrapping paper since that's all I seem to buy and I forget about the gifts!"

"I just wanted to do something normal."

"What is normal anyway? You bought what you needed to; you did well. Congratulate yourself for that, at least."

I nodded and missed his embrace as he stepped back. He walked to the passenger door and opened it for me. He placed his hand on my lower back as I climbed in and a shiver ran up my spine. It confused me, I felt conflicted.

"Do you want me to take you back home?"

"Is there an alternative?"

"We haven't eaten."

"I'm hungry."

Miller smiled over to me. "Food it is then," he said.

He drove for a while in silence. I spent the time trying to clear my head. Did I have feelings for Miller? I wasn't sure what was going on. I enjoyed his company, I felt my skin prickle when he'd held me, even though that hold was in sympathy and not romantic. I closed my eyes and shook my head gently.

I was being daft. I was overly emotional and needy. I was confused and lonely. Miller was just a friend, nothing more, and I had to respect those boundaries.

Miller took me to a beach café with a difference. Nestled on the edge of a cliff, the view while sitting outside on the veranda was just amazing.

"I don't think I've ever been here before," I said, as a waiter placed a couple of menus on the table.

"It's a real hidden gem. We'll have to come back at night, it's a proper restaurant then," he said with a laugh.

I picked up the menu and scanned. To call it a beach café was probably the wrong description, there was not one mention of fish and chips or burger on the menu. I chose an Asian seafood salad, and was assured that the seafood was all local.

"This is owned by an Australian guy. He came here to surf and never left," Miller said.

The menu had a modern feel; it was way more up market than the average beach café locally.

"China supplies the smoked meats and fish," Miller said, still deciding what to order.

"I meant to ask, why is he called China?"

"Rumour has it he's the son of a Duke, turned his back on his inheritance to live a life in a caravan and to be one with nature, as the entitled with a large trust fund usually do. Anyway, years ago, he would pretend to be really common, cockney even, and started calling everyone 'me old china.'"

"Me old china?"

"China plate, mate. Or so he said. He said it so often he ended up being nicknamed China. His real name is Lord Henry something or the other. Probably adds 'the third' after that as well. We all had nicknames given to us."

Miller looked up at the waitress and ordered a platter of smoked meats and two glasses of wine.

"So…" he said, smiling at me.

"So?"

"How are you feeling now?"

"As if it hadn't happened. And embarrassed, very embarrassed."

"Why are you embarrassed?"

"You came to build my barn and end up with me sobbing all over you, a few times."

"I don't mind, never could resist a damsel in distress," he replied.

I wasn't entirely sure of his meaning but laughed along with him. The waiter returned with our wine and we clinked glasses.

"Here's to building barns and sobbing damsels," I said.

"I'll drink to that."

Once I'd placed my glass back on the table, I turned slightly in my seat. The veranda was built, sturdily I hoped, right at the edge of the cliff, an infinity veranda it felt like. Above us, and secured to the ceiling, were heaters that I was very thankful of. At either end, the veranda was shielded from the elements by wood panelling.

"If you're chilly, we can always go inside," Miller said.

"No, I'm fine. The heaters are keeping me warm, and it's nice out here."

Not that the café was overly busy, it wasn't the right time of year for tourists, but I wanted the fresh air for as long as possible.

"It's an amazing view. I didn't take too much notice of where we are, how far round is our beach?" I asked.

"Couple of bays over, I think. I know I've sailed round to here and it took about an hour. It's probably further than we think it is."

"Do you sail a lot?"

"No, not since…"

"Since…?"

"Just haven't for a long time," he said, and then picked up his wine.

"I remember going out in a boat when I was a kid, I can't remember who with, though. I'm sure there was a few of us, there must have been an adult as well."

Miller stared at me for long enough to have me feel a little uncomfortable.

"You don't remember?" he asked very quietly.

I slowly shook my head. There was something in the way he asked that had me thinking I should know, and he was disappointed that I hadn't.

The waiter, returning with our meals, interrupted us from any further conversation. A large round white bowl was placed in front of me and the smell that wafted up had my mouth watering. I inhaled a fusion of Asia, of the saltiness of the sea, and herbs. I already knew the meal would be delicious without having to taste it. I picked up my fork and pierced a prawn. I let my tongue taste it before popping it into my mouth and then closing my eyes as I savoured it.

Miller laughed. "I take it you're enjoying that? You look like you're about to do a *Meg Ryan* scene."

I opened my eyes and once the initial shock had worn off, I laughed.

"That is better than any…You know what I mean."

"Then you've never had a mind-blowing orgasm."

My mouth hung open and I felt my eyes widen.

"Sorry, that was so far off base," Miller said.

"It was, sort of, I think."

He raised his eyebrows and smirked. "Only *sort of* and *you think*?"

"Eat your lunch, Miller."

Was he flirting with me? I didn't think anyone had flirted with me, not even Trey. When Trey asked me to date him, it had all been matter-of-fact, not far short of a business proposal, and at the time, I thought it was his shyness and rather cute.

I remembered him stumbling over his words as he invited me to the cinema. We'd spent plenty of time with each other in uni, of course, and as he was an overseas student, it had been nice to show him the sights of London. On our first *real* date, however, I'd seen a very different side to him. He had been the ultimate gentleman, insisting I walked on the inside of the pavement, giving me his jacket when it had rained, and shaking my hand once he'd walked me to my front door after the film.

"Earth to Dani," I heard.

"Sorry, I was thinking."

"Do you want another wine?"

I hadn't realised I'd finished the large glass of Pinot.

"Oh no, I'll be drunk. I really can't handle my alcohol," I said with a laugh.

"Coffee then," he said, turning in his chair to catch the waiter as he passed.

Miller order two coffees and I pushed my bowl away, having eaten only half of my meal.

"I've enjoyed being here, thank you," I said.

"You're welcome. It's nice to get out and do something normal every once in a while."

"Tell me a little about you. I don't know much," I said.

"Not much to tell, really. I was born here, lived here until my late teens, I think. Went off the rails for a while and eventually, once I'd straightened out, I came back."

"Went off the rails?"

"Yeah, you don't want to know all that shit."

"What made you want to get involved in buildings? You said you were an architect, where did you study?"

"Prison, Dani."

I sat there, not sure I'd heard him correctly. I guessed the look on my face had him worried.

"Spoiled the day, have I?"

"Erm, no. I was just surprised. Why…No, you don't have to tell me anything."

In that moment I was so annoyed to have drunk all my wine, I needed something to do, to break the moment. Thankfully our coffee arrived.

"My mum died, I told you my dad was a priest, didn't I? Anyway, I guess I just didn't deal with it how I should have. I distanced myself from my dad, because I didn't think he was supporting me. Like Daniel, they chose prayer instead of practicalities. I fucked up, did some dumb stuff, and got caught. I spent two years in prison, and while I was there I took an online course for something to do, at first. I've always been fascinated with buildings, loved them in fact."

"I thought you said your dad was a carpenter?"

Had he said that, or had I imagined it?

"He was, as a hobby I guess. He made cabinets, boats, you name it; he could do it. I used to work alongside him when I was a kid, and then when I straightened myself out, I came home. I decided an office job wasn't for me, not that I would have gotten employed at that time, so I started doing small renovations and it grew from there."

"Do you…?"

"Still do the dumb stuff? No, trust me, I learned a very harsh lesson by going to prison. I shouldn't have told you, to be fair. I don't want you to think any less of me. It was a long time ago."

"It's fine, I'm glad you have," I smiled reassuringly at him.

Once the initial shock had worn off, I found that it didn't bother me. I didn't know anyone who had been to prison, but as he said, it was a long time ago.

We sipped on our coffee but his earlier *spark* had gone. I reached forward and touched his hand.

"It's okay, Miller. So you went to prison, you're not that person now."

"My ex-wife loved the notoriety of being married to an ex-con, as she told everyone I was. It was fucking annoying. I just wanted to get on with my life and put it all behind me. She didn't seem to want me to. In fact, she's now with someone who's doing time." He laughed as he picked up his coffee cup.

"I guess there are plenty of women around who like that kind of thing."

"What about you? Would you date someone who'd been in prison?" he asked, staring intently at me.

"I'd date someone who had been in prison, providing they weren't doing anything that would take them back there," I replied.

He nodded slightly and warmth spread over me. I wasn't sure I wanted that warmth, but I liked it. It was a boost to my very bruised ego to think, or assume, he might be interested in me beyond the client relationship.

"Time to get going," he said, standing as the waiter handed him the bill.

"Let me give you something towards lunch," I said reaching for my bag.

"What kind of a man would I be if I let a lady pay, even half, for lunch?"

He paid the bill and we walked back towards his truck. He opened the door for me and reached to pull the seatbelt forwards for me to grab.

It was a torturous drive home. Not because there was any tension but I didn't want my time with him to end. Yet, I wanted my time with him to end because I wanted to get in my room and try to make sense of the feelings coursing through my body.

He dropped me off at the top of the drive.

"I won't join you at Christmas, but thank you for the offer. I meant to say earlier. I'd like to call though, to wish you and your dad a happy day. Or as happy as it's going to be…"

He sighed.

"Fuck it, Dani. I want to talk to you every day, okay. I'm just going to come out and say it. I want to check on you, make sure you're coping. I feel…"

I placed my hand on his arm.

"Thank you, I appreciate that, and I'd like for you to check on me."

I leant forwards and gave him the briefest kiss to his cheek before sliding from my seat and closing the passenger door. I walked to the front door, only turning once to give him a quick wave before stepping into the house. I leant my back against the door and my heart was hammering in my chest.

"I can't believe I just did that," I said, to myself.

"Can't believe what?" Dad said as he walked out of the living room.

"Oh, nothing. I'm just going to put these upstairs.

I walked up the stairs as quickly as I could and fell backwards on my bed.

"Bloody hell," I whispered. Then I laughed.

CHAPTER EIGHTEEN

I never got to wrap Dad's gifts in fancy paper, and we never got the tree that we'd said we would. We did, however, string some decorations around the yucca plant that had stood looking miserable in the corner of the living room for as long as I could remember.

Christmas morning was way better than I imagined it would be. I woke to the smell of bacon being grilled, carols playing on the radio, and Dad whistling along. I laughed when I joined him and saw him wearing plaid pyjama bottoms, a Christmas themed jumper that had seen better days, and a Santa hat. I hugged him, because I wanted to and because I wanted him to know I was okay.

We sat and ate our breakfast, planning our day. Unbeknown to me, Mrs. Hampton had invited herself for a drink later in the afternoon. I told Dad to call her and invite her for lunch. The old girl was on her own, and the thought of anyone spending that day alone saddened me. His smile was broad as he bustled off to the hallway.

I set about to prepare the vegetables and stuff the turkey. I turned the radio up and even Lucy seemed to get into the Christmas spirit with a couple of barks, as if singing along.

"She was thrilled. Said she'd be here in a half hour with wine," Dad said when he returned to the kitchen.

"I think it's nice that she wants to spend time with you."

"Oh, I don't know about that."

"She does, and you want to spend time with her. It's great, Dad."

"It's nice to have her company. I mean, I love spending time with you…"

I cut him off. "Dad, it's fine. You're allowed to have a *companion*," I said.

"Well, before she gets here, I want to give you something."

Dad left the room and I could hear the under stairs cupboard door open. He returned with a large package wrapped in brown paper.

"Oh, you didn't have to," I said, taking the package from him.

"It's not much, because we said we weren't going to bother but…Open it."

I unwrapped to find a wooden plaque. Carved into the plaque were two words.

The Hayloft

I looked up at Dad. From behind his back he presented me with a small book.

"I did some research, on the interweb. The barn was known as The Hayloft and since you'll need an address, I thought it might be nice to go back to that. I made a book of all the research I'd found."

"You made a book?"

"I found a website thingy that made it for me. It was all quite easy really."

I opened the book and read the dedication on the first page.

To my darling daughter,

This is your new home, and the start of your new life. A life that, I hope, will be filled with new adventures and new memories to carry you forward.

You'll never forget your old life, but now is the time to let it all go and start afresh. I hope The Hayloft will help you do that.

I love you, Dani,

Dad xx

I quickly rubbed at a tear that had dripped to the page.

"Oh, Dad, it's amazing, I love it. Thank you so much."

He wrapped me in his arms and held me tight. "I've missed you, Dani. For the past year, I've missed the woman that I know, but I can see she's on her way back, and I'll forever be thankful for whoever, or whatever, has helped that to happen."

"I don't know what to say," I said.

"Nothing, Dani. You don't need to say anything. Just start living again."

I placed the book on the table and picked up the plaque.

"It's a piece of driftwood I found on the beach. I thought it was something that was lost and now it has a home," Dad said. That made me tear up again.

"Where did you get it done?" I asked, running fingers over the intricate cursive letters.

"Miller carved it for me."

"Did you know he'd been in prison?" I asked.

"Yes, I think it's common knowledge, to be honest. Man's paid his dues, there's some who won't hire him because of it. I think that's bloody daft."

"What did he go to prison for?"

"Fighting, stealing cars, and driving drunk, I think. Rumour has it, people paid him to collect debts and not in the way you see on the TV."

"Crikey. Anyway, I have a couple of gifts for you, too."

I'd left a small bag on the seat of one of the chairs.

"It's not much but…"

Dad waved my sentence away and opened the perfume. For a while he was silent, but then he smiled.

"She always wore this, from our wedding day to the day she died. She'd say, 'I can be wearing the scruffiest clothes, no makeup, and my hair a mass of tangles, but I feel like a beautiful woman with a dab of perfume behind my ears.'"

I could imagine my mum saying something like that.

"I know it seems silly, but I like to spray it on her pillow. It helps me remember her," he added.

He placed the perfume on the table and opened the jumper.

"Just what I needed, thank you," he said with a laugh.

"I think we should have a glass of something bubbly," I said, heading for the fridge.

A knock on the front door meant I pulled three glasses from the cupboard.

"Happy Christmas," I heard Mrs. Hampton call out, as she walked down the hallway.

I smiled as she came into the kitchen and handed her a glass of bubbly. "Happy Christmas, Mrs. Hampton," I said.

As she took a sip of her Prosecco, she waved her hand in my direction. "Call me Colette," she said.

We clinked glasses and while Dad and Colette made their way into the living room, I continued to prepare our lunch. Between basting the turkey and preparing the vegetables, I sent Christian a text message to wish him a happy day, he didn't reply.

I had tried to call him first thing but the call had gone to his voicemail. I knew Dad had done the same. We didn't know where he was staying, other than it was with a friend. Christian had many friends, most of whom I didn't know.

Colette spent most of the day keeping us entertained, enough for the sadness that bubbled within me to be kept under the surface, ensuring we had an enjoyable time. We ate, way too much, we drank a little too much, and when the olds dozed on the sofa after the Queen's Speech, I decided to get some fresh air.

There were some walkers on the beach, trying to counteract the calories they'd eaten, I imagined. I wandered along the cliff until I came to the bench. I sat for a while and just watched the walkers below, and the strangers out on surfboards testing out their Christmas gifts, I thought. Why someone would want to dip their toes, let alone surf in December in Cornwall, was beyond me. I shivered at the thought of the water temperature.

I enjoyed the peace, the cold breeze that freshened my skin and blew the sadness from my mind. Part of me wanted to visit Hannah, the other part wanted to stay as far away as possible. I hadn't thought much more about the conversation I'd had with Daniel, but I knew I ought to. I should make my mind up on what I wanted to do. There was also Patricia to consider.

Trey had been born in California; he'd come to England many times over his childhood, having a father in the military. It was why, he'd told me, he wanted to study in the UK. Patricia and Dad had been instrumental in the funeral arrangements for Trey and Hannah. I wondered how crass it would be if I offered to cremate him and then send his ashes back to her. Could I pretend he'd always wanted to go home?

The thought not only surprised, but also horrified me. Patricia had always been so wonderful to me, supportive, and the best mother-in-law I could have wished for.

I shook the thoughts from my mind and headed home. Maybe I shouldn't spend too much time on my own over the festive period, or after a glass of bubbly and a glass of wine.

We finished the day with cold turkey sandwiches. Dad decided to walk Colette back to her house and I sat with a cup of tea. A half hour or so later, I remembered a conversation with Miller. I ran to the kitchen to retrieve my mobile. Sure enough, there were two missed calls and one text message.

Hey, just checking in. How has your day been so far? Miller

I wasn't sure whether to call or text back. I decided a text might be better in case he was busy.

I'm sorry to miss your call, I guess I'm not used to keeping my phone near me. It's been great, much better than I was expecting, to be honest. Mrs. Hampton joined us. I went for a walk after lunch, now I'm chilling on the sofa. Dad has walked Mrs. Hampton home, I think there might be a budding relationship going on there! Dani

I'd just placed the phone on the seat beside me when it rang.

"Hi, so you've had a good day?" Miller said. For a moment I let his low toned voice just wash over me.

"I have. I didn't expect to. And thank you so much for the house name plaque. It was a wonderful surprise. I absolutely love it."

"It was all your dad's idea. I think it's a perfect name for the barn. I was very impressed with his research," Miller chuckled.

"He said he found the wood on the beach, I think it's just a wonderful idea. I've been drifting along for so long, now we both have a home. Or hopefully we both have a home."

"I'm pretty confident you will. I wondered what you were planning to do tomorrow?"

"Nothing really, I guess. Why?"

"I'll be at a loose end in the afternoon, maybe you'd like to go for a walk, or something?"

"At a loose end? So your invitation is just to fill in a few hours?" I teased, hoping that he could hear the smile in my voice.

"Yeah, something like that," he retorted.

I chuckled. "I'd like that, thank you."

"Great, I'll call by mid-afternoon, if that's okay. I can't say an exact time, it depends on my dad."

"I'll be here."

"See you then," he said.

I replaced the phone on the sofa and found myself smiling at the thought of spending some more time with Miller. As I rested back, I closed my eyes.

Should I be happy about spending time with Miller?

How long should I grieve before I could move on?

I guessed, it wasn't as simple as losing my loving husband. Did the fact that he cheated on me, that I hated him so much right then, justify spending time with another man?

What were we actually doing? Was it a date? Or were we just friends spending time together? Was I reading way too much into this friendship?

Those thoughts, and more, ran through my mind. I doubted I'd be able to Google the mourning period for someone in my situation. I took a deep breath in and let it out slowly. I had to stop overthinking it all.

My mobile vibrated beside me, disturbing me. I was certainly popular that day.

"Hello?" I said.

"Dani, hi. It's Daniel."

"Hi, how was your day?"

"Really good. We had a great service; you missed some cracking hymn singing. I then had a rather disgusting lunch, consisting of an indescribable meat, boiled to death cabbage, and something I think might have been mash at the old people's home."

"I think your day tops mine by miles," I said with a laugh.

"Anyway, as it is a rather important Christian date on our calendar, and all that, I'm busy tomorrow as well but wondered if you'd have a few hours free the day after? I could do with some younger company and a pint or two."

"Gosh, I seem to be the fall back, or fill in, go-to person lately," I said, laughing again.

"I'm not following."

"Your brother invited me out for a walk tomorrow because he was at a loose end, and you need younger company to get over all the old people, or doing God's work, or whatever you call it."

Daniel laughed. "Ah, yes, I guess us Copeland boys aren't the best at asking a lovely lady on a date."

"So you're asking me on a date?"

"Daniella, I'd like to invite you to join me for a pint or two at the local public house the day after tomorrow, for an official date."

I didn't answer immediately, and wondered how he knew to call me Daniella. I didn't recall telling him that was my full name. However, I guessed there was no harm in joining him at the pub.

"Thank you, Daniel, I'd be thrilled to join you."

I wouldn't think of it as a real date, I was sure he was just joking. He was a vicar; he didn't have time to date, did he?

"Now I'm going to get my sloppy joggers on, eat some proper food, like sweets and ice cream, and catch up on all the crap Christmas movies I've missed today."

"It was good to talk to you, see you in a couple of days," I said.

The front door opened and although I was in the living room, off the hallway, I felt the dip in temperature as a cold blast of air blew through.

"I'm back," Dad called out. "I'm making a cup of tea, do you want one?"

"No, thank you. If it's okay with you, I'm going to get an early night. I think all that overeating has exhausted me."

I followed him into the kitchen and gave him a hug. "Thank you for today. It hasn't been as awful as I imagined it to be," I said.

"I did wonder how you'd feel but I thought it was best not to keep asking, to keep reminding you."

"I feel guilty that I didn't go to see her, but I just can't right now."

"I can understand that. Go on up, get yourself some sleep. Maybe we'll both take a walk up there tomorrow morning, or another day, whenever you're ready."

I hadn't been back to Hannah's grave since the day I found out about Trey, and although that was just a few short weeks ago, it seemed like months. Despite my earlier words, and the fact that I'd had an enjoyable day, a wave of sadness washed over me. What kind of a mother was I to ignore my child on what should have been her first Christmas, just because I hated her father?

A little voice popped up in my head—A hurt one, it said.

I was up early the next morning. I guessed the early night had the desired effect, as I felt very refreshed. I sat at the table and decided to write to Lincoln. I hadn't replied to his last letter and I felt bad as if I'd neglected him of late.

Lincoln,

I hope that you had a wonderful Christmas Day and I want to thank you for your last letter. I'm still deeply hurt by Trey's affair, although I do believe it now. I received a letter from a solicitor wanting to discuss her child receiving part of Trey's estate. I did a little Googling, he's entitled, but I think there could be lots of complications, because Trey wasn't British, he was American.

Anyway, I'm not focussing on it for a while. I've decided to put it all to the back of my mind for a couple of days.

I want to tell you something interesting. I met a gentleman in the cemetery the other day; his name was Lincoln as well. How strange to have two gentlemen in the same village with the same name. He was a lovely and humorous, man. I'd love to meet up with him again. He said he lived in an old people's home…

I paused writing. Daniel had spent Christmas Day in an old people's home. I couldn't imagine the village was large enough to support two. In fact, the more I thought about it, the more there seemed to be so many connections, and overlaps.

Daniel, our local vicar, spent Christmas Day in the local old folks' home, I wonder if he might know that Lincoln.

I had hoped the man I met would have been you, but I guess not. Anyway, I made a decision to go to the cemetery on Thursday, I don't want to ignore my child, and I'll just have to get over the fact he's with her. I had spoken to Daniel about exhuming him, but now my mind is a little clearer, I guess that's a little extreme. A total overreaction I imagine. I think I shocked Daniel to hell and back!

I'm going to spend New Year's Eve on the beach, I remember doing that as a child for so many years. We'd watch the fireworks exploding from all different directions and then the boats tooting their horns at midnight. I'm hoping it will remind me of better times, and give me a future to look forward to.

Dad had a wonderful plaque made for my new home. It was known as The Hayloft in the past, so I hope I can get the planning and it can return to being called that. The name is carved into a piece of driftwood, Dad felt we were both lost but now we have a home. I thought it was a wonderful idea. I feel like I have something to be excited about, and the guilt I feel is lessening each day, for that, I'm thankful.

I'm also thankful for you, Lincoln. I'm not sure what I would have done without having you read my ramblings and taking the time to reply.

Your friend, always.

Dani.

I read back through my words and started to remember certain things said by both Miller and Daniel. I began to think that one, or both, knew of my Lincoln. Daniel had been vague on the 'Anna' issue. Surely he'd know, or have access to records of, who was buried in the cemetery? Miller seemed shocked when I'd told him about the Lincoln I'd met. Like I'd thought before, what were the chances of two Lincolns in the same small village?

I folded the letter and placed it in the envelope, I wasn't sure how long that envelope was going to last. It had long since lost the ability to stick and we'd given up on using tape. Instead, I tucked the flap into the back of the envelope and pulled on my boots and jacket. I took a slow walk up the lane to the honesty box.

Another thought hit me. There wasn't a defined time between letters. Did that mean Lincoln walked this lane frequently, daily even? How else would he know there was a letter waiting for him?

Only once had anyone seen me near that honesty box, and that was Mrs. Hampton. It was just a broken wooden box, nestled in a hedge, which most people would walk past without noticing.

"Been for a walk?" Dad said when I returned.

"Just posting a letter. You know those ones I get from Lincoln? I leave them in the honesty box up the lane."

"I didn't know it was still there. Old Fred Samuels used to own that farm. He died a year ago, I think."

"Who owns it now?"

"His son, he rents it out, though. He doesn't even live in the UK, I don't think. I'm sure someone said he's emigrated to Australia, or it might have been America."

"I've been thinking about this Lincoln person. I'm wondering if that's not his real name. I met a man called Lincoln in the cemetery. How likely is it to have two men with the same name in the village?"

"It's not the most common of names, I guess. Have you asked him?"

"I don't want to, really. If he felt the need to use a fake name, I guess there's a reason for that. It's a shame though, because I'd love to know who he really is."

"He puts a letter through our door, doesn't he?"

"He does."

"We could get one of those camera things," Dad said.

"CCTV? You know, although I really want to know who he is, what if I'm disappointed? He said once that he'd known me as a child. I wonder if he was teacher at my old school."

"That won't be hard to work out. I'm sure all your old school reports are in the barn. Although you'd need to know his surname, but we might be able to work out who's still alive at least, narrow it down a little."

I paused, thinking about something Miller had said.

"Do you remember Miller as a child? He said something, I can't remember his exact words, but I told him I'd been on a boat, when I was kid, and he…Oh, what did he say?"

I racked my brain for the words. "It was as if I should remember who the other kids were, I think."

"I do, I'm sure you might have played with him. All the kids used to gather on the beach. Things were easier back then, you kids had way more freedom than perhaps you should have. You'd go out in the morning and come home when you were hungry. Maybe he was on that boat with you. I know a few of their parents had boats, you used to moan that we didn't but your friends' dads did."

"I don't really remember him, I wonder why."

"Who do you remember from your childhood?"

We sat while we chatted.

"I remember Katy, I wonder what happened to her. She had brown pigtails and was always crying if someone messed with her hair. The boys used to pull it all the time. Then there was, George, I think he was called. He was a snotty kid, always up for a dare."

"He died, in his teens," Dad said.

"How?"

"Cliff diving, so I was told."

"Bloody hell! There's nowhere local for that."

"Oh, I don't think it was here. I can't remember the facts. You know who you should ask? Colette is the font of all that goes on in his village. There's not much she doesn't remember, I'm sure."

I wondered if that was an excuse to invite her down again.

"I think that might be a good idea. Maybe she'd like to visit later, for dinner?"

"She has family visiting today, she told me. But I'll give her a call and invite for the day after. I'm sure we'll still have some of that turkey left over."

I grinned at the smile Dad displayed.

"I don't know why you two don't make it official," I said.

"Whatever do you mean by that?"

"Well, you're both single, you have a fondness for each other, so call it what it is."

"Call it what it is? I'm not following. We're friends, nothing more."

"Dad, you'd love for it to be more than 'nothing more,' I can tell," I said with a laugh.

"Well, young lady, you might be right, but at my age, friends is what we call it."

He laughed as he made his way to the hallway, no doubt to call her. I started to prepare us some breakfast. It had surprised me not to remember many children from my childhood. I struggled to remember anyone from secondary school, so I guessed I couldn't blame myself, or my memory, for not going back even further.

CHAPTER NINETEEN

*M*iller arrived earlier than I'd expected. I could hear the truck rumbling on the drive outside. I opened the front door and gave him a wave. I pulled a coat off the rack and shouted out to Dad that I'd see him later.

"Hi, what a nice day for a walk," I said, as I climbed into his truck.

The sun was out and the wind had died down to a gentle breeze. Although cold, it was a perfect day for a stroll.

"So you had a good day yesterday?" Miller asked.

"I did, I think Dad did all he could to take my mind off other things. The only sad thing was not hearing back from Christian. I know Dad was a little upset over that."

"He's not in a good place, I guess he's avoiding the season and probably anyone who reminds him of the situation."

'Maybe, but the least he could do is call his dad."

"People do strange things when they're in such a shitty situation, I guess. I'm sure he'll call at some point."

"Mmm, not sure. Where are we going, anyway?" I asked.

"Somewhere I played as a kid, maybe you did, too."

Miller gave me a smile as he turned the truck around and we drove off down the lane. It wasn't long before we bumped down a lane that hadn't seen a vehicle in years. Grass had grown through the cracked tarmac in the centre, and rain had carved ditches either side. I held on to the handle on the door as we dodged potholes. Eventually, we came to a grassed area on top of a cliff. Miller turned off the truck.

"Look familiar?" he asked.

"It does, there's a staircase carved into the rock down to the beach, isn't there?"

"There is, but that's not the way we're going. Come on, put your coat on."

He reached behind to retrieve a jacket from the back seat and then opened his door. I struggled into my coat before stepping out. Being on the edge of the cliff meant the wind whipping off the sea was a little stronger. I fiddled around in my coat pocket for a hairband.

"This way," Miller said.

I followed him down a small bank and to a brook that emerged from the rock and flowed to the sea. We walked alongside it for a few minutes until I saw a path carved between the bushes. Miller took the path and the mud squelched beneath my boots. I was glad I'd worn them. After a few minutes, we came to an opening. In front of me was a derelict cottage.

"Wow, I remember this place. Wasn't it supposed to be haunted or something?"

"I imagine, as kids, we thought every empty house was haunted," Miller said with a laugh.

I watched as he pulled a key from his pocket and opened the front door.

"I bought this place a few years ago. I've never gotten around to doing anything with it. Well, I've not had the inclination to do anything about it, to be honest."

We stepped inside the empty building.

"It's gorgeous, or could be. Look at that view," I said.

From the window, I could see miles of uninterrupted land and sea.

"I decided, when I've finished your barn, I'm going to take some time out to work on this. I think it could make a great holiday rental, if I can sort out that access, of course."

"It would. Imagine sitting outside on a nice summer's evening."

"Follow me," Miller said.

He walked into what I assumed would be a living room and to the back wall. He pointed to something written on the wall. When I stepped closer, I could see the faint list of names.

"That's me, isn't it?" I asked.

"Yes, I think so. And that's me," he said, pointing the name directly underneath.

"So we played here together?"

"Yes. And that boat you said you went out on? That was my dad's, I was on it."

"I wonder why I don't…"

"Remember me?"

"I wasn't going to say that, but now you mention it," I lied.

Miller didn't answer immediately, instead he walked around the room as if inspecting the whitewashed brick walls, rattling the windowpanes to check they were secure, and occasionally stamping on the bare wooden floorboards.

"You'll go through if one of those is rotten," I said with a chuckle.

He looked up at me and smiled.

"How about I say something that might have you running for the hills?"

"I'm not sure I'd be able to run anywhere, and if you already think it's something I might not like, should you?"

"It's just a kid thing. You were my first ever crush. I used to follow you around a lot; I think it started when I was about ten or so. Like I said, a kid thing."

"Started?"

Miller just shrugged his shoulders and didn't answer my question. I wasn't sure whether to laugh or not.

"Did we play together a lot?" I asked.

"No. I was too shy to join in. You were always so confident and such a tomboy. Your brother used to warn me off," he said, laughing.

"Warn you off?"

"Yeah. I remember him calling me a freak, or something like that, because I used to follow you. Told me he'd give me a punch if I talked to you. I think, because of my dad, most of the kids were wary of me."

"I wouldn't have been wary of you just because your dad was a vicar. And I don't like that Christian did that, at all."

"We'll never know, I guess."

"Tell me about the boat?" I asked. I had vague memories of it.

"Dad wanted to take his boat out, I asked if I could go with him. You were at the harbour, with some girl, I can't remember her name, and because Christian wasn't with you, I took a chance to invite you. You hated it, if I remember."

"I did! I guessed I could swim but I don't think I liked going out of my depth in the sea, and I'm pretty sure that might have been the year we watched *Jaws* on the TV. I know I was terrified of even getting into the bath on my own. You held my hand, I remember that part now."

Miller laughed.

"I know, it was totally irrational but I was absolutely terrified of water," I said, laughing along with him.

"So you had a major crush on me," I added.

"I didn't say *major*, I said you were my first," he replied, smirking at me.

"Major, first, whatever. I never knew. What about when we got older? I don't remember you in my teens," I said, feeling terribly guilty for saying that.

"We left for a couple of years. Dad had to cover another parish for a while. I was about seventeen, eighteen, before we came back."

"And I was off to university at eighteen. That's a shame, we might have been great friends again."

"One of the first things I did when I got back was to look you up. Of course, you'd gone, taken my heart and hopes with you, not that you were aware, of course."

I stared at him. He winked and then laughed. I shook my head and sat on the windowsill looking at him.

"Well, I'm sorry for breaking your heart and dashing your hopes. Whatever can I do to make it up to you?" I said, joking.

"Kiss me."

Miller walked towards me, I was frozen to the spot. He took my face in his hands.

"Just one, for years I've wondered what it would have felt like to kiss you," he whispered.

I opened my mouth to speak but couldn't find the words. I sat staring up at him, in a derelict house, with goose bumps coursing over my skin, with my heart racing, and with my tongue running over my lower lip to moisten it. Whether any of that was conscious or not, I wasn't sure.

He lowered his head very slowly, not taking his gaze from me. I could feel his breath on my lips; he was that close. I closed my eyes and gripped the front of his jacket. Just as his lips were about to touch mine, I found my voice.

"I have a date with your brother tomorrow," I blurted out.

Miller sighed, his breath ghosted across my lips. He rested his forehead briefly on mine.

"Then I guess I'll forever be wondering," he said, and then pulled away.

For the longest moments, we stood in silence just looking at each other. Miller took a deep breath.

"I'm so sorry. That was about the most inappropriate thing I've ever done," he said, no longer meeting my eyes.

"I…"

"It's okay, no need to say anything. That was totally on me and I can't apologise enough. Maybe we should start heading back."

Without waiting for an answer, he turned and walked towards the door. My breath caught in my throat, my heart missed a beat, and sadness washed over me. If I was confused before, I was more so then.

"I don't want you to apologise," I said to his retreating back.

"I have to. I'd hate for you to think badly of me. Shall we?" He held the door open for me.

The walk back to the truck was in silence. My legs felt heavy, I felt weary, and I wanted to reach out to him. I wasn't sure if that was physically or verbally. I didn't want his apology, because deep down, I knew I wanted his kiss. I needed him to understand, it had absolutely nothing to do with my date with Daniel, and I wasn't even sure why I'd mentioned that. The *date* part was a joke, I thought. I wanted Miller to understand that although it had been nearly a year since Trey had died, and at that moment I hated Trey, a part of me felt I was betraying my marriage.

Miller held the truck door open, he gave me a smile but I saw that it didn't reach his eyes; there was no sparkle to them. I thanked him as I climbed in. I watched him walk around to the driver's side. He removed his jacket and threw it into the back before taking his seat.

"So where are you off to tomorrow?" Miller asked as he turned the truck around.

"It's not a date, I'm not sure why I even said that. I just agreed to go to the pub with him, that's all. Why don't you join us?" I asked.

Miller laughed, although it wasn't in humour. "No, but thank you for inviting me."

He mumbled something under his breath and I didn't ask what it was. I guessed it wasn't intended for my ears.

I didn't want for anything to sour our friendship but I was at a loss as to what to say. I'd had one boyfriend, and I'd married him. I had no idea what to do in that situation, but I knew I had to make amends; I had to get our relationship back on track.

We arrived home way quicker than I was prepared for. Miller climbed from the truck but I stayed put in my seat. He opened my door for me, expecting me to climb out also.

"Miller..."

"It's okay. I did something stupid, I should have kept my mouth shut."

"Well, I wish you'd keep your mouth shut for a moment now," I said.

He raised his eyebrows at me.

"Miller, I would have loved nothing more than to have kissed you back then. I need to tell you why I didn't. It has absolutely nothing to do with Daniel; there is nothing other than friendship between us. I'm confused. I hate my husband, yet just as your lips were about to touch mine, guilt washed over me. I'm pissed off at that guilt because I don't think I have anything to feel guilty for. That's where the confusion comes. Why should I feel guilty about wanting to kiss another man, when my husband spent two years fucking another woman? And it's not like he's alive, I'm not cheating on him, but..."

I didn't get to finish my sentence. Miller pulled me from the truck and I stumbled into his chest. Before I could get a breath, he had one hand wrapped in my hair and pulled my face to his. His lips crashed down on mine with enough force for me to know they'd bruise. His tongue swiped across my lips as if requesting access. I gave it to him. I kissed him back as furiously as he was kissing me. My tongue tangled with his, I tasted him, and I inhaled him. Our teeth clashed and I could hear my ragged breath trying to pass between the seal his mouth had made. I could feel my heart beat so hard in my chest, and I could feel his as he pulled me closer. His hand tightened in my hair and I felt his other cup my chin, holding me in place.

I raised my hand and gripped the hair at the nape of his neck. I wanted to force him closer to me, not that it was possible. I wanted to feel his body against mine, and I cursed the bulky coat I wore. I heard the low moan as it left my lips and it startled me enough to pause my assault on his mouth. I was aroused, so very aroused. More than I think I'd been in many years. I wanted to cross my legs to quell the ache, the need that pulsed through me.

Miller stopped kissing me, but not abruptly. Although I'd stopped moving, my mouth partly closed, he gently kissed my lips. First my upper lip, then my lower one. He gently kissed across my cheek before whispering in my ear.

"That was everything. More than I ever dreamed possible."

I released my grip on the back of his hair, all of a sudden conscious that I was standing in the driveway to my house. My dad could very well be staring from the living room window. I swallowed hard as he took a step back. He ran his hand through his hair and looked around. In fact, he looked anywhere other than me. Although I didn't want to, my eyes scanned down his chest. I could see his arousal through his jeans. That sight didn't help to settle the ache between my thighs.

"I think I should go. I just wanted to show you the house," he said quietly.

"Maybe you'll take me back there, please?"

He looked up at me; a ghost of a smile crossed his lips. "If you want to."

"I do."

He nodded, just the once, and then walked around to his side of the truck. I stepped to one side and closed the passenger door. I watched as he drove away without a backwards glance. I stood for a while, even when he'd turned the corner and was out of view. I touched my lips, still warm, with my fingertips and gently ran my hand through my hair where he'd gripped it. My scalp was a little sore.

"Fuck," I said.

I ran my hand through my hair again, retying it neatly before walking towards the front door. I fished around in my pocket for my front door key and before I had it in the lock it opened.

"Good walk?" Dad asked.

I paused before answering, not sure whether he'd seen what happened.

"Yes. Miller bought an old house that we used to play in as kids, I had written my name on the wall. The house is by Harleson Falls, do you know it?"

"I do, you used to run home crying that it was haunted, or that might have been Christian, you were the tougher of the two."

"Well, he bought it a couple of years ago but hasn't done anything with it. He's going to renovate it after the barn," I said, removing my jacket and not making eye contact.

"I'm pleased that you've made a friend in him. You both deserve to have that friendship."

I wondered what Dad had meant by that statement, but I didn't want to talk about Miller. I changed the subject.

"Did you hear from Christian?" I asked.

"No, I tried again, left another message. If I don't hear tomorrow, I might ring around a couple of his friends, find out exactly where he is."

"I think that's a good idea. But I don't think you need to worry. I'm sure he's just hiding out, ignoring the festivities. Did you call Colette?" I asked.

"I did, she invited us both to visit tomorrow."

"I think you should go, I've got plans," I said.

"Plans?"

"Daniel invited me for a drink."

Dad chuckled and shook his head.

"What?"

"Miller and Daniel, now there's a box of fireworks you're about to ignite."

"What do you mean by that?" I asked, following Dad into the kitchen.

"You don't know?"

"No, so tell me."

"Miller's wife, who was having an affair, eventually left him, and it's rumoured, took up with Daniel for a while."

"No way. Hold on, Miller told me his wife had left him for a criminal or someone."

Dad shrugged his shoulders. "Well, that's not what I heard. It's why they don't get on."

"I'm sure he said his ex-wife was with someone who was in prison."

"Maybe she is now, but she ran straight into the arms of Daniel for consoling, told him a bunch of lies, according to Colette, then she divorced Miller and took his dog. Or was it his record collection, I can't remember."

"His dog."

Miller had told me his wife had an affair; he omitted the part about Daniel, if it was true of course. Mrs. Hampton was either the font of all village knowledge, or a terrible gossip.

"They only started talking again a few months ago and I think it's still very strained."

"He told me that he met someone else after his divorce," I said.

"He did, that was tragic. She died, can't remember from what. Now, do you want cold meat and mashed potato?"

"That would be lovely. Why don't I get that sorted, you go and pour us a glass of wine each."

As soon as Dad left the kitchen, I sat to think. Miller had lost his partner yet he hadn't said a word about that. I wondered why. Wouldn't that have given us a connection, something in common? Or maybe he didn't want to talk about it at all. The more I knew about Miller, the more I realised I knew nothing at all. Yet his kiss had been so consuming, so connecting, and passionate. It had felt so natural but he was effectively a stranger. How could that be?

There was something in the back of my mind that I just couldn't grasp. Some knowledge that was wriggling its way to the front. It frustrated me, but all I could do was to concentrate on something else and hope whatever it was, would come to me.

I set about to prepare dinner and put Miller out of my mind. His kiss though, was there thanks to the tingle still on my lips.

Dad and I decided to eat off our laps in front of the TV. It wasn't something we'd normally do, but there was a movie that we both didn't want to miss. Dad moaned at the unreality and I gawked at the leading man in his ripped t-shirt and oil stained skin. We had fun and it was another day that I didn't feel overwhelmed with Trey, Hannah, Christian, Helen, affairs, and deceit. When the movie finished, I picked up the plates and took them to the kitchen.

My head felt a little fuzzy just from one, large glass of wine, so I poured myself a glass of water. I was such a lightweight when it came to alcohol. I guessed it stemmed back to uni days when I was always the designated driver. When I should have been out challenging my tolerance, I was sober and sensible.

I stacked the dishwasher, let Lucy out for a ramble around the garden, and topped up her feed and water bowls. She would enjoy some leftover turkey and warm gravy. It was as I let her back into the kitchen that a thought came to me.

I rushed upstairs and retrieved all the letters I'd received from Lincoln and returned to the kitchen. I scanned through them.

Knew you as a child.

My wife died a couple of years ago.

Reconciling, of sorts.

I have many wrongs to right.

I shook my head. They were just a few words in a sea of hundreds. Was it just coincidence that Miller had either told me similar things, or I'd found out similar things? I'd convinced myself for such a long time my Lincoln was an elderly gentle-man, who sat at a scratched old desk, in front of an open fire with a dog by his feet. My Lincoln resembled the man in the cemetery that day, the man caring for Anna's grave, even though that wasn't his wife. And, of course, Miller wasn't called Lincoln.

...son called Lincoln...

Those words, said by the man at the cemetery floated through my mind.

"No way," I said, aloud.

"No way, what?" Dad said, bring the empty glasses into the kitchen.

"Is Miller his real name?"

"I guess so, why do you ask?"

"I'm beginning to think the man who writes these letters to me is Miller."

I showed Dad the passages in the letters and explained some things that either Miller or he had told me.

"I don't know, Dani, that's a pretty obscure conclusion to come to. I mean, I know I said his partner died, I don't know if they were married or not. So he knew you as a child, but this is a small village, everyone knows everyone. Are you sure you're not just grasping at straws because you want to know who this Lincoln is?"

"The man at the cemetery said he had a son named Lincoln, yet no one knows of two Lincolns living in this village."

"Well, I don't have an answer for that. What would you do if this was Miller?"

"I don't know. I think I'd be upset, if I'm honest. I've poured my soul out in these letters, told Lincoln things I've not been able to tell anyone, even you. I'd feel cheated, deceived, again."

"I guess all you can do is ask him but I hope you're wrong. And you'll need to be careful, you don't want to alienate him. Those letters have been a comfort to you, is it really so important to know who wrote them? Let's say it was Miller, wouldn't you want to focus on the fact that you have two, as such, people that support you? And who's to say that what he's written aren't, like you, words he can't express in person?"

I didn't answer because I couldn't.

"Can I borrow your car?" I asked. I'd made a decision.

"You can, obviously, but I'm not sure you're doing the right thing," Dad replied.

"I don't know if I'm doing the right thing, but something changed between Miller and me today, and I now need to know if this is him," I said, waving the letters in front of me.

Dad opened a cupboard and retrieved his car keys. I pulled on a jacket and gave him a kiss on his cheek.

"Thank you. Don't wait up for me, but I'll call if I need you," I said, knowing that was want he'd want to hear.

Dad nodded and walked me to the front door. He watched as I opened the barn and drove his car onto the drive. I hadn't driven in a long while, but it didn't take long to find the headlights and head off down the lane.

My palms started to sweat and the closer I got to Miller's house, the more nervous I became. As I rounded the corner, and his cottage came into view, I slowed the car.

"This is daft," I said to myself.

I scanned the lane, looking for somewhere I could turn around but the only place was Miller's drive. I saw lights on in the room at the front of the house, if I pulled onto his drive, he'd see the headlights. If I killed the lights, I was sure that he'd still hear the car. I was committed.

I pulled onto his drive and turned off the car. I sat for a moment, taking some deep breaths before opening the door and walking to his front door. Before I could change my mind, I knocked.

Miller opened the door wearing a pair of jeans and a crumpled t-shirt. His hair was wet, as if he'd recently showered.

"Dani?"

"What's your name?" I asked, probably more abruptly through nerves than was necessary.

"Sorry?"

"What's your name," I repeated.

"Do you want to come in?" He stepped to one side and I walked into the hallway.

"Are you Lincoln?"

He didn't answer immediately. "Can I get you a glass of wine, or tea, since you're driving?"

"I don't want a glass of wine, or tea, I want to know if you are the one who wrote me these letters." I held them in front of me.

"Come through," he said, walking away.

I followed him into a living room. There were two standard lamps lit, and a fire roaring in the hearth. A book was placed face down on a brown leather sofa, and a small glass filled with a brown liquid and ice sat on a wooden table in the centre of the room.

"Take a seat," he said, indicating with his hand towards the sofa.

"Did you write these letters?" I asked again, while standing in the middle of the room.

He sighed. "Can I read them?"

"No. Answer my question, please?"

Miller sat on the sofa; he leant forwards and picked up the glass, taking a sip of the liquid. He rested his head back and closed his eyes for a moment. I wasn't sure if that was him savouring his drink, or contemplating what to say.

Without opening his eyes, he answered me.

"Yes."

Just one word was all he gave me, and I deflated. I sat at the other end of the sofa, my legs all of a sudden so weary.

"Why?"

"Because you needed me to."

"I didn't need *you* to," I said.

"You needed someone to answer you. I found your letter, in fact, I saw you place it in the bottle. I was curious."

"And you just decided to write back?" I could hear the sarcasm in my voice.

"Is that so terrible? Your letter tore at my heart, and you know what? Maybe I needed someone to write to as well."

He stared hard at me.

"All this is a bloody lie. You've deceived me, just like…"

"I am nothing like your shit of an ex-husband, Dani. Don't insult me by comparing me to him. There is not one lie in those words, so I'm not sure how you got to deceit."

"You called yourself Lincoln. I met a man…"

"You met my father, he told you he had a son called Lincoln, and he wasn't lying to you. My name is Lincoln Miller Copeland. I have gone by the name, Miller, since primary school. I got fed up, even at that age, of being called by my father's name, of both of us answering when someone called us, of not having my own identity."

"He lives in an old people's home. You told me he lives at the bottom of your garden."

"I told you he lived, past tense, at the bottom of my garden. He moved into a home just a few months ago, because he prefers that and it's better for him. I can't care for him the way he needs, or so he thinks."

"You said, in your *letter*, that your wife died of breast cancer."

"So she did, two…well, three years ago now."

"But you divorced…"

"I've been married twice, for my shame, and both fucked off and left me."

"Fucked off?"

"Abandoned, whatever words you want to use. It's all the same."

I could see the anger and sadness mixing in his eyes. His features hardened, and the tension was palpable. His jaw worked from side to side, and his fist had clenched around his glass to the point his knuckled were white.

"I feel exposed. I've said things in my letters that I haven't told anyone, yet all the time you pretended to be someone else."

"How have I pretended to be anything other than who I am?"

"You didn't tell me you'd written those letters, you fucking kissed me, you…"

"None of that connects, Dani. And you kissed me back just as fucking passionately, didn't you? You wanted me as much as I wanted you. Deny that."

I opened my mouth to speak but couldn't. Miller shuffled up the sofa, I pulled my knees up to block him.

"I wrote those letters, not expecting to ever meet you. I knew who you were, like I told you earlier today, I've known you for years. I've thought about you a lot over those years. It was a childhood crush, I knew that, but in mind, with every shitty day I lived through, I wondered what my life would have been like had you been in it. You, without knowing it, got me through nights in prison when all-out war was going on, both in my mind and outside the cells. You, Dani, stopped me from killing myself when life was so fucked up and I was so drunk nothing made sense. So I found your letter and I thought I could give back some of the help you, unknowingly, gave me."

"But…"

"But then your dad asked me to quote for your barn. What was I to do? I could have refused, I could have said I was too busy, but I didn't want to."

I watched his shoulders rise and fall faster than they should have. I saw a pulse beat frantically in the side of his neck. His eyes, however, had softened. Gone was the darkness, instead I saw a pleading. I shook my head.

"I think it was a shitty thing to do," I said, quieter as the fight had left my body.

"Shitty? Shitty would have been to ignore your cry, no, scream, for help. Shitty would have been to have stopped replying to you earlier, when you still needed to hear those words and read those letters. Shitty would have been to have abandoned you, when you needed me."

"I don't need you," I said, my voice rising.

"You don't need *me*, Miller, the man sitting here now, watching your heart rate increase, watching your pupils dilate, watching your body start to shiver even though it's fucking warm in here? Or Lincoln? Because we are one and the same, and every word written in those letters was healing, cathartic, freeing, for both of us. And from the heart, Dani. From. The. Heart."

Without me realising he was so close, his body had pushed my knees to my chest. I was squashed into the corner of the sofa with nowhere to go.

"From the heart," he whispered.

I stared at him, all the while trying to slow my heart down, trying to stop the shiver that raced over my body. Miller placed his hand on the outside of my thigh; he slid it to my waist.

"You needed me, and you know what? I needed you. And that has nothing to do with some silly childhood crush. We were both grieving, hurting; don't tell me you didn't find those letters a comfort. Don't tell me you didn't want to receive them, that you didn't look forward to receiving them."

"It's creepy," I said, not sure where the word had come from. "You said you'd followed me around when I was a kid, and this kind of feels like you've taken advantage of me."

"Taken advantage of you?"

"Yes." I straightened my back in defiance.

"Anything I've ever done has been because I care. But if you feel differently, then I guess you ought to leave."

He sat back so abruptly it was as if I'd slapped his face. And I guessed I had. He stood and paced for a moment, before picking up his glass, and draining his drink. I was about to stand when he threw the glass into the fire. It shattered, it hissed, sparks flew out covering the stone hearth. I cried out in shock.

"I'm sorry, I didn't mean to scare you," he said, not looking at me.

I stood, not sure what to do.

"Let me drive you home, it's dark out. I can bring the car back in the morning."

"I'm capable of driving in the dark, it's how I got here," I said.

He kept his back to me. "How did you find out?" he asked, his voice so quiet it was difficult to hear at first. "Was it Daniel?"

"Daniel? No. Does Daniel know?"

He nodded his head. "My brother the *saint that ain't* found one of your letters. Guess that's why he decided to step in and protect you from me." His laugh was bitter.

"Did your first wife have an affair with Daniel?"

"No. She was having an affair, just not with Daniel. She then had the decency to leave me and ran to Daniel, her confidant. She told him I'd abused her, verbally, emotionally, whatever. He believed her because he thought I was a fuck-up anyway. I guess

254

they got close, super close. Close enough for me to walk in on them one time. See, Dani, I know about betrayal and deceit, which is why I thought I was doing a good thing by replying to your letters."

He walked from the room, leaving me standing there. I walked to the living room door.

"What about your wife? You told me she was called Anna. Your dad was visiting Anna's grave. How coincidental is that?"

"Very coincidental. My wife was called Annabelle. My dad picked a grave that didn't look like anyone had visited it for years. I thought it was a strange thing to do, but it gave him some comfort. My mother is in Devon. I told you we moved away, yes? My mother died there. My dad never envisioned coming back here; it was too painful. But he, we, did, and he couldn't bring her with him. She was cremated and her ashes were scattered."

By the direction of his voice, I took it that Miller was in the kitchen. I could hear the clink of glass and wondered if he was pouring himself another drink.

"I don't know what to say or think," I said.

"Say nothing, think nothing. I'm not going to apologise, Dani. I don't think I've done anything wrong but try to do good. If you can't see that, you need to leave."

I couldn't, at that moment, see that. My thoughts were shrouded with confusion. I was attracted to Miller; I was enthralled with Lincoln. I couldn't reconcile them. I walked to the front door and gently closed it behind me. I got in the car, and with tears blurring my vision; I drove home.

CHAPTER TWENTY

*A*lthough the hallway light was on, there were no others. I opened the front door leaving the car in the driveway. I locked the door behind me and crept up the stairs. I could hear the gentle snores coming from Dad's bedroom as I tiptoed past. I shrugged off my clothes, not bothering to shower, and pulled on a pair of shorts and a tank top. I climbed under the duvet, leaving the side light on and read through the letters again. It wasn't the elderly gentleman that I pictured but a tortured Miller. It was obvious when I thought about it. He had actually told me some of the things he'd written about, just not as elaborately. Maybe he'd wanted me to figure it out. Perhaps he'd been calling out for help as loudly as I had been. If what I knew was true, he'd been to hell and back, several times. He hadn't told me a great deal about Annabelle, but I figured they hadn't been together for long before she'd died. I imagined that to be so hard. He'd had a second chance with her and it had been wrenched away.

I felt awful for some of the things I'd said, things that, in hindsight, didn't make sense. I was angry, disappointed, yet as I lay in bed and read his words, I realised how much he'd helped me. I understood the pain he had suffered, we had bonded over those letters. We had connected in real life. I had thrown that all back in his face.

I picked up my phone and hovered over his name. Instead of calling, I sent him a text message.

I'm sorry. I'd like to talk some more about the letters, if you wish to, of course. Dani.

I placed the phone on the side of the bed and watched the screen for a while. It faded to black and stayed that way. Eventually, I turned off the bedside light and rolled to my side. I pulled the duvet up around my neck and closed my eyes. All I saw was Miller. I saw his lips as they closed in on mine. I saw the desire in his eyes, the pupils dilate, and the irises darken. I felt his heartbeat increase, and his breath on my skin. I fell asleep to Miller and his low, comforting voice in my mind.

I woke late the following morning. I stretched and rubbed at my eyes. I was warm and content to stay put, but hearing Dad speaking to someone had me climb out of bed. I grabbed a sweatshirt and my slippers and walked from the room. Dad was sitting on the chair in the hallway with the phone to his ear. He looked up at me as I walked down the stairs and he smiled. He gave me a thumbs up and mouthed the word, Christian. I smiled in return. I was pleased he'd managed to contact him, who had called whom, I didn't know, but they were speaking, that was all that counted.

I made my way to the kitchen and poured a cup of tea, thankful the pot was still warm. It was a few minutes later that Dad appeared.

"He's skiing, can you believe that? I tore a strip off him for not letting us know. He said he thought he'd replied to one of your messages but obviously it didn't go through. I'm glad he's safe, I was beginning to get very worried."

"Did he say where he was?

"Somewhere in France. He did tell me the name, but I forget. He seemed quite upbeat, said he was enjoying himself. I asked if he'd seen Alistair but he cut me off, so I'm guessing not. He asked after you and apologised for worrying us both."

"That's good. I'm glad you've spoken to him."

Dad sat at the table. "So, was it him?"

I nodded as I sipped my tea.

"Well, that's a mystery solved. I bet you were pleased."

"Far from it. In fact, I felt quite violated and deceived, which this morning, I think is a little irrational."

"I imagine that it was a shock but you need to remember the kindness in the words, and how much you enjoyed receiving those letters. Does it matter who sent them?"

I shrugged my shoulders. "I don't know, Dad, I just don't feel it was right to keep up two very different personalities."

"Did he, though. I mean, I haven't read the letters, obviously, but from what you've said, and from what I've heard him say to you, it doesn't seem like two personalities. Two names, sure, but not two people."

"His real name is Lincoln Miller Copeland. He dropped the Lincoln in primary school, something to do with wanting his own identity. Would you think that advanced in primary school?"

"If I remember, you insisted on being called Sapphire for a while. You wouldn't answer to Daniella, or Dani, or Dee as Christian called you. It was rather annoying and I don't believe you were much older than about seven at the time."

I laughed at the memory. Sapphire had been the name of a horse at the local riding stables that I had fallen in love with. I'd been besotted with her, until I'd fallen off and never wanted to get back on.

"I think I screwed up with Miller. We might need another builder."

"We all screw up, he has as well. I'm sure he's professional enough to continue his job, if you still want him to, of course."

"God, I feel like a bloody teenager. All this angst is tiring. I'm going to shower and get dressed."

After my shower, I lay on the bed. I thought back over the past few months and the turmoil I'd been through. I still had a long way to go before I felt I could move on with my life, there was the matter of the solicitor's letter hanging over my head. Yet there was something inside that felt so clear and vibrant. For the past day or so, I'd felt more alive than I had in years.

Dad was planning on spending the evening with Colette and I was due to meet Daniel. I didn't feel like going to the pub, or socialising, at all. I hadn't heard back from Miller and resigned myself to the fact he was very pissed off. I still believed I had a right to be upset and the more his silence stretched, the angrier I became. Sure, he'd done what he had with my best interests at heart, but he should have either stopped the letters or confessed when we grew closer. The thought startled me. Were we close? I guessed we were since we'd shared a kiss.

I sighed and pulled on a clean pair of jeans, then buttoned up my shirt. I ran a brush through my hair, which desperately needed a cut, and tied it back in a ponytail. I stared in the mirror. Dragging my fingertips down my cheeks did nothing to flatten the bags under my eyes, yet I'd been getting plenty of sleep. I pulled my cosmetics bag off the dresser and applied some concealer, a little foundation, mascara, and then a swipe of lip gloss. It was the most makeup I'd worn in ages.

I opened the wardrobe and scanned my footwear. I had walking boots, wellingtons, or Converse. I was sure I had some high-heeled shoes at one point and wondered if they'd ended up in storage. I could hardly remember the day I packed a suitcase and left my house. Or maybe I hadn't packed at all. I remembered Helen helping me. In fact, it was both Christian and Helen that had packed up my house. I guessed that would put pay to finding any letters Trey had received from her. If she had any sense, she would have destroyed them.

A toot of a car horn outside brought me out of my thoughts. I walked down the stairs and pulled a thin jacket from the hook. Dad had already left to visit Colette. I locked up the door behind me and walked towards Daniel's car.

"Hi, I'm a little late, I'm so sorry," he said when I'd opened the door and climbed in.

"I didn't realise the time, so no need to apologise," I replied.

"How are you?" he asked.

"A little pissed to discover Miller was the one writing letters to me, you knew, and it was your dad I met in the cemetery that time. I'm guessing you knew he visited Anna's grave, which is why you were so vague when I asked about her." I decided to get it out of the way.

"Ah, yes. I imagine I owe you a huge apology. Will you let me explain when we get to the pub?"

"I'll be interested in your explanation. I'm sorry, I still a little pissy about it all."

"I can imagine you are."

"Shall we go?" I asked, buckling up my seatbelt.

"Certainly, ma'am," he replied, trying to hold back the chuckle I could hear in his voice.

"So other than being totally, and rightly, pissed off at us Copelands, how have you been?"

"Good. Christian finally rang Dad today; I was annoyed at him as well. He's skiing in France and didn't think to let us know. Mrs. Hampton joined us Christmas Day, I'm not sure if I told you. Anyway, Dad is visiting with her this evening. I think there's a budding relationship starting there."

"I think there's been a budding relationship there for a while," he said, laughing.

"Probably. I'm pleased for him, though. Everyone deserves a second chance at a nice relationship."

Daniel glanced over to me. I caught sight of him from the corner of my eye, but I kept my gaze firmly on the road ahead.

"Are there any bands playing tonight?" I asked.

"No, thankfully. We'll be able to chat in peace without the wailing. I imagine it might be quiet, which will be nice."

We pulled into the unmade car park and Daniel reversed into the only spot that didn't have a puddle beside it. The clouds had darkened overhead and the air felt damp.

"I think we might have a storm tonight," Daniel said, as he left the car.

"Glad I didn't wear heels," I said, eyeing the muddy car park.

"I would have laid my coat down for you to walk over, if you had," he said, laughing some more.

"You are always the gentleman, Daniel. Which will bring me to my first question when we get inside."

"Why do I get the feeling I'm about to get a roasting, or at least an inquisition?"

"Because you are a very astute man." I smiled and led the way to the door of the pub.

I walked straight to the bar and had my purse at the ready. I ordered a bottle of wine and two glasses; not remembering what Daniel had drunk the last time we were there. When I'd turned, Daniel had found a table in a nook with only the one bench seat. For my 'inquisition' I would have rather been facing him. I guessed he was thinking tactics as well.

I placed the wine bucket with the bottle and glasses on the table then slid in beside him.

"Shall I pour?" he said.

"Please, I wasn't sure what you wanted and since you bought last time, I thought it only right I did this time."

"That's okay, wine is fine with me. I suspect this will be much better than what we have at the church."

"I thought only communion served wine?"

"We have Holy Communion in the Church of England, Dani. I suspect the Catholics got the better wine, though," he said, taking a sip from his glass.

I couldn't help but laugh. No matter how mad I was with him, he did cheer me up. He placed his glass on the table, made the sign of the cross on his chest, and then bowed his head in silent prayer.

"Right, I've asked the boss to look after me should you kill me. Fire away," he said.

I rested back in my seat and twirled my glass around in my fingers.

"I think I have a right to be pissed off about all this. Yet there's a part of me that feels bad for being pissed off."

"Because you are the most empathic person I've ever met, Dani."

"Don't interrupt me."

He held up in hands in surrender.

"I needed those letters. Those words were such a comfort to me; I really believe they got me through some very tough times. Now I feel cheated of them. And I can't explain exactly what I mean. I guess the anonymity was part of the thing that helped. I didn't know Lincoln, that Lincoln. I visualised him, and there were times I wanted to meet him, but I poured my soul out in those letters and now I feel violated because everyone knows. It's as if the trust I had in *my* Lincoln has been broken."

"Not everyone, Dani. I don't know what's in them, just that they were written."

"I'm confused. In hindsight, Miller had told me some of what he'd written; I just didn't pick up on it. And I can't even sit here now and say 'I had a light bulb moment.' There was just something in the back of my mind, and when I read through the letters again, I connected some of the things he'd said. It seemed too coincidental so I confronted him. He wasn't happy."

I picked up my glass to take a sip.

"I want to ask you, did you have an affair with his ex-wife?"

I turned to face him, searching his eyes for the truth.

"No. Although that's what he believes, regardless of how many times I've told him it's not true. I'll tell you exactly what happened. Miller and I fell out when we were younger. I don't know what you know about him, but he went completely off the rails when our mum died, and I don't blame him for that. He drank too much, smoked weed, got in with the wrong crowd.

You name it; he did it. He disappeared for weeks on end, sending Dad into a frenzy. The man had lost his wife; I didn't think it was fair to then have to put that grief aside to deal with Miller. I was wrong in my thinking at the time."

I didn't think my eyes could have gotten any wider.

"We tried to help him, he wasn't having any of it. It was Dad who called the police one night when Miller had arrived in a stolen car and without a licence, drunk and stinking of weed. It was the hardest thing my dad had ever done. He cried when they arrested him, Dani. But he thought it was the only thing he could do. Of course, Miller didn't see it that way for a very long time. Prison was the best thing that could have happened to him, though. When he was released, he disappeared for a little while, but then he came home and announced he was married. She wasn't what we thought a suitable partner. I know that sounds terrible, but she was just as bad as him. She encouraged him to drink too much; she loved the notoriety of being with an ex-con. She was also about fifteen years older than him. He vowed to clean up his act; I guess his wife didn't like that. She came to see me and confessed to an affair, and in hindsight, it was to cause trouble. She wasn't religious, never attended a service, so to want to confess was strange. However, I thought she wanted some form of counselling." Daniel chuckled sadly at the thought.

"What happened after that?" I asked.

"One day she came to the church and threw herself at me. I pushed her away but somehow her blouse got torn. And guess what happened next?"

"Miller walked in?"

"Miller walked in. Unbeknown to me, she had left him, a day or so before I think, but he took one look at the situation, came to the wrong conclusion, and freaked out. He kicked over a couple of pews and I didn't see him again for weeks."

"Did he ever let you explain?"

"No. Well, sort of. When I caught up with him, I tried hard to tell him what had happened. I mean, come on, I'm a vicar! I don't doubt there are some very dodgy vicars out there, but I'm not one of them. Anyway, we did manage to chat and a lot of things came out. Miller felt he hadn't been supported enough when Mum died. And he wasn't, if the truth were known. He's the youngest and I guess I concentrated on Dad, who had broken down. Miller got left on the outside."

"I imagine that was hard for him," I said.

"It was. Don't get me wrong, he doesn't use Mum's death as an excuse for his behaviour, he's totally able to accept it was all him."

"Tell me about his last wife," I asked.

"That was a very sad state of affairs. Annabelle was just what Miller needed a long time ago. She was a free spirit but sensible at the same time, I don't know if that makes any sense. She loved the sea. She was going to move to Australia to take up a position as a marine biologist, but she fell in love instead."

"In the letters, there's something about him blaming himself for her not doing that," I said.

"He did, maybe he still does. Miller is so closed, you know more about how he feels than I do. He didn't want to go with her so she gave up her dream job. He also got very angry when she discovered she had a tumour. She didn't tell him at first, her reasoning was that Miller isn't always the best at handling bad news; I guess you've witnessed that. She wanted all the facts before she told him. He found out and flipped. I think, and this is just my opinion, he never dealt with Mum's death and now his wife was about to die of the same thing. He couldn't deal with it. Annabelle died quite quickly, which is a blessing, and he went off the rails again."

"He drank a lot, I understand."

"Yes. It worried Dad and me for a while, we thought he might fall back so far he couldn't claw his way back out, but he did. He threw himself into work, built Dad a bungalow and closed down, emotionally."

"And now?"

"Now he seems to be in turmoil again," Daniel said.

"And that's my fault."

"Not necessarily. It's Miller's fault for not being able to deal with his emotions. Which brings me straight to the letters. I found one on his table; it had your name, and his, on the front. I'm sorry, Dani, but what could I do? He's my brother and I'm not going to betray him, no matter what he thinks about me. I tried to encourage him to tell you but I think, by then, he was in too deep. He's always had a soft spot for you and when you came back, I think he thought he could save you while you were, without knowing, saving him."

"Does your dad know about the letters?"

"I doubt it. He moved into the home a little while ago. He has early onset dementia and he knows. He wanted to get everything sorted while he was still able to make the decisions."

"Why is Miller always on edge when I talk about you, or when he sees me with you?"

"I guess he thinks I might tell you about the letters."

"What would he say if we were in a relationship?" I asked.

Daniel laughed and patted my knee. "As much as I'd be very flattered, and I know you're not inviting a relationship, but I'd be more interested in your brother, if you know what I mean."

"You're not!"

"I am. Hence the fact I'm single. It's not the done thing, publically, within the church, to be gay."

"Bullshit," I said, laughing.

"I know, half the vicars I know are gay but we're just not allowed to be in public," he said with a wink.

"Does Miller know?"

"It's not something I've ever sat down and openly talked about with him. Like I said, we don't have the closest of relationships anymore, and that saddens me, to be honest."

"Could you get that closeness back?"

"That's up to him. I tried and after so many pushbacks, I gave up. Not very Christian of me, was it?"

"Not really. You're supposed to love your flock, flaws and all, didn't you say that once?"

"Ah, I say a lot, I need to learn to take my own advice someday. Now, as much as this wine is okay, it's a bit too girly for me, and I have a butch reputation to fake. Mind if I get a beer?"

I watched Daniel walk to the bar. I was glad he'd told me what he had. It had also saddened me further. Daniel led a life of lies; Miller led a life of lies. Yet they couldn't find a way to connect, even through those lies.

It took Daniel ten minutes or so to walk the few steps back to the bar. He was a popular guy, and although there weren't many visitors to the pub that night, each one wanted to talk. He'd drunk a quarter of his pint by the time he made it back to the table.

"So," he said.

"So."

"Are we forgiven?"

"We?"

"Miller at least, he needs your forgiveness. I'd like it, of course, but right now, he's more important. I'm going to ask you a favour that maybe I don't have a right to. Please forgive him. Think about the reasons why he did this. He honestly had your best interests at heart. I don't think he ever thought he would be spending time with you. It's blown up in his face at the worst possible time."

"What do you mean?"

"It the anniversary of Annabelle's death. Like I said before, he doesn't deal with loss very well."

"What about my feelings, Daniel?"

I wasn't about to be dismissed just for the sake of Miller's feelings.

"Look, keeping Miller's secret, my brother's secret, is about the only thing I've done wrong, and I don't believe it to be a wrong. I understand how you feel, I really do, but can you also look at the good intention? Miller never lied to you, Dani. Not once. He never denied it, either, did he?"

"No, he didn't. Do you think I've been too harsh?"

"I'm not going to answer that. I do think that you've had the worst time yourself over the past year. I can see why you'd feel betrayed because you are still vulnerable, and I don't mean that to patronise you. But those letters comforted you; they comforted him. Is what he's done so very terrible?"

I couldn't answer him. I sighed heavily.

"I don't know now. It just felt so wrong, like I was being deceived all over again."

"Dani, do you think that had you not been through what you have, with Trey's affair, you might not feel so strongly. I get that you're upset, no one would expect less, but…"

"Am I overreacting, you're going to ask me. Yes, and no. I don't know."

I took a large gulp of the wine, now tepid. I reached into the wine bucket and pulled out a couple of pieces of ice, which I deposited in the glass.

"I thought I had every right to be upset, now, although I'm still a little disappointed, I guess it's not as awful as I initially thought. Especially now you've explained Miller's situation a little more."

"Miller is a good man, Dani. He's not good at verbally articulating his feelings. He does that through his work, and I guess, letters."

I remembered back to Miller visiting the barn that very first time and his appreciation of the wooden beams; how he wanted to keep them exposed because they told a story, the history of the barn was engrained in the wood.

"I did send him a text yesterday, he hasn't replied. I'll try calling him tomorrow," I said.

Daniel smiled. "Now, shall we get back to our *date*? Remember, I've got a fake reputation to keep up."

"I don't know why you do that. Why not come out?"

"Because this is a small village of mostly old folks. And I like to keep my private life, private. It's hard to have a life outside the church at the best of times, and it's not like I get a lot of spare time to have a relationship. I'm married to my job, and I quite like it."

I raised my glass, "Well, here's to fucked up Copelands, old folk, and the church."

"I'll drink to that."

We didn't mention the letters for the rest of the evening. In fact, we chatted about absolutely everything from village and vicar life, to my time in London. At the mention of London and a life that was so far removed to what I had now, it was a sense of nostalgia instead of remorse that flowed over me. I was pleased about that. I wanted to remember that period of my life with fondness, excluding Trey, of course. My level of empathy didn't extend to forgiving my cheating husband.

"Have you thought any more about your plans for the exhumation?" Daniel asked as we walked out to the car.

"No. I guess at some point I'll be able to visit Hannah and just learn to ignore him. I don't think I can put myself through the stress of it all right now. I've got a letter at home to deal with. A solicitor wrote to me on Helen's behalf. They want to invite discussion on Alistair inheriting part of Trey's estate."

"Can they do that?"

"They can invite me to a discussion, whether they can get any money from me, I have no idea. I found out a child, even an illegitimate one is entitled to part of its father's estate. I'm banking on the fact Trey was American to complicate things."

"Is that…?"

I held up my hand. "Don't go there, Daniel, please. Right now, I don't care if it's fair or not. It's bloody poor timing and it's come about because Helen is desperate for money, not because she truly believes Alistair should be entitled to anything. She's looking out for herself, not her child."

"Okay," he said, opening the car door for me.

We drove home while still chatting, mainly about Daniel's love of his job.

"I've had a lovely time, thank you for our *date*," I said with a laugh.

"So have I, and if I've upset you in any way, I am truly sorry."

"It's okay, I'm pretty sure I'll survive. You might have to buy me dinner sometime to make it up to me."

"Anytime. It's nice to get out and have a friend," he said.

I said goodbye and walked to my house. All the lights were blazing so I guessed Dad was back from his *date* with Colette.

"I'm home," I called out as I walked through the front door.

"In the kitchen, do you want a cup of tea?" Dad replied.

"Yes, please," I said, as I kicked off my shoes and hung my jacket up.

"Did you have a good time?" he asked.

"It was interesting. I learned a lot about Miller and Daniel. I think I'll call Miller tomorrow and see if we can meet up."

"We've got some storms coming in over the next couple of days, maybe you should arrange for him to visit you here. I'm not sure my old car is suitable for driving in the rain."

"I will, but I'm sure you're car is waterproof," I replied with a chuckle.

"I'm thinking more of you aquaplaning into a hedge. I'm rather fond of Mertle."

"Mertle?"

"Mertle the Mercedes," he said, smiling as he handed me a cup of tea.

His car was, I guessed, a classic and he'd owned *Mertle* for many years.

"I'll be sure to invite Miller here. I wouldn't want to hurt Mertle if I can help it."

"Good girl. Now, I'm off to bed. Colette can talk the hind legs off a donkey, my poor brain needs to just chill in the dark for a while."

Dad walked away and my laughter followed him. I sat at the table in the silence and thought. I hadn't laughed so much in ages. It surprised me not to feel the usual guilt that followed any miniscule period of happiness. Maybe I was finally moving forward, as Miller/Lincoln said I would.

I turned off the lights and made my way to bed. Storm or no storm, I was determined to track Miller down the following day and talk. And maybe apologise, depending on how it all went.

CHAPTER TWENTY-ONE

*I*t was a clap of thunder that woke me in the early hours of the morning. Or so I thought. In fact, although there was a storm howling outside, it was the vibration of my phone against the wood of the cabinet. I reached over, initially knocking it to the floor. I cursed as I fumbled with the light.

I reached down for my phone and saw a text message.

Yes, good to talk. I have something to do. Will be in touch. Miller.

It didn't dawn on me for a little while just how unlike Miller that text was. Not only was it very clipped but the time it was sent, just after four in the morning, seemed strange.

I shuffled up into a sitting position and double-checked the time with the clock on the chest of drawers.

Are you okay? I typed.

Letting her go soon, he replied.

Letting her go? I frowned as I tried to work out what he meant. That little niggle that I'd felt before started in the back of my mind. I pulled the letters out from Lincoln.

In one he'd mentioned about cutting off his wife's hair and keeping it. He'd also said that he would throw that hair out to sea at some point. Were we at that *some point*? I looked out the window at the rain lashing down. Although too dark to see the sea, I had no doubt it would be raging. I pictured the boat Miller had taken down to the harbour; it wasn't particularly big, more something to sail for fun on a calm day. I hoped he wasn't thinking of taking that boat out. If he was, I prayed by the time the sun came up, the weather had abated.

I didn't want to call Daniel at that time of the morning, but I was anxious for Miller. I didn't think the weather was right for that boat, and I wondered what his state of mind was.

Are you talking about taking your boat out? Miller, would you wait? At least until this storm breaks. Maybe having company might be a nice thing as well?

I held the phone for ages but no reply came. An hour passed, with me deliberating, until eventually, I decided I needed to call Daniel. It might be an overreaction, but I'd rather that than Miller launching a boat in a storm while mentally in a mess.

The call rang and just as I thought it was about to go to voice-mail, Daniel answered.

"Hello?" Daniel said, groggily.

"Hi, I'm so sorry to call this early but I'm worried about a text I received from Miller," I said.

"What text?" he asked, more alert.

I repeated what Miller had sent me.

"Shit. He was passed out when I looked in on him earlier. There was an empty glass on the table, I think he'd been drinking."

"He had a drink when I visited him. Is he supposed to be sober? He told me he can drink and it doesn't mean he'll want more."

"He was teetotal for a long time. I know he takes a drink every now and again; he seems to be able to control it now. But that still doesn't sound good, especially sending you that text at that time. I'll go over and see what I can find out."

"Will you call me when you get there?"

"Of course, and thank you for letting me know."

Daniel cut off the call and I climbed out of bed. I pulled on my jeans and a jumper and made my way downstairs, there was no way I could stay in bed.

I made myself some tea and sat watching the phone. It seemed that time slowed down, the clock on the screen took forever to change from one minute to the next. Eventually, it lit up and I received a text.

He's not here, and neither is the boat. Daniel.

I typed back. **He took the boat to the harbour a few days ago.**

That's where I am, no boat. The sea is way too rough for that little boat.

I didn't reply but called. It was taking too long to type a message.

"How good a sailor is Miller?" I asked when Daniel answered.

"I don't know the last time he ever took that boat out. I'm surprised it floated. Dani, it hasn't been on the water for at least a couple of years."

"Are you at the harbour still?"

"I am. I'm hoping I might catch a fisherman or two. Or maybe I should call the Coastguard?"

"I would. I'm on my way."

Before he could reply, I cut off the call and started to leave a note for Dad. I grabbed a jacket and slipped on my boots, not bothering with the laces. I picked up the car keys and pocketed my phone. I raced from the house.

The screech as a branch caught the side of the car, in my haste to race down the lane, had me wincing. Whatever damage I'd caused, I'd repair. I took one wrong turn and had to reverse back up the lane to the junction but eventually made it to the harbour. Daniel was without a jacket and soaked through, he was pacing up and down.

I pulled my coat on and left the car. As I flipped up the hood, he noticed me.

"Anything?" I called out. The rain was lashing so hard it was difficult to be heard.

"No. I've tried his phone; it just rings. I've called the Coastguard, they've put a call out for any nearby boats and will launch soon. I'm waiting on a call back from them."

"What can we do?"

"Nothing, we just have to wait."

Even with a jacket and the hood up, I was getting soaked. My jeans chaffed against the skin on my thighs that had goose bumped with the cold. I began to shiver. While we stood, I scrolled through my phone for the local Royal National Lifeboat Institution, wondering if they would be called in to help. A few minutes later, three men walked down the slipway towards us.

"You looking for the missing lad?" one called out.

"We are, do you know anything?" Daniel asked.

"No, but we heard it over the radio, we're going out now to help search."

"Oh God, thank you so much," I said.

"If he had any good sense, he'll have headed into one of the coves for shelter. We're going to stick close to the coastline, there's another boat launching just up the bay. We're coordinating with the RNLI," he said.

"I don't know if good sense is his priority right now," Daniel said. I looked sharply at him. I wasn't sure three strangers needed to know that.

They nodded before walking away to a boat that was moored beside me. It looked a lot more robust and seaworthy than the small thing Miller was out on.

"Why don't we wait in the car?" Daniel asked. I nodded.

"They'll find him," he said, as he climbed into the passenger seat.

"I hope so. He could sail up here any minute and get cross that we've made such a fuss. Can we get arrested for wasting the Coastguard's time?" I asked.

"I doubt it. And if he did rock up here, I'd kick his bloody arse."

Blue and red flashing lights reflected in the rearview mirror. I watched as a police car pulled up behind us. For some reason, seeing the police attend seemed to make it feel way more serious than I hoped it was.

We watched as they donned long waterproof jackets and caps before walking to our car.

"Mr. Copeland?" one asked.

"Yes, and it's Daniel. Thank you for coming out."

"I think it might be best if we talk in here," the officer said as he opened the rear door.

Both Daniel and I turned in our seats.

"Lincoln Copeland is your brother, I take it. Can you give me as many details as you know?" He opened a pad as he spoke.

Daniel relayed all the information I'd given him and our concerns for Miller's welfare. They asked to see the text messages and made notes of the calls Daniel had made to both Miller and the Coastguard.

We couldn't answer any questions as to what he might be wearing, and I wanted to kick Daniel when he mentioned that Miller might have been drinking and that he had a drinking problem in his past.

"He was late teens, early adult, though," I said, hoping to allay the fears they were on the hunt for a drunkard.

"I also think I know why he took the boat out," I added.

Daniel looked at me. I addressed the policeman behind.

"Miller wrote to me, in those letters he talked about his wife. She died of cancer but before she died, he had to cut off her hair. He kept that hair. I think he's sailed out to throw her hair overboard. She wanted to be a marine biologist, loved the sea. I think he thought it would be fitting to let the sea have that little piece of her."

"I didn't know that," Daniel said quietly.

"Were you close, Mr. Copeland?"

"No, not for the past few years."

"What state of mind do you think Lincoln is in?" the officer asked, directing his question to me.

"We had a small falling out, but I'm not sure that was the reason for his decision to take his boat out."

I was desperate to convince them, or maybe it was myself, that he wasn't in a bad way, even knowing that he probably was.

"I understand there are two lifeboats out, and a few fishing boats scouring the coastline. At this moment, all I can say is to hang tight, here or at home, and as soon as we have any news, we'll be in touch."

"If we decide to go home, you have my details, you will call, won't you?" Daniel asked. I could hear the panic in his voice.

"Of course we will. I'd suggest going home, get back into some dry clothes."

The police left and sat in their car. I could see one talking on his radio. The windows in our car had started to steam up with the condensation from our clothes; despite the heating on full blast, I still shivered.

"Do you want to head home?" Daniel asked.

"No, do you?"

"I think we should. Come back to my place. I think I need to call Dad."

"Would the police have checked Miller's house?"

"I imagine so…I don't know, to be honest."

I put the car in gear and we drove slowly towards Daniel's house without speaking. I found myself feeling sick with worry. And full of regret that our last encounter had been so fractious.

I wasn't sure if the shivering that had every limb jolting, was from the cold or fear. Daniel had offered me the use of his shower, but I declined. I did, however, accept a pair of dry joggers and a sweatshirt. I used his bathroom simply to change and bundled up my wet clothes. The dry clothes did nothing to stop the ice that seemed to run through my veins.

We sat and drank endless cups of tea, checked our phones on a regular basis, and Daniel called his dad as the sun was rising.

"How did he take the news?" I asked.

"He's on his way over. I don't like that he still drives, he really shouldn't with his condition, but to take away his car is the last bit of independence he has. So far he hasn't managed to crash it, or worse, knock someone down, but his reaction speed isn't what it should be."

"Maybe you should have offered to collect him?" I asked, wondering why he hadn't done that. I wasn't sure I'd give news that my brother was missing over the phone then expect my dad to drive to me.

"I know, I should; I didn't think."

"I feel responsible," I said.

"How?"

"I don't know. If I hadn't kicked off at Miller he might not be where he is now."

"I don't think that would have mattered. It's that time of year for him, sadly."

"He said he was going to check in with me over Christmas, I wonder how much of that was for him as well. I missed so much of what he'd said now that I think about it. I feel he was reaching out to me for help, as much as comforting me."

"You can't blame yourself. He's a grown man, Dani, responsible for his own decisions, however poor they are."

I thought Daniel's comment was a little harsh and assumed it to be the stress he was under. However, I remembered Miller's words: he'd said that he didn't think Daniel had been very supportive when he'd needed him. Daniel wasn't a bad man; I think perhaps he was also one that wasn't very good with dealing with emotions when under pressure himself.

I watched him sit on the sofa. His fingers were steepled together, his chin rested on them. He closed his eyes and his mouth moved in a silent prayer, I assumed.

I heard a key in a lock and the front door open. I looked up as the man that I'd met in the cemetery walked in. He gave me a small smile and then turned his attention to Daniel.

"What happened?" he asked, as he shrugged off his jacket and sat in a chair.

Daniel gave him all the information we had. Lincoln senior nodded but didn't interrupt. I saw his shoulders rise in a heavy sigh.

"I think this might be my fault," he said.

"I said the same," I answered.

"No, Dani, I really do think this is my fault. He's very keen on you and I know about the letters, Daniel told me. I knew who you were when we met, which is why I rushed off. I felt terrible that you might think I was the narrator of the letters, or that you were being deceived."

"I did, I confronted Miller a couple of days ago."

"Why do you think this is your fault, Dad?" Daniel asked.

"I told him he had to let Annabelle go. He was stuck, don't you see? He was actually desperate to let her go, to move on, and I think he hoped he'd be able to form a relationship with you." The elder Lincoln looked at me.

"But he hardly knows me," I said quietly.

"He knows you well through the letters, and I think he thought there might be another chance at love for both of you. I told him yesterday that all the time he clung on to Annabelle, that was never going to happen."

"What do you mean by clinging on to her?" I asked.

"Until you, every woman he's met, he's compared to her. No one measured up. He talked to me about you a while ago, about how different to Annabelle you are, and how refreshing he found that.

I'm probably not using the right words here, but I guess he saw something in you that he saw in himself, kindred spirits, or whatnot. He seemed to know what he had to do to free himself completely of the tie to Annabelle."

"I don't understand, why would he want to free himself? He loved her, she died, wouldn't he want to keep that?"

"He felt he couldn't fully move on until he'd done all the things she'd asked him to do. She'd asked him to cut off her hair, she'd asked him to throw that out at sea before she died. Don't ask me why, I don't understand her thinking. He told her he had, but he lied to her. He lied with all good intentions. He needed to keep something of hers and it was that. Somewhere in his mind, right now, he wants to right the wrongs."

"He told me that in a letter. He said he had a lot of wrongs to right," I said.

"And he's doing that so he can truly be free from his past self, and capable of moving on, I guess."

I didn't believe for one minute that Miller was doing all that just for me. I thought it coincidence, and perhaps the letter writing had opened some old wounds, the *sticking plaster* no longer able to hold him together. Although he had known me as a child, in adulthood it had only really been a few months. As much as I was fond of him, and he certainly managed to have me aroused on occasions, I wasn't in love with him any more than he was in love with me. I didn't think so, anyway.

Daniel decided to make a pot of coffee, more for something to do, I guessed. Lincoln and I sat in silence. Time moved on so slowly it was agonising. I constantly checked my mobile, hoping that he might text or call. That he might have decided not to take the boat out and was sitting in his truck somewhere.

"Truck!" I said.

"What about the truck?" Lincoln asked.

"His truck wasn't at the harbour. Maybe he didn't take the boat out; maybe someone stole it, or something. You did check the boat wasn't still at his house, didn't you?" I asked Daniel, as he walked back into the room with the coffee pot on a tray.

"Of course. It's usually beside the cottage; there was nothing there. We didn't check the car park, Dani. You can't leave your vehicle at the harbour. You launch, then go and park. But I'm going to call the police and see if we, or they, should check."

He placed the tray on the coffee table, and Lincoln poured coffee while Daniel left to make the call. It seemed so stupid that we hadn't thought to check, or at least Daniel, since he knew parking at the harbour wasn't allowed. It was a few minutes later when Daniel returned.

"Well?" Lincoln asked.

"The police will check the car park, but they verified that they'd been around to his cottage and there was no sign of a boat, or his truck, for that matter."

"There must be something we can do. Do you have a radio? Maybe we could tune into their emergency frequency and listen." I knew I was clutching at straws, but I was becoming desperate for news.

"All we can do is sit tight until someone contacts us," Lincoln said gently. He moved from the chair and sat beside me, taking my hand in his.

"Miller said I went out on the boat when I was young. I don't remember, I wonder why?" I said.

"You were terrified. You kept worrying about sharks so we had to turn back, and I think you were a little embarrassed about that. I remember another child, a girl I think, teased you about it," Lincoln said.

"You were sailing the boat?"

"Of course. Miller used to be an accomplished sailor, Dani. I'm pretty sure that he's safe. He's probably sailed into a cove or something until the storm passes over."

"But how long has it been since that boat has been out? It's reckless of him to do this, and to cause us so much worry," Daniel said.

"I'm sure you, or us, weren't at the forefront of his mind, Daniel. If he's hurting over Annabelle, I can assure you, other people's feelings don't really factor," I said, a little annoyed at his lack of empathy.

"I'm sure that's the case, we just have to pray that he's safe," Lincoln said, diffusing the growing tension and glaring at Daniel.

Maybe Miller had been right about his brother. I'd witnessed a couple of occasions where I'd thought he'd been less than *Christian* towards him. Perhaps Daniel didn't understand what Miller had, or was, going through. As a vicar, I would have thought he should have more empathy. Or was I just being cranky?

Tiredness swept over me, and I tried to conceal the yawn. I curled my feet under me and slumped into the corner of the sofa. I checked the time on my phone, wondering whether I should call Dad before he saw my note. It was only seven in the morning, and yet, I was surprised at how much time had passed. The thought depressed me. It had been two hours without any news.

"How far can that boat sail?" I asked.

"It's just a wooden sail boat. It's not designed for the open sea, as such, just for fun around the coastline."

I knew nothing about boats at all. "So if the sail broke, how would he get home?"

"Miller could probably fix most things. It would have to be a catastrophic failure for the boat not to be able to make it back."

"It doesn't have an engine?" I tried to remember that one time I'd been on it.

"No, without a sail, Miller will just drift. But he has his phone, so I can only assume he's okay, holed up somewhere, and not realising we'd be worrying about him," Lincoln said.

I didn't want to ask the next question but it ran through my mind.

All sorts of reasons ran through my head: he could have left his phone at home, he could have it on silent, or *what if he's fallen overboard?* His phone wouldn't work then.

I stood and paced the room, "Shouldn't we have had an update by now?" I asked.

"I guess they'll get some news to us when they have some. It's frustrating, for sure," Lincoln said.

"Is there something we can do?" Not that I had any idea what that *something* would be.

"Why don't we drive along the coast, as close as we can get?" Lincoln asked.

"I'm up for that. I can take one direction, you the other."

"Don't you think we should leave it up to the experts?" Daniel interjected.

"The experts are checking the sea, what if he managed to get into a small cove and is stuck there?"

There were loads of small coves, or inlets, along the cliffs. Some of those had small beaches that would interconnect while the tide was out. Many a person had to be airlifted off when the tide came in and cut off their exit route. The cliffs were too sheer and unstable to attempt to climb out. I knew of a couple of coves that had small tunnels, they would flood when the tide came in. I remembered years ago a young lad being caught. They knew he'd gone into the tunnel, but he was never found, it was assumed he was washed out to sea.

I shuddered at the thought. "I'll tell you what? You stay here and wait for news. I'm going to take a drive along the coast and check out some of the coves I know about."

I couldn't sit around any longer and do nothing. I picked up my phone and called Dad.

"Hi, did you get my note?" I asked when he'd answered.

"I did, I was about to call you, what's happened?"

I ran through what I knew. "I'm going to take a drive along the coast and see if I get into any coves."

"Come back and get me. Two are better than one and I don't want you getting into trouble."

"Okay, I'll be back as soon as I can."

I picked up my still wet clothes and promised to check in as often as I could, then climbed into the car and drove back home.

Mrs. Hampton was walking towards the front door as I pulled onto the drive. Two men, who I hadn't met before and dressed in bright yellow jackets, climbed down from a Land Rover and greeted her.

"Tell us what happened?" she asked as I left the car.

Again, I recounted what I knew while we walked into the house.

"Okay, this is Peter and Charlie, they know this coastline like no other. In fact, they were part of a team to map out the cliff erosion, so they know all the coves. They've brought maps."

"That's fantastic."

One of them, I wasn't sure which, laid a map on the kitchen table. I told them from where Miller may have launched his boat then left them to go and change. I was back in the kitchen in a matter of minutes, still pulling a jumper over my t-shirt.

Peter, or Charlie, was on the phone to the local RNLI station, informing them of the plan to organise a search party. The other one was calling up his friends. From what I could gather, these guys knew what they were doing. According to Mrs. Hampton, they worked in conjunction with the police for search and rescue. I wondered why the police hadn't notified them.

"Does the RNLI contact you?" I asked one of them, once they'd finished their call.

"Sometimes, but normally only when it's a walker missing that might have taken a tumble off the cliffs. But your dad said you thought your friend might have sailed into a cove for safety."

"I'm not sure he has, it was just an idea. He's not a seasoned sailor, but not a novice either. I just want to do something to help look for him."

"I can understand that. We've got a team of five who know this coastline very well. You're welcome to join us, but I don't recommend getting into the coves; the tide is still in and the currents will be running strong."

I wasn't sure if that should have been a comfort or not.

"Okay, and yes, I want to come along."

"And me," Dad said, pulling on his walking boots.

It was another twenty minutes before we set off. Peter and Charlie were to meet with their friends; before they left I gave them my mobile so we could keep in touch. Dad, Mrs. Hampton, and I drove to the harbour. I thought we'd start there and walk in the opposite direction to the others. Dad unfurled an Ordnance Survey map on the bonnet of the car; he marked out as many coves and inlets as we thought we'd have access to.

"Hello, there. Are you looking for Miller?" I heard. I looked up to see two older men walking towards us.

"We are," I replied.

"Great, we'll join you."

"That's wonderful, thank you."

"Most of the village is coming out to help. Oh, I'm Jim, by the way," he said, extending his hand.

I shook it. "We're really grateful for your help. We don't know where he is, he might not even be in danger, and he'll be so embarrassed he's caused all this trouble," I said.

"Well, better to find him safe and embarrassed," he replied with a smile.

Just before we set off, I checked my phone. I sent two texts, the first to Miller.

Miller, we are all getting really concerned. The lifeboats are out looking for you, some fishermen, and we're going to walk along the coast. If you get this message, please contact me or your brother. Dani.

The second text was to Daniel, to explain what was happening. He replied.

I've just heard. Thank you for all you're doing and if we hear anything our end, I'll ring.

It was Miller that I wanted to hear from; I didn't.

CHAPTER TWENTY-TWO

*M*y legs ached, the skin on my face was frozen from the cold, and although the rain had let up, we were all muddy. The going was treacherous in places, and Mrs. Hampton, Dad, and I let the guys do the climbing down to check ridges and inlets in the cliffs. As the hours wore on, the despondency grew. Fear gripped at my heart and I struggled to keep negative thoughts from overwhelming me. I regularly checked in with Daniel, and I could hear the desperation in his voice each time he told me there had been no news. The police had visited again, they, and Daniel, had gone to Miller's house. It appeared there were two empty whisky bottles in the kitchen, and the consensus was that he had taken the boat out while drunk.

I needed to rest. While the guys kept going, Dad, Colette, and I rested on a bench. For a while we sat in silence and I scanned the ocean in front of me. The sun was up, albeit low in the sky and the sea had calmed. I was at least thankful for that. I wanted to curse Miller, to shout out obscenities and hope he heard how cross I was with him.

"I think we should head back, Dani," I heard Dad say.

I hadn't realised how long we'd sat on that bench, but I knew my backside was numb and my body stiff from the chill. I slowly stood, stretching my limbs, and nodded.

The walk back wasn't with the same amount of enthusiasm we'd been able to muster earlier that day. It seemed to take twice as long, and a couple of times, I had to hold Colette's arm as she stumbled over the loose rocks and wet earth. We hadn't heard from anyone, and by the time we made it back to the car, a feeling of dread washed over me.

Dad drove home and I noticed him look at the scratches along the side of the car, he didn't make mention of it, of course. I slumped in the passenger seat and stared out the side window until we pulled onto our drive and noticed a police car waiting there.

At first, I didn't want to leave the safety of the car. The presence of the police didn't bode well at all. Two officers exited their car, different officers to the ones I'd met earlier that morning.

"Mrs. Carlton?" The name threw me. I hadn't been called by my married name for a while.

"Yes, I'm sorry, I'm not..." I shook my head. "Do you have any news on Miller, I mean, Lincoln?"

"Can we come in?"

Just those four words had me rooted to the spot. I'd seen enough TV shows to know that wasn't good news.

Dad unlocked the door and they followed me into the living room. I sat; they stood.

"A boat has been found, Mrs..."

"It's Dani. Miller's boat?"

"It appears so, the family have confirmed the details."

"And Miller?"

"There's no sign of Mr. Copeland, as of yet. The boat was found capsized and heavily damaged. That could actually be good news."

"How?"

"If the damage was caused by rocks, it could be that Mr. Copeland had moored up somewhere and the mooring broke loose."

"Okay, so that's positive, isn't it? What happens now?" I asked.

"The Coastguard has launched a helicopter and are scanning the cliff faces along the coast, obviously there are search and rescue teams out, and it appears a lot of volunteers, as well."

"I know, we met some of them. So you've spoken to Daniel and Lincoln?"

"Yes, Daniel tried to call you, I said we'd call on you as it's on our way back."

I picked up my phone to see a blank screen. "Shit, my battery has died, I think. Miller could have been calling me."

I ran to the kitchen to retrieve my charger.

"If Mr. Copeland gets in touch, you will let us know, won't you?"

"Of course I will. And if you find him, I'll get to know?"

"We have to inform the family first, I hope you understand that."

"Of course, yes, I'm sorry. I'm sure they'll let me know."

The police left and exhaustion overtook me. Colette decided to make a late lunch, although I wasn't sure I'd be able to push a sandwich past the nausea. I curled on the sofa, and no matter how hard I tried, I couldn't keep my eyes open.

The sun had set when I was shaken awake. Lincoln and Daniel stood in the living room and my heart froze.

"What's happened?" I asked, bolting upright.

"Nothing. Dani, they haven't found him." Lincoln's voice hitched as he spoke, and I noticed the tears in his eyes.

"Why? I mean, they found his boat," I said, not believing; yet fully understanding, what he'd said.

"They have to call off the search at some point, until the morning."

"They can't do that! He could be stranded somewhere, he'd be cold and…"

"They can't see, it's getting dark. They've been out all day and so far, nothing," Daniel said.

I angrily wiped at the tears that had formed in my eyes. They couldn't stop searching, not even if just for overnight. He could be hurt.

"Where did they find the boat? They've concentrated on that area, haven't they?" I knew the questions I was asking were probably stupid, but I wanted the answers.

"Yes. The police told you the boat was damaged, didn't they?"

I nodded my head.

"Our thoughts are that he moored up somewhere but the location the boat was found, there isn't anywhere safe that he could be. They've searched the cliff face, much of it is pretty sheer; there wasn't a ledge or anything he could have gotten to."

"Could another boat have run into him?" I asked.

"If that had happened, there's no way that wouldn't have been called in," Lincoln said.

Daniel and Lincoln had sat on the sofa, Colette had left, and Dad was making yet more tea. I was thankful for a hot drink and something to fill my hollow stomach.

Lincoln looked to have aged considerably during the hours Miller had been missing. The skin on his face was sallow and he sat wringing his hands in his lap. Daniel silently prayed, constantly. Maybe I'd been too harsh in how I'd thought of him. Perhaps he was just someone not able to cope with the level of stress I was sure they were suffering without lashing out. I had to thank them though, for keeping me included. I had no right to be in the middle of their drama, yet they'd welcomed me in and kept me informed, as much as they could.

"I can't bear the thought of him out on his own overnight," I said quietly.

"Neither can I, Dani. I just don't know what to do," Lincoln said.

"I can't believe they just give up like that," I said.

"I don't think it's a case of just giving up. They'll go on for as long as they can, I'm sure."

"Can't another boat take over? Search through the night?"

"I honestly don't know. If that was an option, I'm sure we'll get to know."

I wasn't sure if calling off the search soon was a fact or an assumption. I totally got that if the weather worsened it could be dangerous, but at that moment it wasn't raining and the sea was just its usual December self.

Daniel and Lincoln left with a promise to keep me informed if they received any news. Dad and I sat in a silent house.

I hadn't physically known Miller that long, but whether it be via the letters he'd sent or the conversations we'd had, I thought I knew him well. I kept his enthusiasm for my barn, and for his derelict cottage, in the front of my mind. I needed to remember all the times he made me laugh to push away the niggling negative thoughts that fought for dominance.

"Will you eat something?" Dad said.

"I'm really not hungry but I'll make myself a sandwich. Do you want one?" I asked.

"No, but I will. It will give us something to do, I guess."

It was the doing nothing that was the killer. Doing nothing gave the opportunity to think, and my brain hurt from all the thinking.

Dad and I stood side by side and prepared a snack. Lucy whined for her dinner, and then to be let out in the garden. I stood in the garden for a moment while she did her business. I watched the poor thing struggle to walk and wondered just how long she was going to hold on, or rather, just how long Dad was going to hold on to her. I remembered back, not that long ago, when she'd sleep on his bed. When her arthritic legs stopped her from climbing the steep stairs, Dad had carried her for a while.

It was the phone ringing that had me run back into the kitchen. Dad had gotten to the phone before me. He shook his head and mouthed that Christian was calling. I felt my shoulders sink and sighed.

Minutes passed, then hours, and all I could do was sit and watch my phone. Dad turned on the TV at one point, just in time for the local news and an enlarged photograph of Miller. We watched, learning more about the search from the Lifeboat Station Manager than the police. Perhaps Daniel and Lincoln were being brought up to date that way as well. I had texted Daniel as soon as I saw the report. It appeared they had scoured the coastline repeatedly; they had been out to sea, following the current and back again. They commented on the boat and the belief that Miller might be holed up somewhere. They asked for people to be vigilant but to not put themselves in danger on the slippery cliffs. The more I watched, the sicker I felt.

"Why don't you have a lie down? I'll let you know if there's any news," Dad said.

"I might do, thanks. How was Christian, by the way?" I'd forgotten to ask.

"Angry, as usual. We don't need to worry about that right now," he said, obviously keeping something from me.

I nodded, it wasn't that I didn't care about Christian, but I was starting to feel very strange.

As I lay on the bed, with the phone beside me, I focussed on the strangeness that I felt. My body had begun to feel weightless, and my mind was foggy. I didn't believe it to be tiredness as I'd slept earlier on. My fingertips began to tingle, and it was at that point I recognised the same symptoms that day I was shopping. I closed my eyes and took in some really deep breaths, trying to oxygenate my blood and quell the attack.

I pictured Miller in my mind, and the time he held me by the truck. Somehow that image morphed into the one where he kissed me. I wasn't sure if the tingle to my lips was the low oxygen levels, hyperventilation, or just the memory. Those tears pricked at my eyes again. I felt something for Miller; I knew I did, although I had tried to deny that. I'd let guilt override my emotion and it was wrong of me.

Trey had been gone for nearly a year, but should there be a time limit on dating again? If a second chance came along, should I not grab it with both hands? How often do second chances present themselves? I swung my legs over the bed; I wasn't going to miss the opportunity of Miller.

Miller, I miss you. I'm worried about you so much, and I can't bear the thought that you're alone right now. I don't know if you'll get this message but I want you to know that I'll not only kick your arse when I find you, but I'll kiss you so hard, too. You cannot leave me before you've even really

arrived. I won't allow it. Tomorrow I'm going to search for you and I won't stop until I find you. You need me, Miller, and I need you. Come home, please!

I sent him another.

Maybe you can read these but can't reply for some reason. I'm hoping that. I'm praying this will give you some comfort until we find you. When we were at your cottage, the derelict one, I said I didn't remember you, but I did, in a way that might be difficult for me to explain. I can't give you specifics about our childhood friendship, but everything is easy with you. I feel comfortable and I can only assume that's because I was comfortable with you back then. When you held me, it felt right. So right that it scared me. More right than with Trey. When you kissed me, you affected me right to my core. More importantly, you not only affected my body, but my mind, too. I get you, Miller, and you get me. I understand your pain because I've felt it myself.

It was a half hour later that I sent my last text.

I'm going to write one last letter to Lincoln. Please respond to that letter.

I grabbed a pad and pen and without a thought, I wrote.

My dearest Lincoln.

So much has happened these past few days, weeks, even. I know where to begin but I doubt I'm going to be coherent. I met a man, a wonderful man, a damaged man who needs me, and it feels wonderful to be needed.

The last two years of my married life was a total farce; I can see that now. It's only the whirlwind of a man named Miller, who has blown into my life and turned it on its head, that has my vision of the past so clear.

This is my last letter to you, Lincoln, because from now, we won't need them.

We'll talk every day. We'll wake up together, and we'll fall asleep together. You see, I had that light bulb moment that everyone talks about. I'm in love with Miller. I didn't realise until now, and isn't it terrible that it takes a tragedy to understand that? I always liked him, although he irritated me sometimes, but his passion for life and for righting his wrongs makes him a remarkable man. A man I want to spend a long time with. A man that I know can make me happy, and I hope that I can do the same for him.

Shall I tell you when I had that light bulb moment? It was when my heart stopped, when the blood froze in my veins with fear and worry. It was when all I wanted to do was walk and scour the cliffs for him. It was when the thought of never seeing him again was unbearable. It was then, Lincoln, that I realised I was in love.

I want to feel Miller's lips on mine. I want to feel his hands on my body. I want to give myself to him, and I want to take him. I can't do that if he doesn't come back to me.

I'll pray all night, and when the sun rises, I'll walk for however long I have to until I find him. And if I don't find him tomorrow, I'll search the following day, and the one after. I'll ask the sea to give him back to me. Annabelle would want that, I'm sure of it. She'd approve, Lincoln, I just know that in my heart.

So, as I said, this is my last letter to you, Lincoln. It's Miller I need now.

I'll be forever in your debt for bringing him to me.

Dani.

I folded the letter and placed it in a fresh envelope. There was something symbolic about using a new envelope. To me, it represented a new, fresh start.

Then I prayed. For the first time in my life, I placed my palms together and I asked God to keep him safe until he was found. I apologised for my lack of faith in the past, and for the contradiction of what I was doing. However, I was desperate.

I didn't undress and ready myself for bed. I didn't sleep. I checked my phone constantly and resisted the temptation to contact Daniel every hour throughout the night. I watched the sun break over the horizon, and when it did, I made my way downstairs. I was at a loss as to what to do for a while. I picked up the solicitor's letter that I'd received and scanned through it. I decided to deal with that; I wanted all loose ends tied up so I could concentrate on Miller. I also wanted something to occupy my mind until such a time, as it was decent to ring Daniel. Not that I imagined he'd slept any.

I wrote asking for evidence of Alistair's parentage. I believed him to be Trey's son, but I wasn't going to just roll over. I confirmed Trey's nationality and that, as he wasn't a British national, I asked whether that would have an impact on a straightforward claim. I was praying that was the case, and the complication would have Helen back off.

In my mind, I'd already resolved that I would give a sum of money for Alistair, not that I would mention that, of course. I didn't owe Trey, or his child, anything. But Alistair was just a child, an innocent party in his parents' illicit affair. I couldn't move forwards and put all this behind me, if I left it unresolved. It was the right thing to do, for me, and for Alistair.

I addressed another envelope and left the letter on the side ready for posting. Whether I initially thought about it or not, I felt I was closing up all that baggage I held and sending it on its way. I wanted to be clear of my shit so I could help Miller deal with his. Two broken people would get nowhere, in my opinion, but if I could be strong for him, we might stand a chance.

"Any news?" Dad said, when he walked into the kitchen.

"No, nothing. Dad, I've made some decisions. I'm going to sort out this Alistair thing as quickly as possible. I want to be able to help Miller with his issues so I need to let go of mine."

"You like him, don't you?"

"I do. I didn't realise just how much. Is that terrible? Is it too early?"

"There's no time limit on when you can start a new relationship, Dani. And don't listen to anyone that would tell you otherwise. If you've found someone who makes you happy, then don't let go of that chance."

"I think, and I'm sure I'm not going to say this in the right way, but had Trey been faithful, had I not found out what happened, I might believe it was wrong to move on so quickly. But his affair has freed me in one way."

"I can understand that, and I'm pleased for you. Everyone deserves a second chance. It can be very lonely getting old on your own."

"Did you ever want to find another wife?" I asked, as I set the kettle to boil.

"I met someone a couple of years after your mum passed, but my focus was you children. You needed my full attention back then, and I didn't want to share that with someone else."

"That's a sad thing to hear. I'm sure we would have all adapted."

"Maybe, but I wasn't going to take the risk. As hard as this is to hear, you have no ties, Dani. Even if you did, you go for it, if that's what you want. You have an opportunity for a new life, grab that and don't let go. If Miller feels the same way…"

"He does," I interrupted. He did, didn't he? Yes. I wouldn't let a shred of self-doubt cloud my way.

"Then you'd disappoint me if you didn't try to make it work with him. I doubt it's going to be easy, he's clearly a troubled man, but if anyone can help him heal, it's you."

I stepped into my dad's embrace; it felt like all those times from childhood when I'd needed his hug wrapped up in one. His belief in me nearly brought me to tears.

"Now I just have to find him," I said.

"I think we need to let the experts do that. Although I'm up for some more scouting, of course."

I checked the clock on the wall to see it approaching six o'clock. I sent Daniel a text to ask if he had any news. He didn't reply immediately, it was an anxious twenty minutes before he did.

Nothing yet. The search is about to start again, they seem convinced he moored up somewhere, and the boat broke loose, because the mooring line is sheared in half. That is such good news for us. I know we'll find him, Dani. I'm convinced he got to safety until the weather passed and is stuck, maybe until the tide turns. I'm going to an update meeting at the lifeboat station. Dad will stay at home. I don't think he's doing so good. Did you get any sleep?

I sent him my reply.

Not really. I want to walk the coastline again, maybe he might have moved in the night.

Okay, let us know what you're doing so I can tell the police. Daniel replied.

I showed Dad the text messages while I unfolded his Ordnance map.

"Where did we get to?" I asked.

Dad pointed to a red line he'd drawn. We didn't know for sure where the boat had been found but that could have drifted for miles. The currents in that area could be ferocious.

"I think we drive to here and walk ten miles that way. The problem we have with some parts is we can't get close enough to the cliff edge. Here is too dangerous, and this part is farmland."

I ran my finger along the coastal path, a designated path for walkers. It made its way inland. We'd either have to trespass and run the risk of angry farmers or cattle, or miss out huge sections of the cliff face. We were banking on Miller being conscious as we had been calling out to him. If he wasn't; we'd never see him.

"This isn't going to work, is it?" I said, disappointed.

"No, I don't think so. If we could get close enough, there are overhangs all along this part from the erosion, and there's no way we should be getting close enough," Dad replied.

The only other option was to persuade someone to take me out on a boat and sail along the cliffs. I assumed the fishermen were back out, as well as the lifeboat, and perhaps the Coastguard with their helicopter. Realistically, I didn't think I was going to be much help at all.

"I feel so frustrated, I just want to do something," I said.

"You know what you could do? Lincoln is going to be pretty lonely, maybe you could offer to sit with him?"

"Good idea."

I texted Daniel back and told him I'd sit with his dad while he went to his update meeting.

I'd appreciate that, I didn't want to leave him at mine on his own, and he doesn't want to go back to the home. He hasn't slept; he might if you're there with him.

It was settled then. I grabbed an oversized handbag and stuffed it with a clean t-shirt and jeans, just in case I ventured out and got muddy or wet. I put in my phone charger and phone, then kissed Dad on the cheek. The first thing I did was to post the letter to Lincoln in the honesty box. Then I drove the Mercedes to Daniel's, hoping that by the time I arrived, there'd be news. I hated the fact I was out of contact, even if it was just for the ten-minute drive. The car wasn't advanced enough to have Bluetooth or some way of connecting my phone to a loudspeaker.

I knocked on the front door and waited. Lincoln answered and it took all my resolve not to gasp at the sight of him. His shoulders were so hunched; he'd lost inches in height. His eyes were dull, the whites were tinged with red from either lack of sleep or crying, I thought. His hands shook as he reached out for me. I wrapped my arms around him and he openly cried into my shoulder.

"Let's get inside," I said gently.

I ushered him in, closing the door behind me. I held his arm and helped him into the living room. A blanket was strewn over the floor and the curtains were still closed. Lincoln perched on the edge of the sofa, while I opened the curtains and picked up the blanket. I folded it and placed it on the back of the sofa.

"Have you eaten, Lincoln?" I asked. He slowly shook his head.

"I'm going to make you something, and a drink. You need to keep your strength up for when Miller returns."

"He's not coming back," he whispered.

"He is, Lincoln. I know he is."

Lincoln looked up at me while slowly shaking his head. He patted his chest, near his heart. "I don't feel him anymore."

I clenched my jaw together initially; I sat beside him and held his hand in mine.

"Lincoln, we have to believe he's out there somewhere. Please don't give up on him, not yet. The boat had been moored up, he got to safety; we just need to find him."

"I abandoned him when he needed me the most. I should have helped him more. I know both Daniel and I got so frustrated with him over the years, yet we missed that he was grieving himself. He threw himself in a *gang* because he didn't have a *family*. I'm solely to blame for that."

"No you're not, Lincoln. Miller was old enough to know right from wrong, and you are talking about a lifestyle he led many years ago. It's not relevant today. He took that boat out to let go, finally, of Annabelle, so he could move on with his life. That has nothing to do with what happened in the past. If *he* blamed you for anything, why would he have built that bungalow so you could live close to him? That doesn't sound like a man who held a grudge, does it?"

Lincoln sighed.

"You lost your wife, maybe you lost your way for a little while, and that's totally understandable. I've been there myself. Okay, I wasn't married for as long as you were, but I bet you did the best you could. We are all adults, Lincoln, way beyond blaming our childhood for our poor decisions. Miller made stupid decisions; he knows that. But that's all on him, not you."

I could see what Lincoln was doing, but Miller's life prior to prison had no bearing, in my mind, on why he took that boat out. I wanted Lincoln to understand that Miller made the choices he made, and perhaps they stemmed from the loss of his mother and the fact he felt abandoned by his family, but that was then. I didn't want him to confuse the two.

I guessed it was quite normal, in times of utter despair, to question everything, to tear yourself apart, and I didn't know the family during those troubled times. I wanted to concentrate on the Miller I knew, the man he'd become despite his past. I hoped I could convince Lincoln to do the same.

"I'll make you some breakfast, Lincoln, and I wonder if you should try to get some sleep?"

He didn't answer except to nod his head.

Daniel had a small kitchen, very old-fashioned, but then the church owned the house he lived in, and I guessed modernisation wasn't in their budget. I opened cupboards and found tea and some mugs. I filled the kettle and let it boil, while I opened the fridge. Someone had stocked it with fresh food; at least I assumed it was someone other than Daniel. I decided to make Lincoln an omelette.

With the mugs in one hand and the plate in the other, I walked back into the living room. Lincoln had rested himself into the corner of the sofa and was sleeping. I placed the plate and his mug on the wooden coffee table and decided to leave him be. I imagined he felt comfortable enough to sleep with me being there. I sat in one of the chairs and placed my phone on the arm.

I hated the quiet. Silence allowed for my mind to wander to places I didn't want it to go. I tried to think of books that I'd read, of songs that I'd loved, I wanted to fill my mind of anything other than my fears or Lincoln's words.

I drank my tea, removed the plate and cup from the coffee table, and washed up. I cleaned the kitchen, not that it needed it, but I wanted to occupy myself. When I returned to the living room, Lincoln stirred. His panic and disorientation were evident, and I wondered if, in times of high stress, his early dementia was intensified.

"It's okay, you fell asleep. There's no news. Let me get you a fresh cup of tea," I said.

I made Lincoln tea and another omelette. I was pleased to see that he ate it.

"I can't bear all this waiting around, Dani," he said as he sipped on his tea. "He's been out all night, all day yesterday."

"I know, but he's a strong man. If he got to safety, which we believe he did, he'll make it through one night and day."

I had only just finished my sentence when my phone rang. Daniel was calling.

"Hi," I said as I answered it.

"They've found him…" The phone crackled making it difficult to hear.

"Daniel! Where? Is he okay?" I looked over to Lincoln who had stood.

"They've found him but I can't hear Daniel very well," I said to Lincoln.

"Dani? Can you hear me?…hospital…hypothermia."

I'd heard enough to let the sob I'd been holding in for so long escape. The call cut off.

"All I got was hospital and hypothermia. That means he's alive, Lincoln," I said.

Lincoln collapsed to the sofa and covered his face with his hands. He sobbed. I sat beside him and placed my arm around his shoulder. I cried along with him.

"Which hospital is he in?" he asked, eventually.

"Let me text Daniel."

Daniel replied with the details, letting me know that they should arrive at the hospital in a few minutes. I wondered if he was travelling with Miller.

"Do you want to leave now?" I asked Lincoln.

"Yes. Yes, of course. I need to get to my boy. Oh, God, thank you, thank you," he said.

It took us a half hour to get to the hospital; I texted Daniel when we arrived and was given instructions on where ICU was. Lincoln held on to my arm as we walked towards the department and the nurses' station.

"Hi, this is Lincoln Copeland's father. Can you tell us where he is?" I asked.

"His brother is in the family room, just down the hall. Why don't you join him? I think a doctor will be coming to see you soon," I was told.

Lincoln struggled to walk the short distance to the family room. His legs wobbled and I wasn't sure it was relief or fatigue. I opened the door and helped him in. Daniel jumped up from the chair he sat in and caught Lincoln just as he started to fall.

"Dad, come and sit down," he said, taking Lincoln from me.

"What happened?" Lincoln asked.

"They found him near the falls. He'd managed to get part way up the cliff and just behind the falls was a small cave. He's broken his arm, they think, and has hypothermia. They're stabilising him, warming him up or whatever they do. The doctor will come and find us as soon as he can."

Harleson Falls was where Miller's cottage was. It was where the river deposited into the sea via a waterfall. In winter, that river had often flooded, causing devastation to the local properties. I remembered the local council widening the banks and funnelling excess water off the cliff top. As a kid we'd play in the river, but I'd never attempted to get behind the waterfall.

"Did you get to speak to him?" I asked.

"No, he's pretty much out of it at the moment."

"How did they find him?" Lincoln asked.

"One of the search team remembered the cave. I know that area was searched thoroughly."

"Not thoroughly enough," Lincoln said, echoing my thoughts.

"Well, he's been found, and for that we need to be thankful," Daniel said.

We were then back to the waiting. I texted Dad to let him know the news, he replied that he'd just been told himself and was about to call me.

The door opening woke me, I hadn't realised I'd fallen asleep, and the stiffness in my neck and back suggested I'd fallen asleep where I'd been sitting.

"Mr. Copeland's family?" a man asked, looking at some notes in his hand.

"I'm his father, this is his brother and his friend," Lincoln said, not looking at us.

The doctor sat. "Your son suffered severe hypothermia, Mr. Copeland. He's undergone what we call cardiopulmonary bypass, which basically means removing his blood, heating it, before pumping it back in. We're continuing to, slowly, get his temperature raised, but at the moment, I'm afraid you're son is classed as critical."

"I don't understand; is he going to die?" Lincoln asked.

"His temperature was so low that, from what I understand, the paramedics couldn't detect a pulse. His body was shutting down. The process to *warm him back up*, I guess is the basic term, is slow. There is a risk he could go into cardiac arrest, his body has been through a lot of trauma. But he's a fit man. I've seen plenty of people in his condition pull through."

"Why was he half-naked?" Daniel asked. I saw Lincoln stare at him with a frown.

"There are a few theories behind that. Our best guess is that your brother might have experienced what we'd call paradoxical undressing. During that process, the muscles relax through exhaustion from the shivering. There would be a surge of blood to his extremities; confusing him into thinking he was overheating. Add that to the fact he was found in the small cave, which could have been terminal burrowing, your brother was very lucky to have survived."

"Burrowing? What does that mean?" I asked.

"It's often the case, and it's believed to be a primitive reaction, the casualty will 'burrow' into a small space. It's also referred to the hide and die syndrome."

Silence followed the doctor's statement. Miller must have been so close to death. I covered my mouth to hide the sob.

"Will there be any permanent damage?" Lincoln asked.

"Until we've got his temperature up and he's conscious, I can't tell you with any certainty. However, as I said, he's a fit and healthy man, so I think there's a possibility for a full recovery."

"When can I see him?" Lincoln asked.

"He's in ICU, so one family member at a time, but you can pop in now if you like. Our ward sister is a little ferocious; she'll tell you if she thinks you've been in there too long. We don't generally have restricted visiting for our ICU guests, but Lincoln isn't the only patient on that ward, so we'd ask that you keep that in mind."

The doctor rose and shook Lincoln's hand. He nodded towards Daniel and me, and then left.

"Dad, do you want to visit him?" Daniel asked.

Lincoln nodded and Daniel gave me a smile before escorting his dad from the room. I wasn't sure what to do. I decided to hang around for a little longer and then, I guessed, I would have to leave for home. As the doctor had said, only family were allowed around his bedside. I'd have to wait until he was moved to a ward before I could visit him.

I sat for about an hour before a weeping Lincoln was helped back into the room. I stood and took his arm, leading him to a chair.

"He looks so frail," he said quietly.

I looked up at Daniel. "He's very pale still but that's to be expected according to the nurse."

There was no offer for me to visit him, and I didn't expect to. "I'll make my way home, you will keep me informed, won't you? And as soon as he's up for visitors, I'd like to come back," I said.

Maybe there was a little part of me hoping one of them would have said to go visit, even if for a few minutes, but all I got was a nod from Daniel.

I left the hospital totally thankful that Miller had been found and was alive, and entirely exhausted. The past couple of days seemed to hit me like a truck. I slumped into the car seat and rested my forehead on the steering wheel. I let the tears drip to my thighs. After a minute or so, I turned the car on, put it into gear, and reversed from my parking spot. I drove home much slower than I had recently.

I pulled onto the drive and Dad was already at the front door, I guessed having heard the car.

"How is he?" Dad asked.

"I didn't get to see him but he's alive. They're warming him up, doing something with this blood, bypassing it, or whatever."

"Why didn't you get to see him?"

"I think it's family only and Daniel didn't offer for me to."

Dad raised his eyebrows. "After all you've done? If it wasn't for you, he wouldn't have known where to start."

I couldn't disagree, but I wasn't family, so that was that. Obviously, had it been the other way around, I would have encouraged Daniel to stay and given him the opportunity to see whomever for a few minutes.

"I'm exhausted, thirsty, and hungry. I'll give them this morning then call Daniel this afternoon to see if there are any developments," I said.

Dad nodded and led the way to the kitchen. "I told Colette, she was thrilled with the news."

"She's very fond of him, I bet she was pleased."

I sat at the kitchen table and let Dad wait on me. He had a cup of tea and a sandwich ready in minutes. I burnt my tongue on the tea but was grateful to have something warm inside me.

"I need to have a shower, and I think, a lie down," I said, putting my mug and plate in the sink.

"Leave your mobile here. I'll answer it if it rings. I'm sure I read somewhere that it wasn't good to take your mobile device to bed with you, and I'm sure you'll just keep looking at it."

I smiled at him, not disbelieving him, and left my phone on the table.

My legs felt heavy as I slowly climbed each tread of the stairs. I stripped off my clothes and stepped under the shower. I stood for a few minutes, just letting the warm water flow over my head and down my body. The sting in my eyes was the only indication I was crying, my tears mingled with the shower water.

When my skin was wrinkled, and the water cooled, I wrapped a towel around my head and another around my body and walked to my bedroom. Still in the towels and slightly damp, I climbed under the duvet. I was asleep within seconds.

—

CHAPTER TWENTY-THREE

J slept through the day and night, waking before the sun had risen. I reached over to my bedside cabinet for my phone, feeling very disorientated. Of course, the phone wasn't there. I was tangled in the towel and duvet; the one on my head had long since been discarded. I swung my legs over the edge of the bed and stretched out my back. I ached from sleeping so long. I caught sight of myself in the dressing table mirror as I crossed the room for my robe. I looked an absolute fright. My normally curly hair was frizzy and standing on end in places. I chuckled to myself.

I grabbed the robe and made my way to the kitchen. As I put the kettle on to boil, I looked around for my phone. I couldn't see it and could only assume Dad had done what he'd told me not to, and taken it to bed with him. I made two mugs of tea and carried them back upstairs.

I slowly opened Dad's bedroom door. Although asleep, he was propped up with pillows and my phone was on the side of his bed. I crept in and placed the tea on his bedside table, then picked up my phone. Whether Dad sensed me or not, I wasn't sure but he startled.

"Dani, what's wrong?" he asked.

"Nothing, I just wanted my phone. I'm sorry to wake you. I've left you a cup of tea," I said, backing away towards the door.

"Oh, thank you. I must have drifted off."

"What do you mean? You haven't tried to stay awake all night have you?"

"I tried, but I don't think I even managed that when I was in my teens," he said with a chuckle.

"That's daft. I would have heard the phone, I think. The ring tone is set to loud. Have a couple of sips of tea and then see if you can get some sleep."

I left Dad and headed to my own room. I didn't want to climb back in bed, as tempting as that was, because I knew I was likely to doze. Instead I sat in my chair, looking out to a calm sea and cursed it.

Mother Nature had decided to have the sea raging while Miller was out in his boat, to have the clouds darken and the rain to lash down. Now he had been found, she'd decided to calm the sea, clear the clouds, and let the sun shine. It dawned on me then that it was also New Year's Eve.

I spent the morning moping around the house, checking the time, letting Lucy in and out of the garden, whether she wanted to or not. I called the hospital but because I wasn't family, I wasn't told anything. Eventually, as lunchtime came, I called Daniel. He didn't answer so I left a message on his voicemail.

"Daniel, it's Dani. I wondered how Miller was doing. Could you call me back when you have a spare minute? Thank you."

In my frustration, I slammed the phone back on the kitchen table. I'd been involved right from the beginning, and I knew I had no right to be updated the minute Miller went into hospital, but being notified of his progress shouldn't be too much to ask. I had to check myself. It hadn't been long since Miller had been found; I needed to give them time.

I spotted the letter I'd written to the solicitor on the side and rifled through my purse for a stamp. A walk to the post box would give me something to do. I pulled on my coat and left the house. As I came to the end of the lane, I paused beside the honesty box. I was tempted to look inside and see if my letter had been taken, I knew it couldn't have been, of course. I sighed and carried on walking. I deposited my letter in the small post box situated in the wall of Colette's shop. I was about to walk away when I heard her call me.

"Dani, how are you? Is there any news on Miller?" she asked, rounding the corner of her building.

"No, I left a message for Daniel but I haven't heard back."

"Want to come in for a cup of tea?"

"That would be nice, thank you."

I followed her around the side of the building to the door at the back that took us into her cottage attached to the rear of the shop. I had never been inside her house and was surprised by how modern it was. The door took us straight into an open-plan kitchen diner. I envied her light oak and stainless steel kitchen with its modern appliances.

"This is a beautiful kitchen," I said.

"Miller designed it, made and fitted it as well. He's a very talented man. So sit and tell me what you know."

She made the tea and I told her all I knew.

"And they didn't let you see him? My, that's not nice, or very Christian, either. I think I'd be mightily pissed off at that," she said, startling me with her curse word.

"It's family only at the moment."

"Semantics. That boy is in love with you, they know that."

"I don't know about that," I said.

"Dani, I've seen the way he looks at you, how often he speaks about you. I only had to mention that you'd returned, and that you were thinking of the converting the barn, for him to ask me to recommend him. Not that I wouldn't have, of course. He's a fantastic builder and he'll do an amazing job."

"I'm very fond of him, too. I have to say, I am a little hurt but I understand they probably have way more on their mind than to worry about me."

Colette huffed and waved a hand to dismiss my words. "They should have let you see him, period. He was always a little shit."

"Who was?"

"Daniel. I'm surprised he got made the vicar of this parish after his history."

I frowned. "What history?"

"Oh, I bet he didn't tell you. And of course, it's rumour, but…"

"But what?"

Colette sighed and delayed answering by taking a sip of her tea.

"Did you know that Miller was convicted of stealing cars and selling them? Daniel was, sort of, involved in that."

"What?"

"From what I know, Miller took the fall because Daniel was training to be a vicar, or whatever they call it."

"I don't understand."

"Daniel had a friend, one of the gang that Miller got involved in. Miller only got involved because of Daniel."

"But how was Daniel involved in stealing cars?"

"Daniel allowed his friend to hide a car at his dad's house. Now, whether Daniel truly knew what was going on is questionable, however, he definitely knew the guy was a wrong 'un. Maybe he thought he was doing good, I don't know. Miller drove home drunk and in another stolen car. I think Lincoln had come to the end of his tether; he called the police. When they came, they arrested Miller and also found the hidden stolen car. Lincoln told them he thought that belonged to Daniel. The police arrested Daniel for, what's it called...?"

"Aiding and abetting?"

"Yes, I think so. Anyway, Miller stepped up, he was already arrested, and said that he'd put the car there. He *confessed* to stealing it and was about to sell it. I think that might have been his final nail in his proverbial coffin."

"Wow, Miller didn't tell me anything like that."

"I don't suppose he did. My assumption is, not once did Daniel acknowledge what Miller did. In fact, he publically criticised him, distanced himself when Miller went to prison. That is where their problem stems from."

"I didn't know any of that. So Daniel presents himself as the good guy all the time, when in fact, he might have been on the fringes of the same criminal activity Miller was involved in."

Colette slowly nodded her head. "I imagine Daniel thought he'd be able to save souls and all that rubbish, despite not being an actual vicar at the time."

Dad had been right, Colette seemed to be the font of all knowledge.

"I need to get back, thank you for the tea," I said, pulling my coat from the back of the chair and putting it back on.

I walked slowly back to the house, digesting what she'd said. I couldn't remember exactly what Miller had said as to why he'd been in prison, but I knew there had been no mention of Daniel.

"Hi, you've been gone a while," Dad said, when I walked into the house.

"I had a cup of tea with Colette. I never know whether to call her by her first name or Mrs. Hampton," I said with a laugh.

"I think she answers to anything nowadays."

"Anyway, she told me something interesting." I repeated what I'd learned.

"Interesting, I certainly never knew that. I don't know if honourable would be the right word, but what he did, to save his brother's humiliation and possible loss of his career certainly warrants some respect. More so from Daniel."

"I thought so, too. Most of the time when he talks about Miller, it's with fondness, but just every now and again he'll say something that has my hackles up. I'm not sure that sometimes I get to see the real Daniel, or the Daniel that's doing *public service*. Does that make sense?"

"It does. So what are you going to do with that knowledge?"

"Nothing, I guess. But it just gives me a better understanding of why they don't get on."

I picked up my mobile to check for the umpteenth time. There was no reply from Daniel.

"Do you want to do anything tonight?" I asked Dad.

"Get drunk and pray the new year will be better for you than the past one?"

I laughed. "Drunk? I don't think so. But I will pray with you for a better new year."

As the day wore on, I became more despondent and desperate for news.

"Do you mind if I pop out for a little while?" Dad asked.

I assumed he wanted to spend a little time with Colette. I smiled at him. "Of course, you don't need my permission."

Dad left and I settled on the sofa. I tried to read a book, but the words just didn't hold my attention. I tried to listen to music but it was just wailing and made me feel very old. I did some house-work, but I drew the line at ironing the pile of clothes that was growing.

I didn't know how much time had passed, but eventually, I heard my mobile ring. I panicked, not remembering where I'd left it. I ran to the kitchen and grabbed it from the counter.

"Hello?"

"Dani, it's Lincoln. I'm sorry not to have been in touch. We sort of got caught up with…well, you know. Anyway, Miller is doing great, he's conscious and is asking to see you. They moved him to Ward J today, it's right off ICU, so how about you come and visit him?"

"Oh, God, I've been so worried. Thank you, I'll do that."

"No, I'm sorry. We should have thought about you and we didn't. I didn't know about your…friendship. Daniel didn't mention it at all."

"There's a lot, Lincoln, that Daniel hasn't mentioned, I'm sure. I'll pop in to see Miller straight away. Will you be there?"

"No, and neither will Daniel. I think you could do with some alone time with Miller."

"I appreciate that, thank you. I'll call you as soon as I leave and let you know how he is. I'm sure I'm able to capture your number from this call."

"I'd appreciate that. I'll say goodbye now."

After saying goodbye myself, I laid the phone down. My interpretation of that call was that Daniel seemed to have deliberately decided to keep me out of the loop, and I wondered why. Maybe Miller had said something to his dad and that was why I'd received that call. Whatever the reason, I was just pleased to be informed of his progress.

I rushed upstairs to change and brush my hair.

"Balls," I said aloud. Dad had the car.

Was it fair of me to call and ask if he could come back? Trying to get a taxi was out of the question; I doubted there were any taxis within ten miles of the village as it was New Year's Eve. As for public transport? That was non-existent. My heart stopped for a second when I heard a car pull onto the drive. I rushed downstairs and to the front door. A second car, my Dad's, pulled on behind a small red car.

"Dad?" I said, as I watched him get out and thank the driver of the red car who then walked away.

"I thought you'd need your own set of wheels, and this lady is a little too precious to be driving through hedges."

"What? You got me a car?"

"Well, technically you've got yourself a car. I made the assumption that you'd pay the garage. It's cheap, reliable, and will bounce off anything you care to drive into," he said with a laugh. "Now, I understand you have somewhere to be?"

I frowned at him. "How did you know that?"

"Because I just reminded Lincoln Copeland of a few of the things you've done to find his son, of the fact you two are more than friends, and how shitty it was to keep you out of the loop."

"Dad, you didn't!"

"I bloody well did. Now, get your purse, or whatever you call them nowadays and get going. I'm having dinner with Colette and I need to get freshened up."

Dad strode into the house, depositing the car keys in my hand. "Oh, I've insured it," he added.

"I'll pay for a respray," I called out after him.

"Nothing that a good polish hasn't solved. I guess I need to get Miller to erect a garage. You tell him he has an extra job when he's ready, so he better get back on his feet super quick."

I grabbed my bag and left the house. The car took a little while to get used to, and I found myself grinding through the gears on occasion. It was small, nippy, and I loved it. My little red Citroen would do me wonders for getting around.

I parked at the hospital and nerves hit me. I felt my palms become clammy and my heart rate increase a little as I walked towards the ward. I checked in with the nurse and she pointed to a door along the corridor. Miller had his own room. I guessed this was the place they put the patients that had recently come off the critical list. I looked through the glass panel in the door before I opened it. Miller had his eyes closed. I gently opened it and crept in. I sat in the chair beside the bed and picked up his hand in mine.

He slowly turned his head towards me and opened his eyes. I smiled at him. It was hard for him to smile back; his lips were bruised and cracked.

"Hey," he said, his voice a little croaky.

"Hi. How are you feeling?" I asked.

"Awful, sort of like I slept in an icy cold waterfall in the middle of winter without a jacket."

I chuckled; he winced as he tried to.

"Are you in pain?"

"Only my throat. I understand they shoved some tube down it. I don't think they were particularly gentle when they took it out. Can you help me up?"

I raised the back of his bed slightly and then picked up a glass of water for him. He took it and it was then that I noticed his other arm was in plaster. I guess he'd had it under the sheet at first.

Miller took a sip from the glass before holding it out for me. I replaced it on the cabinet. He sighed and also took hold of my hand again.

"What happened, Miller?" I asked.

"Well, I wasn't drunk, fuck knows where Daniel got that from. I've had the lecture from the police about wasting their time with my drunken antics."

"Lecture?"

"It sure felt like it. Anyway, I've sailed in weather like that night before, and I knew I was going to be quick. I wanted just to get around to the cove, where they found me and..."

"To let her go, I know. You told me in a text."

"Yes. To let her go. I moored up the boat, climbed onto the rock, and then fell. I broke my arm and it hurt like anything. I knew I wouldn't be able to sail back with a broken arm so decided to wait it out. The weather got worse and then the boat broke loose. I was sort of fucked. I remembered the cave behind the falls and thought I'd be dry there and could wait until the following day when the tide went out. I got it wrong. I didn't realise just how wet I was, and how cold it was. I was of perfectly sound mind,

Dani. I just made a wrong call. I should have sailed straight back."

"Are you sure you were of sound mind, Miller?"

He shrugged his shoulders a little.

"I mean, wouldn't it have been better to have waited? You gave me such a fright with that text."

"I guess so, and okay, maybe I wasn't of sound mind. Maybe I was feeling like shit because I'd made a mistake. Perhaps I was consumed with guilt and sadness because I thought I might have lost you, as dramatic as that sounds. And no, you weren't to blame, it was all me. I chose to do what I did, I just didn't think it through before I actually did it."

"Well, none of it matters now. You're safe, and I'm so bloody thankful."

He smiled at me and my heart skipped a beat. I raised my hand and brushed away an unruly curl that threatened to sneak into one eye.

"Dad bought me a car, well, technically I've bought it; I just haven't paid for it yet. Anyway, he said to tell you he needs a garage built and would you hurry up and get back on your feet."

Miller laughed and the sound was medicine to my battered heart.

"My dad took a call from your dad earlier. I think there were *words* said. I guess Daniel hasn't been as honest as he should have been, but then…"

"That's nothing new? I know about the stolen car thing. I was hurt that he seemed to keep me away from you and I don't know why."

"Daniel doesn't like me getting close to anyone, scared I might tell them the truth. Not that it's much of a secret. How did you know?"

"Mrs. Hampton, Colette as I'm allowed to call her."

"Ah, she should have been a detective, or a barrister. She's certainly my champion and guardian."

"When will you be able to come home?" I asked.

"A couple of days, I think. They warmed up my cold heart, I expect to be a completely different person," he joked.

"I don't want you to be a different person. I want you to be the Miller that kissed me. I wrote a letter, my last letter to Lincoln. You should read it sometime."

"I'll have my courier deliver it first thing in the morning."

"Your courier?"

"Colette, my champion. Trust me, there isn't anything that woman doesn't know. She saw me picking up a letter from the box one day. She asked me who it was from. I didn't tell her, of course. The following day, or it might have been a couple of days later, I drove to the shop and there she was with a purple envelope in her hand. I called her a nosy cow, but it worked well."

"No way. I'm surprised she didn't say anything to me, she's such a gossip."

"She's a great keeper of secrets also."

"She's a good friend to you, isn't she?"

"Yes, she always has been. She was my mother's friend, and I guess she took over looking after me until I didn't want to be looked after any more. Trust me, I pay for that looking after. I think I've practically rebuilt her house at my own cost!"

I smiled at him.

"Can I ask you something? Something that might make you want to run for the hills?"

"I'm not sure I'll be running anywhere, and if I'm going to be scared of what you want to ask, should you?"

He hadn't quite got the words I'd used right but then, I couldn't remember them exactly either.

"Kiss me?" I asked.

"With pleasure."

Miller reached out with his hand and slid his palm across my cheek. He pulled me towards him. His kiss was gentle, tender, yet held the same passion as before. I felt a tear run down my skin. I felt his rough lips on mine and I tasted the blood as they cracked slightly. When he pulled away, he smiled.

"That was everything, and more," he whispered.

"How bad is it for me to tell you, I'd love to climb in that bed with you right now?"

"Very bad, so bad that I want you to. Not sure what Nurse Happy might have to say about it though. But, do it. Lay with me, Dani."

Miller shuffled over and I slid on the bed beside him. He wrapped his arm around my shoulders and held me close. I placed my hand on his chest and my head on his shoulder. He kissed the top of my head.

"I was so scared," I whispered.

"I can imagine. I'm sorry for scaring you. I tried to call but holding the damn thing with one hand and dialling wasn't in my skill set. I dropped the phone into the sea."

"Who is Nurse Happy?" I asked.

He didn't need to answer. A nurse bustled into the room and ordered me off the bed. She gave me a lecture about germs or something. Miller laughed and I stood and smiled, nodded my head when appropriate, and then apologised. She bustled out again.

"I better go. I can't tell you how happy I am to see you," I said.

I leant down and kissed Miller again.

"Happy New Year," I whispered.

"It's going to be," he replied.

It was a further week before Miller was released, and I waited at his house while Daniel brought him home. I'd visited Miller every day and avoided Daniel as much as I could.

"There's my girl," I heard, as Miller climbed from the car, I smiled the broadest smile I think I had in years.

I walked forwards and was engulfed in his embrace.

"Thanks, Daniel. We've got it from here. I'll call you later," Miller said.

I walked with Miller into his house while Daniel drove away.

"Is he pissed off at me?" I asked.

"Who cares? I have a list of instructions from the hospital. I'm to take it easy for a few more days. I intend to break every one of those instructions. Do me a favour. Grab a couple of blankets and drive us to the cottage?"

I cocked my head. "Should you? I think you ought to rest for a while."

"Please? There's something I need to do."

"Okay, but we won't be out long, will we?"

"Just grab a couple of blankets, maybe a pillow or two. You'll find them in the bottom of the wardrobe."

I left him standing in the hallway and collected what he needed.

"Now we go to the cottage."

"You can't walk that far," I said.

"Dani, I was rather cold, I got warmed up. I only have a broken arm, and I'm not disabled. It's important to me."

I wasn't sure but I made him put a coat on anyway. We drove the short distance to Harlson Falls and walked the path to the derelict cottage. He unlocked the door and we entered. Miller shook out the blankets and laid them on the floor, and he placed one on the windowsill. He took my hand and led me to it.

"Sit," he said.

He positioned himself between my thighs and used his good hand to brush hair from my eyes. He tucked it behind my ear and took a deep breath. I held mine.

"I fell in love with you in this house. I sort of lied and told you it was a kid crush, because that's what I thought it was at the time. But I never stopped thinking about you. Some say a youngster can't possibly know anything about love, and what I felt then, bears no resemblance to what I feel now. I want to kiss you so bad in here, because for me, this is where it all started. It all sounds a little stalkerish, but I can promise you that it isn't. I loved Annabelle, but you were also always in my mind. Maybe it was because whenever I thought of you, the fun you had, the smile you always shared, you reminded me of a better life, of hope.

"You still remind me of that. You're like a rain shower in the middle of a hot summer, the first flowers of spring. Even in your darkest times, you managed to find a smile. You struggled with dignity and courage, and I fell more in love with you then."

I didn't get a chance to reply.

His kiss started slow, his tongue swiped over my lips until I parted them. I raised my arms and placed them around his neck. I drew him close by wrapping my legs around his waist. I wanted to feel his body against mine. Our hearts beat in tune with each other.

As his kiss deepened, so my hold on him tightened. When he broke away it was as if part of me was missing. He stepped back and let his hand run down my arm to catch my hand. He pulled me into a standing position and then led me to the blankets he'd laid on the floor.

I knelt as he did. He stared at me for a long while, running his fingers over my face and through my hair.

"I love you, Dani," he said before kissing me again.

That time it was with such passion he took the air from my lungs. That one kiss took all the pain and hurt I'd felt for months away, he absolved me of any guilt I might have felt. He healed me with his lips and his tongue, with his strength and his courage.

Lincoln Miller Copeland became mine then, and I became his. We were a perfect fit, as if we'd been designed to be together. I could have cursed the years we'd been apart, but I didn't. We wouldn't have been there, in that moment, if we hadn't travelled the paths we did; had life not shaped us to be the people that we were.

As he laid me down, and his hand slid down my side, gently caressing the skin under my jumper, I stared into his eyes.

"I love you, too, Miller."

"I'm not going to make love to you here, as much as I want to. Trust me, I'm desperate to. What I want to do is discover you. I want to know every inch of your body before I make it mine."

He did just that. With his hands, and his mouth, he explored my body. He tasted and caressed every inch of skin, removing my clothes as he did. He licked, nipped, and kissed, and I struggled to keep hold of myself.

"Miller, please," I whispered, as I ran my lips over his neck.

I slid my hand up his jumper and ran it over his bare chest, feeling his heart beating a rapid rhythm. I felt his chuckle against my skin.

"I've waited years for this moment, I'm not going to rush it," he said.

"You're going to kill me," I said, frustrated.

"I'll give you this," he replied, as his mouth trailed down my stomach.

His fingers hooked under the side of my panties and pulled them down. His mouth followed. As his tongue swiped over my clitoris, I lost control. I cried out his name, and I let my tears flow. The release was overwhelming. Not just the release of an orgasm but the pent-up frustration, anger, and sadness, it all flowed from inside me in that moment.

CHAPTER TWENTY-FOUR

$\mathcal{W}$e lay together wrapped in the blankets for warmth for a while without speaking.

"What happens now?" I asked, eventually breaking the silence.

"I read your last letter to Lincoln. And then we decide what we want from each other."

"I want you, Miller. I want a relationship, if that's what you want, too." Uncertainly washed over me.

"Would we be here right now if I didn't?" He chuckled. "Dani, I want you to live with me, where we live, we'll have to decide. However, I want you to give me a couple of weeks to deal with some shit in my head. Will you do that for me?"

I propped myself up on one elbow. "I'll give you all the time you need, as long as you don't shut me out, you let me help you."

"Deal. I want to start a relationship with you without any baggage. I want to be totally honest with you and to do that I need to reconcile some things. I love you, Dani; I respect you enough to know that I need to sort myself out before I give you my all. I don't want to do this half-arsed."

I smiled in appreciation.

"I'm not sure after that taster, I can keep away for two weeks," I said.

"Just think how much sweeter it will be," he winked at me.

"When do we start?" I asked, trailing my fingers around the waistband of his jeans.

"Baby, I'm only just holding on to my control here, as it is. But I want to do this right. For the first time in my life, I want to get it right, from the beginning. You're my future and I need to clear some things so that future can't be disturbed."

I nodded, disappointed, but accepting his reasoning. What was two weeks anyway? I'd waited a long time for Miller, as he had for me. I could do that.

I drove Miller back to his cottage and his kiss goodbye had me in tears.

"Just two weeks, that's all. I'll call you every day, and if I need you, or you need me, then fuck the two weeks, okay?"

I walked to my car and tried my hardest not to look back. I didn't need to ask what he had to do in those two weeks. I guessed he wanted to deal with his relationship with Daniel, with his father. I imagined he wanted closure for Annabelle and his mother.

The first three days were awful. Miller called me twice a day, but the temptation to ring him hourly was so strong. He told me that he'd sat with his father and told him how he'd come to be put in prison. He was protecting Daniel. Although he confessed he knew it wasn't long before he'd be put away, anyway, and he welcomed it. He told me that had he not been convicted, he didn't think he'd have been able to break away from that lifestyle.

He also told me that he talked to his doctor about some counselling. I was pleased that he had decided to do that; his past was obviously of concern to him, not that it was to me. I didn't care about prison, or the lifestyle he'd chosen, because I knew the man I was in love with was a far cry from that person.

We never made it to the full two weeks apart, and I didn't think we would. Miller arrived at my house one morning, and although I told him off for driving one-handed, he placed his fingers over my lips and took my hand to walk me to his car.

"I can't wait any longer, and I don't think your dad will appreciate me fucking you in his house."

I laughed at his coarseness but allowed myself to be led to the passenger door. I climbed in, ignoring that he struggled to drive with one arm in plaster. In silence, we drove back to his cottage.

Before we'd even got the front door closed, he gently pushed me against the wall and he kissed me hard. His hand fisted in my hair and he pushed his body against mine. His breathing was ragged and his moan caused my core to tighten. I could feel the wetness between my thighs as my desire for him escalated.

When he took a step back, I grabbed the front of his shirt. My shaking hands fumbled to undo his buttons. Before I'd managed to unbutton it fully, he pulled it over his head and wrenched it past the plaster cast on his arm.

He took hold of the hem of my jumper and pulled it over my head. The urgency caused me to stumble a little. I undid my jeans and let them slide to my feet; I kicked off my Converse and stepped out of them. He lowered his head to my chest, and his tongue ran over the lace of my bra until he bit down on my puckered nipple. He sucked on it through the material. I gripped his head, tangling my fingers in his hair, and holding him to me.

"Not here," he whispered into my skin.

He stepped away and led me to his bedroom. "We do this right. Don't get me wrong, I'll fuck you against that wall, I'll fuck you everywhere in this house. But I want you in my bed first."

He led me upstairs and to his bedroom. I slipped off my socks and then stood in front of him. He reached behind to unclip my bra and slowly crouched as he pulled my panties to my ankles. All the while he kept looking straight in my eyes. His gaze was intense, his intention so obvious. He held my hips as his gently kissed my lower stomach and across the scar that blighted my skin. When he stood, he walked me backwards until my legs hit the bed and I sat. I watched him remove his jeans and then his underwear. I shuffled on the bed as he crawled towards me. I saw his brow furrow in pain, at the weight of him on his broken arm, but he brushed away my concern.

I lay and he held himself above me. He didn't speak at all, just stared. I parted my legs and wrapped my heels around the back of his legs. When Miller pushed inside me and then stilled, he took my breath away. Not from pain, but the connection I felt to him. A lone tear ran down the side of my face as he made love to me. Not once did he stop looking at me, not once did he close his eyes. Every movement of his body was slow and measured.

When he lowered his head to kiss me, I wrapped my arms around his back. I dug my fingers into his skin and tightened my legs around his. He let go then. The slow and measured was replaced with fast and furious. He slammed into me over and over, deeper with each thrust. He bit down on my shoulder and groaned out my name. I screamed out his as my orgasm built. My body convulsed and I raked my nails down his sweaty back.

Miller's body stiffened under my touch, he raised his head, and with his eyes closed, he bit down on his lower lip as he came. I felt him pulse inside me and I didn't care. I wanted everything he gave me. I wanted his cum to run down my thighs and for his sweat to drip onto my skin.

When Miller rolled to one side, I turned to face him. I placed my hand on his chest and felt his heart. He extended his arm and pulled me into him.

"Thank you," he whispered.

We slept for an hour or so, and then when we woke, we made love again. In fact, we didn't leave the bed for the rest of the day. The sheets were tangled around us, the room smelled of our arousal; it was musky and intoxicating.

At some point during the night, while I was dozing, Miller stirred. I opened my eyes to see him staring at me. He smiled.

"Marry me, Dani," he said.

"Marry you?"

"Yes. I know we agreed we'd live together but I'm an old-fashioned kind of guy. Marry me." It wasn't so much of a question, more a statement.

"Mr. Copeland, I've know you what, a year, if that?"

"So?"

He climbed from the bed and walked naked around to my side. He lowered himself to one knee.

"Dani, I love you. Would you do me the honour of becoming my wife?"

I opened my mouth to speak but I couldn't find the words. Instead I slid my legs over the bed so I was sitting. I nodded my head, eventually uttering the words he wanted to hear.

"Yes, I'll marry you," I said, just as his lips closed on mine.

EPILOGUE

$\mathcal{I}$ thought I'd found my soul mate in Trey, I'd been so very wrong. Just a few months later, as I walked up the aisle of the church towards Miller, I knew the man standing nervously in front of me was the one I was always destined to be with. Daniel presided and he smiled at us both as he gave the service. In fact, he looked more like the proverbial Cheshire cat than a vicar about to marry his brother and his friend.

We'd decided on a very small ceremony, just family and a handful of his friends. It was perfect: more so when Patricia flew over to act as mother of the bride. I'd called her when Miller had asked me to marry him, and at first I thought her silence was disapproval. However, the tears in her voice when she told me how happy she was for me brought a lump to my throat.

My relationship with Christian was still a little fractured and that saddened us both. He was a proud man, too proud to admit he'd caused the rift. However, he was at my wedding, sitting with his new partner, Jennifer. She'd been instrumental in making sure Christian had booked therapy to cope with his level of anger. She'd also made sure he and I sat and talked through how we felt. I had high hopes for their relationship, she was tough, considerate, and I thought we'd become good friends.

We'd decided to live in the barn, the planning permission had come through and with some minor adjustments; it was going to be perfect. We were to create our perfect home. Miller built Dad a garage for Mertle, and a workshop for himself. He put his cottage up for sale but kept hold of the one at Harlson Falls.

We visited that cottage regularly; we made love on the dusty floor many times. We never got around to start its renovation, though. One day, maybe, but for now, that cottage was where it all started, when we were children. We didn't want to disturb that memory or erase the fantasy that had occurred there.

"How do you feel?" Miller asked, as we walked hand in hand to Hannah's grave. I wanted to lay my wedding flowers there for her to share.

"Amazing. I can't believe we're actually married, if I'm honest," I said with a laugh.

"I feel annoyed we don't get to honeymoon just yet," he said.

"I want the house done, then we can lock the door, close the curtains, and pretend we are anywhere in the world."

"Mmm, that doesn't sound too bad."

"Anyway, I don't want to holiday just yet. I want our first holiday to be as a family."

I had knelt down beside Hannah's grave, I no longer thought of Trey being there with her. I kissed my fingertips and placed it over her name before looking back up at Miller. He held a frown on his forehead.

I stood and took his hand. I placed his hand on my stomach.

"Our first holiday will be in about a year, when our baby is a few months old."

He cocked his head to one side.

I sighed. "I'm pregnant, Miller."

He didn't speak, and I watched the tears roll down his cheeks. He knelt and held my hips. He placed a kiss on my stomach, through my wedding dress.

"My baby is in here," he whispered. "Hey, baby, Daddy here."

He stood so abruptly he startled me. He grabbed my shoulders and turned towards our guests that were leaving the church.

"I'm going to be a dad!" he shouted.

At first there wasn't a response, but then the whooping and cheering began.

"I'm going to be a dad?" he said quietly to me.

I nodded.

"Not just any old dad. You're going to be the most amazing father any child could ever wish for," I said.

"Fuck me," he said before laughing out loud.

Miller was the worst expectant parent I could have ever wished for. I wasn't allowed to do anything for myself. He worked, and he finished our house. He panicked at every single wince I made and he rubbed the soles of my feet when they hurt. He read every book, argued with the *useless* doctors who, in his opinion, knew nothing about childbirth, and I banned him from antenatal classes after he lay on the mat that should have been for me, and fell asleep.

A week before my due date, he led me into the spare bedroom that he'd begged me to stay away from. Standing in the middle of a soft cream painted room was an ornately carved oak cot, a matching crib stood beside it. To one side was a large dresser with a changing mat on the top. Miller had made them all.

"You're not cross I wanted to do this myself, are you?" he asked. I guessed my silence had worried him.

I shook my head slowly. "Miller, it's absolutely perfect." There were many other words I wanted to say but I was just so choked they wouldn't form.

Or perhaps it was the pain that ripped through my stomach and stole my ability to speak.

"Dani?"

I panted to quell the pain and pointed to the bag that had been packed for the past month, silently thanking that Miller had been so bloody anal about being prepared.

"It's time?" he asked.

I nodded, biting down on my lower lip.

"Holy fuck. Oh my God."

He ran around the house, placing the bag in the boot, grabbing coats and phones before escorting me to the sensible car we'd had to buy on his insistence.

Isabelle Hannah Copeland was born a few hours later by C-section.

She was a healthy and very cross baby, and she brought Miller to his knees. He cried when he held her and the love that poured from every part of him brought tears to not only my eyes, but the midwife and nurses as well.

"Hey, Izzie," he whispered. "It's so good to finally meet you."

He sat on the edge of the bed and placed her on my chest. I kissed her head and we both cried gentle tears as we welcomed our baby into the world.

"That is everything. More than I ever dreamed possible," Miller said, echoing the words he'd told me the very first time he'd kissed me.

My family was complete. My husband and my daughter were my world, but I'd never forget the angel that I was desperate to visit.

꧁

On the day we were allowed to take Izzie home, we made a detour to the cemetery. I wanted Izzie to meet her sister, Hannah, as soon as possible. We sat on the grass and I winced at the pull across my stomach as I did. We placed Izzie, in her car seat, beside the headstone, and not that it was deliberate of course, but Izzie stretched out her arm, her tiny fingers just touching the headstone beside Hannah's name.

I cried at that moment.

Hannah's photograph sat on a shelf in Izzie's bedroom, not that she was ready to use that room, of course. It comforted me to know she'd be there, looking after her baby sister.

Miller would sit with Izzie in a chair in her bedroom and I'd overhear him talking to his daughter. He always included Hannah in those conversations.

Lincoln Miller Copeland was truly the most amazing man I'd ever encountered. He was a doting father, an annoying father at times. He was the husband I could have only wished for, had my life not taken the turns it had. And for that reason, I was able to reconcile my feelings towards Trey. Silently, I even thanked him for his betrayal. Had he not had the affair, I would not have been standing at the partially open bedroom door, concealed, but listening to my amazing man whispering all the things he planned for his daughter and me.

I never heard back from Helen's solicitor. However, I did set up a trust for Alistair, using part of the settlement I'd received and after gaining confirmation that Trey was the father. It opened those old wounds but not enough that Miller couldn't soothe them closed again. Patricia had formed a 'relationship' with Helen, albeit a very strained one. I was pleased, though. She got to meet her grandson, and when she came to visit us, she got to meet her 'granddaughter' as well.

The End

ABOUT THE AUTHOR

Tracie Podger currently lives in Kent, UK with her husband and a rather obnoxious cat called George. She's a Padi Scuba Diving Instructor with a passion for writing. Tracie has been fortunate to have dived some of the wonderful oceans of the world where she can indulge in another hobby, underwater photography. She likes getting up close and personal with sharks.

Tracie likes to write in different genres. Her Fallen Angel series and its accompanying books are mafia romance and full of suspense. A Virtual Affair is contemporary romance, and Gabriel and A Deadly Sin are thriller/suspense. The Facilitator is erotic romance.

BOOKS BY TRACIE PODGER

STALKER LINKS

https://www.facebook.com/TraciePodgerAuthor/
https://twitter.com/TRACIEPODGER
http://www.TraciePodger.com

Lightning Source UK Ltd.
Milton Keynes UK
UKHW022240130522
402993UK00012B/354/J